About the Author

ISAAC ASIMOV is regarded as one of the greatest science-fiction writers of our time, as well as a valid contributor to the world of science. He holds a Ph.D. in Chemistry from Columbia University (1948) and, though he no longer lives in the Boston area, is an Associate Professor of Biochemistry at Boston University. He has received numerous awards for his inspiring scientific articles covering a wide range of subjects.

Fawcett Crest and Premier Books
by Isaac Asimov:

Fiction:

THE EARLY ASIMOV, *Book One*
THE EARLY ASIMOV, *Book Two*
PEBBLE IN THE SKY
THE STARS, LIKE DUST
THE CURRENTS OF SPACE
THE CAVES OF STEEL
THE END OF ETERNITY
THE MARTIAN WAY
THE NAKED SUN
EARTH IS ROOM ENOUGH
NINE TOMORROWS
NIGHTFALL
THE GODS THEMSELVES
THE BEST OF ISAAC ASIMOV
TALES OF THE BLACK WIDOWERS
MURDER AT THE ABA

Non-fiction:

EARTH: OUR CROWDED SPACESHIP
REALM OF ALGEBRA
REALM OF NUMBER

Edited by Isaac Asimov:

BEFORE THE GOLDEN AGE, Book 1
BEFORE THE GOLDEN AGE, Book 2
BEFORE THE GOLDEN AGE, Book 3
THE HUGO WINNERS, Volume 1
STORIES FROM THE HUGO WINNERS, Volume 2
MORE STORIES FROM THE HUGO WINNERS, Volume 3
WHERE DO WE GO FROM HERE?

ASIMOV'S MYSTERIES

by

Isaac Asimov

A FAWCETT CREST BOOK

Fawcett Publications, Inc., Greenwich, Connecticut

ASIMOV'S MYSTERIES

Publishing History of the Stories

1–"The Singing Bell": Published in *The Magazine of
Fantasy and Science Fiction*, January 1955. Copyright 1954,
by Fantasy House, Inc.

2–"The Talking Stone": Published in *The Magazine of
Fantasy and Science Fiction*, October 1955. Copyright 1955,
by Fantasy House, Inc.

3–"What's in a Name?": Published under the title
"Death of a Honey-Blonde" in *The Saint Detective Magazine*,
June 1956. © by King-Size Publications, Inc.

To all the nice people

at Doubleday

Contents

Introduction

There is a tendency for many people who don't know any better to classify science fiction as just one more member of the group of specialized literatures that include mysteries, westerns, adventures, sport stories, love stories, and so on.

This has always seemed odd to those who know science fiction well, for s.f. is a literary response to scientific change, and that response can run the entire gamut of the human experience. Science fiction, in other words, includes everything.

How does one differentiate between a science fiction story and an adventure story, for instance, when so much s.f. is so intensely adventurous as to leave the ordinary stories of the type rather pale? Surely a trip to the moon is first of all an adventure of the most thrilling kind, whatever else it is.

I have seen excellent science fiction stories that fall into unusual classifications and bring great enrichment to what it had touched. Arthur C. Clarke wrote a delightful "western" —but it took place under the sea, and it had dolphins in place of cattle. Its name was "Home on the Range," however, and it fitted.

Clifford D. Simak wrote "Rule 18" which is a pure sports story, but one that involved time-travel, so that the coach of Earth's team could collect all-time greats with whom to win the annual game with Mars.

In "The Lovers," Philip José Farmer struck a telling variation on ordinary romance by writing a sober and moving tale of love that crossed the boundary line, not of religion or color, but of species.

Oddly enough, it was the mystery form that seemed most difficult to amalgamate with science fiction. Surely this is unexpected. One would think that science fiction would blend easily with the mystery. Science itself is so nearly a mystery and the research scientist so nearly a Sherlock Holmes.

And if we want to reverse things, are there not mysteries that make use of the "scientific mind"? R. Austin Freeman's Dr. Thorndyke is an example of a well-known and successful (fictional) scientist-detective.

And yet science fiction writers seemed to be inhibited in the face of the science fiction mystery.

Back in the late 1940s, this was finally explained to me. I was told that "by its very nature" science fiction would not play fair with the reader. In a science fiction story, the detective could say, "But as you know, Watson, ever since 2175, when all Spaniards learned to speak French, Spanish has been a dead language. How came Juan Lopez, then, to speak those significant words in *Spanish?*"

Or else, he could have his detective whip out an odd device and say, "As you know, Watson, my pocket-frannistan is perfectly capable of detecting the hidden jewel in a trice."

Such arguments did not impress me. It seemed to me that ordinary mystery writers (non-science-fiction variety) could be just as unfair to the readers. They could deliberately hide a necessary clue. They could introduce an additional character from nowhere. They could simply forget about something over which they had been making a great deal of fuss, and mention it no more. They could do *anything*.

The point was, though, that they *didn't* do anything. They stuck to the rule of being fair to the reader. Clues might be obscured, but not omitted. Essential lines of thought might be thrown out casually, but they were thrown out. The reader was remorselessly misdirected, misled, and mystified, but he was *not* cheated.

It seemed, then, a matter to be taken obviously for granted that the same would apply to a science fiction mystery. You *don't* spring new devices on the reader and solve the mystery with them. You *don't* take advantage of future history to introduce *ad hoc* phenomena. In fact, you carefully explain all facets of the future background well in advance so the reader may have a decent chance to see the solution. The fictional detective can make use only of facts known to the reader *in the present* or of "facts" of the fictional future, which will be carefully explained beforehand. Even some of the real facts of our present ought to be mentioned if they are to be used—just to make sure the reader is aware of the world now about him.

Once all this is accepted, not only does it become obvious that the science fiction mystery is a thoroughly acceptable literary form, but it also becomes obvious that it is a lot more fun to write and read, since it often has a background that is fascinating in itself quite apart from the mystery.

But talk is cheap, so I put my typewriter where my mouth was, and in 1953 wrote a science fiction mystery novel called *The Caves of Steel* (Doubleday, 1954). It was accepted by the critics as a good science fiction novel *and* a good mystery and after it appeared I never heard anyone say that science fiction mysteries were impossible to write. I even wrote a sequel called *The Naked Sun* (Doubleday, 1957) just to show that the first book wasn't an accident.

Between and after these novels, moreover, I also wrote several short stories intended to prove that science fiction mysteries could be written in all lengths.

These shorter science fiction mysteries (including some borderline cases) are included in this volume in order of publication. Judge for yourself.

The Singing Bell

Louis Peyton never discussed publicly the methods by which
he had bested the police of Earth in a dozen duels of wits
and bluff, with the psychoprobe always waiting and always
foiled. He would have been foolish to do so, of course, but
in his more complacent moments, he fondled the notion of
leaving a testament to be opened only after his death, one
in which his unbroken success could clearly be seen to be
due to ability and not to luck.

In such a testament he would say, "No false pattern can
be created to cover a crime without bearing upon it some
trace of its creator. It is better, then, to seek in events some
pattern that already exists and then adjust your actions to it."

It was with that principle in mind that Peyton planned
the murder of Albert Cornwell.

Cornwell, that small-time retailer of stolen things, first
approached Peyton at the latter's usual table-for-one at
Grinnell's. Cornwell's blue suit seemed to have a special
shine, his lined face a special grin, and his faded mustache
a special bristle.

"Mr. Peyton," he said, greeting his future murderer with
no fourth-dimensional qualm, "it is so nice to see you. I'd
almost given up, sir, almost given up."

Peyton, who disliked being approached over his newspaper
and dessert at Grinnell's, said, "If you have business with
me, Cornwell, you know where you can reach me." Peyton
was past forty and his hair was past its earlier blackness,
but his back was rigid, his bearing youthful, his eyes dark,
and his voice could cut the more sharply for long practice.

"Not for this, Mr. Peyton," said Cornwell, "not for this. I
know of a cache, sir, a cache of . . . you know, sir." The
forefinger of his right hand moved gently, as though it were

a clapper striking invisible substance, and his left hand momentarily cupped his ear.

Peyton turned a page of the paper, still somewhat damp from its tele-dispenser, folded it flat and said, "Singing Bells?"

"Oh, hush, Mr. Peyton," said Cornwell in whispered agony.

Peyton said, "Come with me."

They walked through the park. It was another Peyton axiom that to be reasonably secret there was nothing like a low-voiced discussion out of doors.

Cornwell whispered, "A cache of Singing Bells; an accumulated cache of Singing Bells. Unpolished, but such beauties, Mr. Peyton."

"Have you seen them?"

"No, sir, but I have spoken with one who has. He had proofs enough to convince me. There is enough there to enable you and me to retire in affluence. In absolute affluence, sir."

"Who was this other man?"

A look of cunning lit Cornwell's face like a smoking torch, obscuring more than it showed and lending it a repulsive oiliness. "The man was a lunar grubstaker who had a method for locating the Bells in the crater sides. I don't know his method; he never told me that. But he has gathered dozens, hidden them on the Moon, and come to Earth to arrange the disposing of them."

"He died, I suppose?"

"Yes. A most shocking accident, Mr. Peyton. A fall from a height. Very sad. Of course, his activities on the Moon were quite illegal. The Dominion is very strict about unauthorized Bell-mining. So perhaps it was a judgment upon him after all . . . In any case, I have his map."

Peyton said, a look of calm indifference on his face, "I don't want any of the details of your little transaction. What I want to know is why you've come to me."

Cornwell said, "Well, now, there's enough for both of us, Mr. Peyton, and we can both do our bit. For my part, I know where the cache is located and I can get a spaceship. You . . ."

"Yes?"

"You can pilot a spaceship, and you have such excellent contacts for disposing of the Bells. It is a very fair division of labor, Mr. Peyton. Wouldn't you say so, now?"

Peyton considered the pattern of his life—the pattern that already existed—and matters seemed to fit.

He said, "We will leave for the Moon on August the tenth."

Cornwell stopped walking and said, "Mr. Peyton! It's only April now."

Peyton maintained an even gait and Cornwell had to hurry to catch up. "Do you hear me, Mr. Peyton?"

Peyton said, "August the tenth. I will get in touch with you at the proper time, tell you where to bring your ship. Make no attempt to see me personally till then. Good-bye, Cornwell."

Cornwell said, "Fifty-fifty?"

"Quite," said Peyton. "Good-bye."

Peyton continued his walk alone and considered the pattern of his life again. At the age of twenty-seven, he had bought a tract of land in the Rockies on which some past owner had built a house designed as refuge against the threatened atomic wars of two centuries back, the ones that had never come to pass after all. The house remained, however, a monument to a frightened drive for self-sufficiency.

It was of steel and concrete in as isolated a spot as could well be found on Earth, set high above sea level and protected on nearly all sides by mountain peaks that reached higher still. It had its self-contained power unit, its water supply fed by mountain streams, its freezers in which ten sides of beef could hang comfortably, its cellar outfitted like a fortress with an arsenal of weapons designed to stave off hungry, panicked hordes that never came. It had its air-conditioning unit that could scrub and scrub the air until anything *but* radioactivity (alas for human frailty) could be scrubbed out of it.

In that house of survival, Peyton passed the month of August every subsequent year of his perennially bachelor life. He took out the communicators, the television, the newspaper tele-dispenser. He built a force-field fence about his property and left a short-distance signal mechanism to the house from the point where the fence crossed the one trail winding through the mountains.

For one month each year, he could be thoroughly alone. No one saw him, no one could reach him. In absolute solitude, he could have the only vacation he valued after eleven months of contact with a humanity for which he could feel only a cold contempt.

Even the police—and Peyton smiled—knew of his rigid regard for August. He had once jumped bail and risked the psychoprobe rather than forgo his August.

Peyton considered another aphorism for possible inclusion in his testament: There is nothing so conducive to an appearance of innocence as the triumphant lack of an alibi.

On July 30, as on July 30 of every year, Louis Peyton took the 9:15 A.M. non-grav stratojet at New York and arrived in Denver at 12:30 P.M. There he lunched and took the 1:45 P.M. semi-grav bus to Hump's Point, from which Sam Leibman took him by ancient ground-car—full grav!—up the trail to the boundaries of his property. Sam Leibman gravely accepted the ten-dollar tip that he always received, touched his hat as he had done on July 30 for fifteen years.

On July 31, as on July 31 of every year, Louis Peyton returned to Hump's Point in his non-grav aeroflitter and placed an order through the Hump's Point general store for such supplies as he needed for the coming month. There was nothing unusual about the order. It was virtually the duplicate of previous such orders.

MacIntyre, manager of the store, checked gravely over the list, put it through to Central Warehouse, Mountain District, in Denver, and the whole of it came pushing over the masstransference beam within the hour. Peyton loaded the supplies onto his aeroflitter with MacIntyre's help, left his usual ten-dollar tip and returned to his house.

On August 1, at 12:01 A.M., the force field that surrounded his property was set to full power and Peyton was isolated.

And now the pattern changed. Deliberately he had left himself eight days. In that time he slowly and meticulously destroyed just enough of his supplies to account for all of August. He used the dusting chambers which served the house as a garbage-disposal unit. They were of an advanced model capable of reducing all matter up to and including metals and silicates to an impalpable and undetectable molecular dust. The excess energy formed in the process was carried away by the mountain stream that ran through his property. It ran five degrees warmer than normal for a week.

On August 9 his aeroflitter carried him to a spot in Wyoming where Albert Cornwell and a spaceship waited. The spaceship, itself, was a weak point, of course, since there were men who had sold it, men who had transported it and helped prepare it for flight. All those men, however, led only as far as Cornwell, and Cornwell, Peyton thought—with the trace of a smile on his cold lips—would be a dead end. A very dead end.

On August 10 the spaceship, with Peyton at the controls and Cornwell—and his map—as passenger, left the surface of Earth. Its non-grav field was excellent. At full power, the ship's weight was reduced to less than an ounce. The micropiles fed energy efficiently and noiselessly, and without flame or sound the ship rose through the atmosphere, shrank to a point, and was gone.

It was very unlikely that there would be witnesses to the flight, or that in these weak, piping times of peace there would be a radar watch as in days of yore. In point of fact, there was none.

Two days in space; now two weeks on the Moon. Almost instinctively Peyton had allowed for those two weeks from the first. He was under no illusions as to the value of homemade maps by non-cartographers. Useful they might be to the designer himself, who had the help of memory. To a stranger, they could be nothing more than a cryptogram.

Cornwell showed Peyton the map for the first time only after takeoff. He smiled obsequiously. "After all, sir, this was my only trump."

"Have you checked this against the lunar charts?"

"I would scarcely know how, Mr. Peyton. I depend upon you."

Peyton stared at him coldly as he returned the map. The one certain thing upon it was Tycho Crater, the site of the buried Luna City.

In one respect, at least, astronomy was on their side. Tycho was on the daylight side of the Moon at the moment. It meant that patrol ships were less likely to be out, they themselves less likely to be observed.

Peyton brought the ship down in a riskily quick non-grav landing within the safe, cold darkness of the inner shadow of a crater. The sun was past zenith and the shadow would grow no shorter.

Cornwell drew a long face. "Dear, dear, Mr. Peyton. We can scarcely go prospecting in the lunar day."

"The lunar day doesn't last forever," said Peyton shortly. "There are about a hundred hours of sun left. We can use that time for acclimating ourselves and for working out the map."

The answer came quickly, but it was plural. Peyton studied the lunar charts over and over, taking meticulous measurements, and trying to find the pattern of craters shown on the homemade scrawl that was the key to—what?

Finally Peyton said, "The crater we want could be any one of three: GC-3, GC-5, or MT-10."

"What do we do, Mr. Peyton?" asked Cornwell anxiously.

"We try them all," said Peyton, "beginning with the nearest."

The terminator passed and they were in the night shadow. After that, they spent increasing periods on the lunar surface, getting used to the eternal silence and blackness, the harsh points of the stars and the crack of light that was the Earth peeping over the rim of the crater above. They left hollow, featureless footprints in the dry dust that did not stir or change. Peyton noted them first when they climbed out of the crater into the full light of the gibbous Earth. That was on the eighth day after their arrival on the moon.

The lunar cold put a limit to how long they could remain outside their ship at any one time. Each day, however, they managed for longer. By the eleventh day after arrival they had eliminated GC-5 as the container of the Singing Bells.

By the fifteenth day, Peyton's cold spirit had grown warm with desperation. It would have to be GC-3. MT-10 was too far away. They would not have time to reach it and explore it and still allow for a return to Earth by August 31.

On that same fifteenth day, however, despair was laid to rest forever when they discovered the Bells.

They were not beautiful. They were merely irregular masses of gray rock, as large as a double fist, vacuum-filled and feather-light in the moon's gravity. There were two dozen of them and each one, after proper polishing, could be sold for a hundred thousand dollars at least.

Carefully, in double handfuls, they carried the Bells to the ship, bedded them in excelsior, and returned for more. Three times they made the trip both ways over ground that would have worn them out on Earth but which, under the Moon's lilliputian gravity, was scarcely a barrier.

Cornwell passed the last of the Bells up to Peyton, who placed them carefully within the outer lock.

"Keep them clear, Mr. Peyton," he said, his radioed voice sounding harshly in the other's ear. "I'm coming up."

He crouched for the slow high leap against lunar gravity, looked up, and froze in panic. His face, clearly visible through the hard carved lusilite of his helmet, froze in a last grimace of terror. "No, Mr. Peyton. Don't—"

Peyton's fist tightened on the grip of the blaster he held. It fired. There was an unbearably brilliant flash and Cornwell was a dead fragment of a man, sprawled amid remnants of a spacesuit and flecked with freezing blood.

Peyton paused to stare somberly at the dead man, but only for a second. Then he transferred the last of the Bells to their prepared containers, removed his suit, activated first the nongrav field, then the micropiles, and, potentially a million or two richer than he had been two weeks earlier, set off on the return trip to Earth.

On the twenty-ninth of August, Peyton's ship descended silently, stern bottomward, to the spot in Wyoming from which it had taken off on August 10. The care with which Peyton had chosen the spot was not wasted. His aeroflitter was still there, drawn within the protection of an enclosing wrinkle of the rocky, tortuous countryside.

He moved the Singing Bells once again, in their containers, into the deepest recess of the wrinkle, covering them, loosely and sparsely, with earth. He returned to the ship once more to set the controls and make last adjustments. He climbed out again and two minutes later the ship's automatics took over.

Silently hurrying, the ship bounded upward and up, veering to westward somewhat as the Earth rotated beneath it. Peyton watched, shading his narrow eyes, and at the extreme edge of vision there was a tiny gleam of light and a dot of cloud against the blue sky.

Peyton's mouth twitched into a smile. He had judged well. With the cadmium safety-rods bent back into uselessness, the micropiles had plunged past the unit-sustaining safety level and the ship had vanished in the heat of the nuclear explosion that had followed.

Twenty minutes later, he was back on his property. He was tired and his muscles ached under Earth's gravity. He slept well.

Twelve hours later, in the earliest dawn, the police came.

The man who opened the door placed his crossed hands over his paunch and ducked his smiling head two or three times in greeting. The man who entered, H. Seton Davenport of the Terrestrial Bureau of Investigation, looked about uncomfortably.

The room he had entered was large and in semidarkness except for the brilliant viewing lamp focused over a combination armchair-desk. Rows of book-films covered the walls. A suspension of Galactic charts occupied one corner of the room and a Galactic Lens gleamed softly on a stand in another corner.

"You are Dr. Wendell Urth?" asked Davenport, in a tone that suggested he found it hard to believe. Davenport was a stocky man with black hair, a thin and prominent nose, and a star-shaped scar on one cheek which marked permanently the place where a neuronic whip had once struck him at too close a range.

"I am," said Dr. Urth in a thin, tenor voice. "And you are Inspector Davenport."

The Inspector presented his credentials and said, "The University recommended you to me as an extraterrologist."

"So you said when you called me half an hour ago," said Urth agreeably. His features were thick, his nose was a snubby button, and over his somewhat protuberant eyes there were thick glasses.

"I shall get to the point, Dr. Urth. I presume you have visited the Moon . . ."

Dr. Urth, who had brought out a bottle of ruddy liquid and two glasses, just a little the worse for dust, from behind a straggling pile of book-films, said with sudden brusqueness, "I have never visited the Moon, Inspector. I never intend to! Space travel is foolishness. I don't believe in it." Then, in softer tones, "Sit down, sir, sit down. Have a drink."

Inspector Davenport did as he was told and said, "But you're an . . ."

"Extraterrologist. Yes. I'm interested in other worlds, but it doesn't mean I have to go there. Good lord, I don't have to be a time traveler to qualify as a historian, do I?" He sat down, and a broad smile impressed itself upon his round face once more as he said, "Now tell me what's on your mind."

"I have come," said the Inspector, frowning, "to consult you in a case of murder."

"Murder? What have I to do with murder?"

"This murder, Dr. Urth, was on the Moon."

"Astonishing."

"It's more than astonishing. It's unprecedented, Dr. Urth. In the fifty years since the Lunar Dominion has been established, ships have blown up and spacesuits have sprung leaks. Men have boiled to death on sun-side, frozen on dark-side, and suffocated on both sides. There have even been deaths by falls, which, considering lunar gravity, is quite a trick. But in all that time, not one man has been killed on the Moon as the result of another man's deliberate act of violence—till now."

Dr. Urth said, "How was it done?"

"A blaster. The authorities were on the scene within the hour through a fortunate set of circumstances. A patrol ship observed a flash of light against the Moon's surface. You know how far a flash can be seen against the night-side. The pilot notified Luna City and landed. In the process of circling back, he swears that he just managed to see by Earthlight what looked like a ship taking off. Upon landing, he discovered a blasted corpse and footprints."

"The flash of light," said Dr. Urth, "you suppose to be the firing blaster."

"That's certain. The corpse was fresh. Interior portions of the body had not yet frozen. The footprints belonged to two people. Careful measurements showed that the depressions fell into two groups of somewhat different diameters, indicating differently sized spaceboots. In the main, they led to craters GC-3 and GC-5, a pair of—"

"I am acquainted with the official code for naming lunar craters," said Dr. Urth pleasantly.

"Umm. In any case, GC-3 contained footprints that led to a rift in the crater wall, within which scraps of hardened pumice were found. X-ray diffraction patterns showed—"

"Singing Bells," put in the extraterrologist in great excitement. "Don't tell me this murder of yours involves Singing Bells!"

"What if it does?" demanded Davenport blankly.

"I have one. A University expedition uncovered it and presented it to me in return for— Come, Inspector, I must show it to you."

Dr. Urth jumped up and pattered across the room, beckoning the other to follow as he did. Davenport, annoyed, followed.

They entered a second room, larger than the first, dimmer, considerably more cluttered. Davenport stared with astonishment at the heterogeneous mass of material that was jumbled together in no pretense at order.

He made out a small lump of "blue glaze" from Mars, the sort of thing some romantics considered to be an artifact of long-extinct Martians, a small meteorite, a model of an early spaceship, a sealed bottle of nothing scrawlingly labeled "Venusian atmosphere."

Dr. Urth said happily, "I've made a museum of my whole house. It's one of the advantages of being a bachelor. Of course, I haven't quite got things organized. Someday, when I have a spare week or so . . ."

For a moment he looked about, puzzled; then, remembering, he pushed aside a chart showing the evolutionary scheme of development of the marine invertebrates that were the highest life forms on Barnard's Planet and said, "Here it is. It's flawed, I'm afraid."

The Bell hung suspended from a slender wire, soldered delicately onto it. That it was flawed was obvious. It had a constriction line running halfway about it that made it seem like two small globes, firmly but imperfectly squashed together. Despite that, it had been lovingly polished to a dull luster, softly gray, velvety smooth, and faintly pock-marked in a way that laboratories, in their futile efforts to prepare synthetic Bells, had found impossible to duplicate.

Dr. Urth said, "I experimented a good deal before I found a decent stroker. A flawed Bell is temperamental. But bone works. I have one here"—and he held up something that looked like a short thick spoon made of a gray-white substance —"which I had made out of the femur of an ox. Listen."

With surprising delicacy, his pudgy fingers maneuvered the Bell, feeling for one best spot. He adjusted it, steadying it daintily. Then, letting the Bell swing free, he brought down the thick end of the bone spoon and stroked the Bell softly.

It was as though a million harps had sounded a mile away. It swelled and faded and returned. It came from no particular direction. It sounded inside the head, incredibly sweet and pathetic and tremulous all at once.

It died away lingeringly and both men were silent for a full minute.

Dr. Urth said, "Not bad, eh?" and with a flick of his hand set the Bell to swinging on its wire.

Davenport stirred restlessly. "Careful! Don't break it." The fragility of a good Singing Bell was proverbial.

Dr. Urth said, "Geologists say the Bells are only pressure-hardened pumice, enclosing a vacuum in which small beads of rock rattle freely. That's what they *say*. But if that's all it is, why can't we reproduce one? Now a flawless Bell would make this one sound like a child's harmonica."

"Exactly," said Davenport, "and there aren't a dozen people on Earth who own a flawless one, and there are a hundred people and institutions who would buy one at any price, no questions asked. A supply of Bells would be worth murder."

The extraterrologist turned to Davenport and pushed his spectacles back on his inconsequential nose with a stubby forefinger. "I haven't forgotten your murder case. Please go on."

"That can be done in a sentence. I know the identity of the murderer."

They had returned to the chairs in the library and Dr. Urth clasped his hands over his ample abdomen. "Indeed? Then surely you have no problem, Inspector."

"Knowing and proving are not the same, Dr. Urth. Unfortunately he has no alibi."

"You mean, unfortunately he *has*, don't you?"

"I mean what I say. If he had an alibi, I could crack it somehow, because it would be a false one. If there were witnesses who claimed they had seen him on Earth at the time of the murder, their stories could be broken down. If he had documentary proof, it could be exposed as a forgery or some sort of trickery. Unfortunately he has none of it."

"What does he have?"

Carefully Inspector Davenport described the Peyton estate in Colorado. He concluded, "He has spent every August there in the strictest isolation. Even the T.B.I. would have to testify to that. Any jury would have to presume that he was on his estate this August as well, unless we could present definite proof that he was on the Moon."

"What makes you think he *was* on the Moon? Perhaps he is innocent."

"No!" Davenport was almost violent. "For fifteen years I've been trying to collect sufficient evidence against him and I've never succeeded. But I can *smell* a Peyton crime now. I tell you that no one but Peyton, no one on Earth, would have the impudence or, for that matter, the practical business contacts to attempt disposal of smuggled Singing Bells. He is known to be an expert space pilot. He is known to have had contact with the murdered man, though admittedly not for some months. Unfortunately none of that is proof."

Dr. Urth said, "Wouldn't it be simple to use the psychoprobe, now that its use has been legalized?"

Davenport scowled, and the scar on his cheek turned livid. "Have you read the Konski-Hiakawa law, Dr. Urth?"

"No."

"I think no one has. The right to mental privacy, the government says, is fundamental. All right, but what follows? The man who is psychoprobed and proves innocent of the crime for which he was psychoprobed is entitled to as much compensation as he can persuade the courts to give him. In a recent case a bank cashier was awarded twenty-five thousand dollars for having been psychoprobed on inaccurate suspicion of theft. It seems that the circumstantial evidence which seemed to point to theft actually pointed to a small spot of adultery. His claim that he lost his job, was threatened by the husband in question and put in bodily fear, and finally was held up to ridicule and contumely because a news-strip man had learned the results of the probe held good in court."

"I can see the man's point."

"So can we all. That's the trouble. One more item to remember: Any man who has been psychoprobed once for any reason can never be psychoprobed again for any reason. No one man, the law says, shall be placed in mental jeopardy twice in his lifetime."

"Inconvenient."

"Exactly. In the two years since the psychoprobe has been legitimized, I couldn't count the number of crooks and chiselers who've tried to get themselves psychoprobed for purse-snatching so that they could play the rackets safely afterward. So you see the Department will not allow Peyton to be psychoprobed until they have firm evidence of his guilt. Not legal evidence, maybe, but evidence that is strong enough to convince my boss. The worst of it, Dr. Urth, is that if we come into court without a psychoprobe record, we can't win. In a case as serious as murder, not to have used the psychoprobe is proof enough to the dumbest juror that the prosecution isn't sure of its ground."

"Now what do you want of me?"

"Proof that he was on the Moon sometime in August. It's got to be done quickly. I can't hold him on suspicion much longer. And if news of the murder gets out, the world press will blow up like an asteroid striking Jupiter's atmosphere. A glamorous crime, you know—first murder on the Moon."

"Exactly when was the murder committed?" asked Urth, in a sudden transition to brisk cross-examination.

"August twenty-seventh."

"And the arrest was made when?"

"Yesterday, August thirtieth."

"Then if Peyton were the murderer, he would have had time to return to Earth."

"Barely. Just barely." Davenport's lips thinned. "If I had been a day sooner— If I had found his place empty—"

"And how long do you suppose the two, the murdered man and the murderer, were on the Moon altogether?"

"Judging by the ground covered by the footprints, a number of days. A week, at the minimum."

"Has the ship they used been located?"

"No, and it probably never will. About ten hours ago, the University of Denver reported a rise in background radio-activity beginning day before yesterday at 6 P.M. and persisting for a number of hours. It's an easy thing, Dr. Urth, to set a ship's controls so as to allow it to blast off without crew and blow up, fifty miles high, in a micropile short."

"If I had been Peyton," said Dr. Urth thoughtfully, "I would have killed the man on board ship and blown up corpse and ship together."

"You don't know Peyton," said Davenport grimly. "He enjoys his victories over the law. He values them. Leaving the corpse on the Moon is his challenge to us."

"I see." Dr. Urth patted his stomach with a rotary motion and said, "Well, there is a chance."

"That you'll be able to prove he was on the Moon?"

"That I'll be able to give you my opinion."

"Now?"

"The sooner the better. If, of course, I get a chance to interview Mr. Peyton."

"That can be arranged. I have a non-grav jet waiting. We can be in Washington in twenty minutes."

But a look of the deepest alarm passed over the plump extraterrologist's face. He rose to his feet and pattered away from the T.B.I. agent toward the duskiest corner of the cluttered room.

"*No!*"

"What's wrong, Dr. Urth?"

"I won't use a non-grav jet. I don't believe in them."

Davenport stared confusedly at Dr. Urth. He stammered, "Would you prefer a monorail?"

Dr. Urth snapped, "I mistrust all forms of transportation. I don't believe in them. Except walking. I don't mind walking." He was suddenly eager. "Couldn't you bring Mr. Peyton to this city, somewhere within walking distance? To City Hall, perhaps? I've often walked to City Hall."

Davenport looked helplessly about the room. He looked at the myriad volumes of lore about the light-years. He could see through the open door into the room beyond, with its tokens of the worlds beyond the sky. And he looked at Dr. Urth, pale at the thought of non-grav jet, and shrugged his shoulders.

"I'll bring Peyton here. Right to this room. Will that satisfy you?"

Dr. Urth puffed out his breath in a deep sigh. "Quite."

"I hope you can deliver, Dr. Urth."

"I will do my best, Mr. Davenport."

Louis Peyton stared with distaste at his surroundings and with contempt at the fat man who bobbed his head in greeting. He glanced at the seat offered him and brushed it with his hand before sitting down. Davenport took a seat next to him, with his blaster holster in clear view.

The fat man was smiling as he sat down and patted his

round abdomen as though he had just finished a good meal and were intent on letting the world know about it.

He said, "Good evening, Mr. Peyton. I am Dr. Wendell Urth, extraterrologist."

Peyton looked at him again. "And what do you want with me?"

"I want to know if you were on the Moon at any time in the month of August."

"I was not."

"Yet no man saw you on Earth between the days of August first and August thirtieth."

"I lived my normal life in August. I am never seen during that month. Let him tell you." And he jerked his head in the direction of Davenport.

Dr. Urth chuckled. "How nice if we could test this matter. If there were only some physical manner in which we could differentiate Moon from Earth. If, for instance, we could analyze the dust in your hair and say, 'Aha, Moon rock.' Unfortunately we can't. Moon rock is much the same as Earth rock. Even if it weren't, there wouldn't be any in your hair unless you stepped onto the lunar surface without a space-suit, which is unlikely."

Peyton remained impassive.

Dr. Urth went on, smiling benevolently, and lifting a hand to steady the glasses perched precariously on the bulb of his nose. "A man traveling in space or on the Moon breathes Earth air, eats Earth food. He carries Earth environment next to his skin whether he's in his ship or in his spacesuit. We are looking for a man who spent two days in space going to the Moon, at least a week on the Moon, and two days coming back from the Moon. In all that time he carried Earth next to his skin, which makes it difficult."

"I'd suggest," said Peyton, "that you can make it less difficult by releasing me and looking for the real murderer."

"It may come to that," said Dr. Urth. "Have you ever seen anything like this?" His hand pushed its pudgy way to the ground beside his chair and came up with a gray sphere that sent back subdued highlights.

Peyton smiled. "It looks like a Singing Bell to me."

"It *is* a Singing Bell. The murder was committed for the sake of Singing Bells. What do you think of this one?"

"I think it is badly flawed."

"Ah, but inspect it," said Dr. Urth, and with a quick motion of his hand, he tossed it through six feet of air to Peyton.

Davenport cried out and half-rose from his chair. Peyton brought up his arms with an effort, but so quickly that he managed to catch the Bell.

Peyton said, "You damned fool. Don't throw it around that way."

"You respect Singing Bells, do you?"

"Too much to break one. That's no crime, at least." Peyton stroked the Bell gently, then lifted it to his ear and shook it slowly, listening to the soft clicks of the Lunoliths, those small pumice particles, as they rattled in vacuum.

Then, holding the Bell up by the length of steel wire still attached to it, he ran a thumbnail over its surface with an expert, curving motion. It twanged! The note was very mellow, very flutelike, holding with a slight *vibrato* that faded lingeringly and conjured up pictures of a summer twilight.

For a short moment, all three men were lost in the sound.

And then Dr. Urth said, "Throw it back, Mr. Peyton. Toss it here!" and held out his hand in peremptory gesture.

Automatically Louis Peyton tossed the Bell. It traveled its short arc one-third of the way to Dr. Urth's waiting hand, curved downward and shattered with a heartbroken, sighing discord on the floor.

Davenport and Peyton stared at the gray slivers with equal wordlessness and Dr. Urth's calm voice went almost unheard as he said, "When the criminal's cache of crude Bells is located, I'll ask that a flawless one, properly polished, be given to me, as replacement and fee."

"A fee? For what?" demanded Davenport irritably.

"Surely the matter is now obvious. Despite my little speech of a moment ago, there is one piece of Earth's environment that no space traveler carries with him and that is *Earth's surface gravity*. The fact that Mr. Peyton could so egregiously misjudge the toss of an object he obviously valued so highly could mean only that his muscles are not yet readjusted to the pull of Earthly gravity. It is my professional opinion, Mr. Davenport, that your prisoner has, in the last few days, been away from Earth. He has either been in space or on some planetary object considerably smaller in size than the Earth—as, for example, the Moon."

Davenport rose triumphantly to his feet. "Let me have your opinion in writing," he said, hand on blaster, "and that will be good enough to get me permission to use a psycho-probe."

Louis Peyton, dazed and unresisting, had only the numb realization that any testament he could now leave would have to include the fact of ultimate failure.

AFTERWORD

My stories generally bring me mail from my readers—usually very pleasant mail, even when some embarrassing point must be brought up. After this story was published, for instance, I received a letter from a young man who said he was inspired by Dr. Urth's reasoning to check on the problem of whether differences in weight would really affect the manner in which an object was thrown. In the end, he made a science project out of it.

He prepared objects, all of the same size and appearance but of different weights, and had people throw them, without saying in advance which were heavy and which were light. He found that all the objects were thrown with roughly equal accuracy.

This has bothered me a bit, but I have decided that the young man's findings are not strictly applicable. Merely by holding an object in preparation to throwing it, one estimates—quite unconsciously—its weight and adjusts the muscular effort to correspond, provided one is accustomed to the intensity of the gravity field under which one is operating.

Astronauts on their flights have generally been strapped in and have not operated under low gravity except for short "walks in space." Apparently these walks have proven surprisingly tiring, so it would seem a change in gravity requires considerable acclimation. And a return to Earth's gravity after such acclimation would require considerable re-acclimation.

So—as of now, at least—I stand pat with Dr. Urth.

The Talking Stone

The asteroid belt is large and its human occupancy small. Larry Vernadsky, in the seventh month of his year-long assignment to Station Five, wondered with increasing frequency if his salary could possibly compensate for a nearly solitary confinement seventy million miles from Earth. He was a slight youth, who did not bear the look of either a spationautical engineer or an asteroid man. He had blue eyes and butter-yellow hair and an invincible air of innocence that masked a quick mind and an isolation-sharpened bump of curiosity.

Both the look of innocence and the bump of curiosity served him well on board the *Robert Q.*

When the *Robert Q.* landed on the outer platform of Station Five, Vernadsky was on board almost immediately. There was an eager delight about him which, in a dog, would have been accompanied by a vibrating tail and a happy cacophony of barks.

The fact that the captain of the *Robert Q.* met his grins with a stern sour silence that sat heavily on his thick-featured face made no difference. As far as Vernadsky was concerned the ship was yearned-for company and was welcome. It was welcome to any amount of the millions of gallons of ice or any of the tons of frozen food concentrates stacked away in the hollowed-out asteroid that served as Station Five. Vernadsky was ready with any power tool that might be necessary, any replacement that might be required for any hyperatomic motor.

Vernadsky was grinning all over his boyish face as he filled out the routine form, writing it out quickly for later conversion into computer notation for filing. He put down ship's name and serial number, engine number, field generator number, and so on, port of embarkation ("asteroids, damned lot of them, don't know which was last" and Vernadsky simply wrote "Belt" which was the usual abbreviation for "asteroid belt"); port of destination ("Earth"); reason for stopping ("stuttering hyperatomic drive").

"How many in your crew, Captain?" asked Vernadsky, as he looked over ship's papers.

The captain said, "Two. Now how about looking over the hyperatomics? We've got a shipment to make." His cheeks were blue with dark stubble, his bearing that of a hardened and lifelong asteroid miner, yet his speech was that of an educated, almost a cultured, man.

"Sure." Vernadsky lugged his diagnostic kit to the engine room, followed by the captain. He tested circuits, vacuum degree, forcefield density with easy-going efficiency.

He could not help wondering about the captain. Despite his own dislike for his surroundings he realized dimly that there were some who found fascination in the vast emptiness and freedom of space. Yet he guessed that a man like this captain was not an asteroid miner for the love of solitude alone.

He said, "Any special type of ore you handle?"

The captain frowned and said, "Chromium and manganese."

"That so? . . . I'd replace the Jenner manifold, if I were you."

"Is that what's causing the trouble?"

"No, it isn't. But it's a little beat-up. You'd be risking another failure within a million miles. As long as you've got the ship in here—"

"All right, replace it. But find the stutter, will you?"

"Doing my best, Captain."

The captain's last remark was harsh enough to abash even Vernadsky. He worked awhile in silence, then got to his feet. "You've got a gamma-fogged semireflector. Every time the positron beam circles round to its position the drive flickers out for a second. You'll have to replace it."

"How long will it take?"

"Several hours. Maybe twelve."

"What? I'm behind schedule."

"Can't help it." Vernadsky remained cheerful. "There's only so much I can do. The system has to be flushed for three hours with helium before I can get inside. And then I have to calibrate the new semireflector and that takes time. I could get it almost right in minutes, but that's only almost right. You'd break down before you reach the orbit of Mars."

The captain glowered. "Go ahead. Get started."

Vernadsky carefully maneuvered the tank of helium on board the ship. With ship's pseudo-grav generators shut off, it weighed virtually nothing, but it had its full mass and inertia. That meant careful handling if it were to make turns correctly. The maneuvers were all the more difficult since Vernadsky himself was without weight.

It was because his attention was concentrated entirely on the cylinder that he took a wrong turn in the crowded quarters and found himself momentarily in a strange and darkened room.

He had time for one startled shout and then two men were upon him, hustling his cylinder, closing the door behind him.

He said nothing, while he hooked the cylinder to the intake valve of the motor and listened to the soft, soughing noise as the helium flushed the interior, slowly washing absorbed radioactive gases into the all-accepting emptiness of space.

Then curiosity overcame prudence and he said, "You've got a silicony aboard ship, Captain. A big one."

The captain turned to face Vernadsky slowly. He said in a voice from which all expression had been removed, "Is that right?"

"I saw it. How about a better look?"

"Why?"

Vernadsky grew imploring. "Oh, look, Captain, I've been on this rock over half a year. I've read everything I could get hold of on the asteroids, which means all sorts of things about the siliconies. And I've never seen even a little one. Have a heart."

"I believe there's a job here to do."

"Just helium-flushing for hours. There's nothing else to be done till that's over. How come you carry a silicony about, anyway, Captain?"

"A pet. Some people like dogs. I like siliconies."

"Have you got it talking?"

The captain flushed. "Why do you ask?"

"Some of them have talked. Some of them read minds, even."

"What are you? An expert on these damn things?"

"I've been reading about them. I told you. Come on, Captain. Let's have a look."

Vernadsky tried not to show that he noticed that there was the captain facing him and a crewman on either side of him. Each of the three was larger than he was, each weightier, each—he felt sure—was armed.

Vernadsky said, "Well, what's wrong? I'm not going to steal the thing. I just want to see it."

It may have been the unfinished repair job that kept him alive at that moment. Even more so, perhaps, it was his look of cheerful and almost moronic innocence that stood him in good stead.

The captain said, "Well, then, come on."

And Vernadsky followed, his agile mind working and his pulse definitely quickened.

Vernadsky stared with considerable awe and just a little revulsion at the gray creature before him. It was quite true that he had never seen a silicony, but he had seen trimensional photographs and read descriptions. Yet there is something in a real presence for which neither words nor photographs are substitutes.

Its skin was of an oily smooth grayness. Its motions were slow, as became a creature who burrowed in stone and was more than half stone itself. There was no writhing of muscles beneath that skin; instead it moved in slabs as thin layers of stone slid greasily over one another.

It had a general ovoid shape, rounded above, flattened below, with two sets of appendages. Below were the "legs," set radially. They totaled six and ended in sharp flinty edges, reinforced by metal deposits. Those edges could cut through rock, breaking it into edible portions.

On the creature's flat undersurface, hidden from view unless the silicony were overturned, was the one opening into its interior. Shredded rocks entered that interior. Within, limestone and hydrated silicates reacted to form the silicones out of which the creature's tissues were built. Excess silica re-emerged from the opening as hard white pebbly excretions.

How extraterrologists had puzzled over the smooth pebbles that lay scattered in small hollows within the rocky structure of the asteroids until the siliconies were first discovered. And how they marveled at the manner in which the creatures made silicones—those silicone-oxygen polymers with hydrocarbon side chains—perform so many of the functions that proteins performed in terrestrial life.

From the highest point on the creature's back came the remaining appendages, two inverse cones hollowed in opposing directions and fitting snugly into parallel recesses running down the back, yet capable of lifting upward a short way. When the silicony burrowed through rock, the "ears" were retracted for streamlining. When it rested in a hollowed-out cavern, they could lift for better and more sensitive reception. Their vague resemblance to a rabbit's ears made the name *silicony* inevitable. The more serious extraterrologists, who referred to such creatures habitually as *Siliconeus asteroidea*, thought the "ears" might have something to do with the rudimentary telepathic powers the beasts possessed. A minority had other notions.

The silicony was flowing slowly over an oil-smeared rock. Other such rocks lay scattered in one corner of the room and represented, Vernadsky knew, the creature's food supply. Or at least it was its tissue-building supply. For sheer energy, he had read, that alone would not do.

Vernadsky marveled. "It's a monster. It's more than a foot across."

The captain grunted noncommittally.

"Where did you get it?" asked Vernadsky.

"One of the rocks."

"Well, listen, two inches is about the biggest anyone's found. You could sell this to some museum or university on Earth for a couple of thousand dollars, maybe."

The captain shrugged. "Well, you've seen it. Let's get back to the hyperatomics."

His hard grip was on Vernadsky's elbow and he was turning away, when there was an interruption in the form of a slow and slurring voice, a hollow and gritty one.

It was made by the carefully modulated friction of rock against rock and Vernadsky stared in near horror at the speaker.

It was the silicony, suddenly becoming a talking stone. It said, "The man wonders if this thing can talk."

Vernadsky whispered, "For the love of space. It does!"

"All right," said the captain impatiently, "you've seen it and heard it, too. Let's go now."

"And it reads minds," said Vernadsky.

The silicony said, "Mars rotates in two four hours three seven and one half minutes. Jupiter's density is one point two two. Uranus was discovered in the year one seven eight one. Pluto is the planet which is most far. Sun is heaviest with a mass of two zero zero zero zero zero zero . . ."

The captain pulled Vernadsky away. Vernadsky, half-walking backward, half-stumbling, listened with fascination to the fading bumbling of zeroes.

He said, "Where does it pick up all that stuff, Captain?"

"There's an old astronomy book we read to him. Real old."

"From before space travel was invented," said one of the crew members in disgust. "Ain't even a fillum. Regular print."

"Shut up," said the captain.

Vernadsky checked the outflow of helium for gamma radiation and eventually it was time to end the flushing and work in the interior. It was a painstaking job, and Vernadsky interrupted it only once for coffee and a breather.

He said, with innocence beaming in his smile, "You know the way I figure it, Captain? That thing lives inside rock, inside some asteroid all its life. Hundreds of years, maybe. It's a damn big thing, and it's probably a lot smarter than the run-of-the-mill silicony. Now you pick it up and it finds out the universe isn't rock. It finds out a trillion things it never imagined. That's why it's interested in astronomy. It's this new world, all these new ideas it gets in the book and in human minds, too. Don't you think that's so?"

He wanted desperately to smoke the captain out, get something concrete he could hang his deductions on. For this reason he risked telling what must be half the truth, the lesser half, of course.

But the captain, leaning against a wall with his arms folded, said only, "When will you be through?"

It was his last comment and Vernadsky was obliged to rest content. The motor was adjusted finally to Vernadsky's satisfaction, and the captain paid the reasonable fee in cash, accepted his receipt, and left in a blaze of ship's hyper-energy.

Vernadsky watched it go with an almost unbearable excitement. He made his way quickly to his sub-etheric sender.

"I've got to be right," he muttered to himself. "I've *got* to be."

Patrolman Milt Hawkins received the call in the privacy of his home station on Patrol Station Asteroid No. 72. He was nursing a two-day stubble, a can of iced beer, and a film viewer, and the settled melancholy on his ruddy, wide-cheeked face was as much the product of loneliness as was the forced cheerfulness in Vernadsky's eyes.

Patrolman Hawkins found himself looking into those eyes and was glad. Even though it was only Vernadsky, company was company. He gave him the big hello and listened luxuriously to the sound of a voice without worrying too strenuously concerning the contents of the speech.

Then suddenly amusement was gone and both ears were on the job and he said, "Hold it. Ho—ld it. What are you talking about?"

"Haven't you been listening, you dumb cop? I'm talking my heart out to you."

"Well, deal it out in smaller pieces, will you? What's this about a silicony?"

"This guy's got one on board. He calls it a pet and feeds it greasy rocks."

"Huh? I swear, a miner on the asteroid run would make a pet out of a piece of cheese if he could get it to talk back to him."

"Not just *a* silicony. Not one of these little inch jobs. It's over a foot across. Don't you get it? Space, you'd think a guy would know something about the asteroids, living out here."

"All right. Suppose you tell me."

"Look, greasy rocks build tissues, but where does a silicony that size get its energy from?"

"I couldn't tell you."

"Directly from— Have you got anyone around you right now?"

"Right now, no. I wish there were."

"You won't in a minute. Siliconies get their energy by the direct absorption of gamma rays."

"Says who?"

"Says a guy called Wendell Urth. He's a big-shot extra-terrologist. What's more, he says that's what the silicony's ears are for." Vernadsky put his two forefingers to his temples and wiggled them. "Not telepathy at all. They detect gamma radiation at levels no human instrument can detect."

"Okay. Now what?" asked Hawkins. But he was growing thoughtful.

"Now this. Urth says there isn't enough gamma radiation on any asteroid to support siliconies more than an inch or two long. Not enough radioactivity. So here we have one a foot long, a good fifteen inches."

"Well—"

"So it has to come from an asteroid just riddled with the stuff, lousy with uranium, solid with gamma rays. An asteroid with enough radioactivity to be warm to the touch and off the regular orbit patterns so that no one's come across it. Only suppose some smart boy landed on the asteroid by happenstance and noticed the warmth of the rocks and got to thinking. This captain of the *Robert Q.* is no rock-hopping ignoramus. He's a shrewd guy."

"Go on."

"Suppose he blasts off chunks for assay and comes across a giant silicony. Now he *knows* he's got the most unbelievable strike in all history. And he doesn't need assays. The silicony can lead him to the rich veins."

"Why should it?"

"Because it wants to learn about the universe. Because it's spent a thousand years, maybe, under rock, and it's just discovered the stars. It can read minds and it could learn to talk. It could make a deal. Listen, the captain would jump at it. Uranium mining is a state monopoly. Unlicensed miners aren't even allowed to carry counters. It's a perfect setup for the captain."

Hawkins said, "Maybe you're right."

"No maybe at all. You should have seen them standing around me while I watched the silicony, ready to jump me if I said one funny word. You should have seen them drag me out after two minutes."

Hawkins brushed his unshaven chin with his hand and made a mental estimate of the time it would take him to shave. He said, "How long can you keep the boy at your station?"

"Keep him! Space, he's gone!"

"What! Then what the devil is all this talk about? Why did you let him get away?"

"Three guys," said Vernadsky patiently, "each one bigger than I am, each one armed, and each one ready to kill, I'll bet. What did you want me to do?"

"All right, but what do we do now?"

"Come out and pick them up. That's simple enough. I was fixing their semireflectors and I fixed them my way. Their power will shut off completely within ten thousand miles. And I installed a tracer in the Jenner manifold."

Hawkins goggled at Vernadsky's grinning face. "Holy Toledo."

"And don't get anyone else in on this. Just you, me, and the police cruiser. They'll have no energy and we'll have a cannon or two. They'll tell us where the uranium asteroid is. We locate it, *then* get in touch with Patrol Headquarters. We will deliver unto them, three, count them, three, uranium smugglers, one giant-size silicony like nobody on Earth ever saw, and one, I repeat, one great big fat chunk of uranium ore like nobody on Earth saw, either. And you make a lieutenancy and I get promoted to a permanent Earth-side job. Right?"

Hawkins was dazed. "Right," he yelled. "I'll be right out there."

They were almost upon the ship before spotting it visually by the weak glinting of reflected sunlight.

Hawkins said, "Didn't you leave them enough power for ship's lights? You didn't throw off their emergency generator, did you?"

Vernadsky shrugged. "They're saving power, hoping they'll get picked up. Right now, they're putting everything they've got into a sub-etheric call, I'll bet."

"If they are," said Hawkins dryly, "I'm not picking it up."

"You're not?"

"Not a thing."

The police cruiser spiraled closer. Their quarry, its power off, was drifting through space at a steady ten thousand miles an hour.

The cruiser matched it, speed for speed, and drifted inward.

A sick expression crossed Hawkins' face. "Oh, *no!*"

"What's the matter?"

"The ship's been hit. A meteor. Lord knows there are enough of them in the asteroid belt."

All the verve washed out of Vernadsky's face and voice. "Hit? Are they wrecked?"

"There's a hole in it the size of a barn door. Sorry, Vernadsky, but this might not look good."

Vernadsky closed his eyes and swallowed hard. He knew what Hawkins meant. Vernadsky had deliberately misrepaired a ship, a procedure which could be judged a felony. And death as a result of a felony was murder.

He said, "Look, Hawkins, you know why I did it."

"I know what you've told me and I'll testify to that if I have to. But if this ship wasn't smuggling . . ."

He didn't finish the statement. Nor did he have to.

They entered the smashed ship in full spacesuit cover.

The *Robert Q.* was a shambles, inside and out. Without power, there was no chance of raising the feeblest screen against the rock that hit them or of detecting it in time or of avoiding it if they had detected it. It had caved in the ship's hull as though it were so much aluminum foil. It had smashed the pilot room, evacuated the ship's air, and killed the three men on board.

One of the crew had been slammed against the wall by the impact and was so much frozen meat. The captain and the other crewman lay in stiff attitudes, skins congested with frozen bloodclots where the air, boiling out of the blood, had broken the vessels.

Vernadsky, who had never seen this form of death in space, felt sick, but he fought against vomiting messily inside his spacesuit and succeeded.

He said, "Let's test the ore they're carrying. It's *got* to be alive." It's *got* to be, he told himself. It's *got* to be.

The door to the hold had been warped by the force of collision and there was a gap half an inch wide where it no longer met the frame.

Hawkins lifted the counter he held in his gauntleted hand and held its mica window to that gap.

It chattered like a million magpies.

Vernadsky said, with infinite relief, "I told you so."

His misrepair of the ship was now only the ingenious and praiseworthy fulfillment of a citizen's loyal duty and the meteor collision that had brought death to three men merely a regrettable accident.

It took two blaster bolts to break the twisted door loose, and tons of rock met their flashlights.

Hawkins lifted two chunks of moderate size and dropped them gingerly into one of the suit's pockets. "As exhibits," he said, "and for assay."

"Don't keep them near the skin too long," warned Vernadsky.

"The suit will protect me till I get it back to ship. It's not pure uranium, you know."

"Pretty near, I'll bet." Every inch of his cockiness was back.

Hawkins looked about. "Well, this tears things. We've stopped a smuggling ring, maybe, or part of one. But what next?"

"The uranium asteroid—uh, oh!"

"Right. Where is it? The only ones who know are dead."

"Space!" And again Vernadsky's spirits were dashed. Without the asteroid itself, they had only three corpses and a few tons of uranium ore. Good, but not spectacular. It would mean a citation, yes, but he wasn't after a citation. He wanted promotion to a permanent Earth-side job and that required something.

He yelled, "For the love of space, the *silicony!* It can live in a vacuum. It lives in a vacuum all the time and *it* knows where the asteroid is."

"Right!" said Hawkins, with instant enthusiasm. "Where is the thing?"

"Aft," cried Vernadsky. "This way."

The silicony glinted in the light of their flashes. It moved and was alive.

Vernadsky's heart beat madly with excitement. "We've got to move it, Hawkins."

"Why?"

"Sound won't carry in a vacuum, for the love of space. We've got to get it into the cruiser."

"All right. All right."

"We can't put a suit around it with a radio transmitter, you know."

"I said all right."

They carried it gingerly and carefully, their metal-sheathed fingers handling the greasy surface of the creature almost lovingly.

Hawkins held it while kicking off the *Robert Q.*

It lay in the control room of the cruiser now. The two men had removed their helmets and Hawkins was shucking his suit. Vernadsky could not wait.

He said, "You can read our minds?"

He held his breath until finally the gratings of rock surfaces modulated themselves into words. To Vernadsky no finer sound could, at the moment, be imagined.

The silicony said, "Yes." Then he said, "Emptiness all about. Nothing."

"What?" said Hawkins.

Vernadsky shushed him. "The trip through space just now, I guess. It must have impressed him."

He said to the silicony, shouting his words as though to make his thoughts clearer, "The men who were with you gathered uranium, special ore, radiations, energy."

"They wanted food," came the weak, gritty sound.

Of course! It was food to the silicony. It was an energy source. Vernadsky said, "You showed them where they could get it?"

"Yes."

Hawkins said, "I can heardly hear the thing."

"There's something wrong with it," said Vernadsky worriedly. He shouted again, "Are you well?"

"Not well. Air gone at once. Something wrong inside."

Vernadsky muttered. "The sudden decompression must have damaged it. Oh, Lord— Look, you know what I want. Where is your home? The place with the food?"

The two men were silent, waiting.

The silicony's ears lifted slowly, very slowly, trembled, and fell back. "There," it said. "Over there."

"Where?" screamed Vernadsky.

"There."

Hawkins said, "It's doing something. It's pointing in some way."

"Sure, only we don't know in what way."

"Well, what do you expect it to do? Give the coordinates?"

Vernadsky said at once, "Why not?" He turned again to the silicony as it lay huddled on the floor. It was motionless now and there was a dullness to its exterior that looked ominous.

Vernadsky said, "The captain knew where your eating place was. He had numbers concerning it, didn't he?" He prayed that the silicony would understand, that it would read his thoughts and not merely listen to his words.

"Yes," said the silicony in a rock-against-rock sigh.

"Three sets of numbers," said Vernadsky. There would have to be three. Three coordinates in space with dates attached, giving three positions of the asteroid in its orbit about the sun. From these data the orbit could be calculated in full and its position determined at any time. Even planetary perturbations could be accounted for, roughly.

"Yes," said the silicony, lower still.

"What were they? What were the numbers? Write them down, Hawkins. Get paper."

But the silicony said, "Do not know. Numbers not important. Eating place there."

Hawkins said, "That's plain enough. It didn't need the coordinates, so it paid no attention to them."

The silicony said, "Soon not"—a long pause, and then slowly, as though testing a new and unfamiliar word—"alive. Soon"—an even longer pause—"dead. What after death?"

"Hang on," implored Vernadsky. "Tell me, did the captain write down these figures anywhere?"

The silicony did not answer for a long minute and then, while both men bent so closely that their heads almost touched over the dying stone, it said, "What after death?"

Vernadsky shouted, "One answer. Just one. The captain must have written down the numbers. Where? Where?"

The silicony whispered, "On the asteroid."

And it never spoke again.

It was a dead rock, as dead as the rock which gave it birth, as dead as the walls of the ship, as dead as a dead human.

And Vernadsky and Hawkins rose from their knees and stared hopelessly at each other.

"It makes no sense," said Hawkins. "Why should he write the coordinates on the asteroid? That's like locking a key inside the cabinet it's meant to open."

Vernadsky shook his head. "A fortune in uranium. The biggest strike in history and we don't know where it is."

H. Seton Davenport looked about him with an odd feeling

of pleasure. Even in repose, there was usually something
hard about his lined face with its prominent nose. The scar
on his right cheek, his black hair, startling eyebrows, and
dark complexion all combined to make him look every bit
the incorruptible agent of the Terrestrial Bureau of Investigation that he actually was.

Yet now something almost like a smile tugged at his lips
as he looked about the large room, in which dimness made
the rows of book-films appear endless, and specimens of
who-knows-what from who-knows-where bulk mysteriously.
The complete disorder, the air of separation, almost insula-
tion, from the world, made the room look unreal. It made it
look every bit as unreal as its owner.

That owner sat in a combination armchair-desk which was
bathed in the only focus of bright light in the room. Slowly
he turned the sheets of official reports he held in his hand.
His hand moved otherwise only to adjust the thick spectacles
which threatened at any moment to fall completely from his
round and completely unimpressive nubbin of a nose. His
paunch lifted and fell quietly as he read.

He was Dr. Wendell Urth, who, if the judgment of experts
counted for anything, was Earth's most outstanding extraterrologist. On any subject outside Earth men came to him,
though Dr. Urth had never in his adult life been more than
an hour's-walk distance from his home on the University
campus.

He looked up solemnly at Inspector Davenport. "A very
intelligent man, this young Vernadsky," he said.

"To have deduced all he did from the presence of the
silicony? Quite so," said Davenport.

"No, no. The deduction was a simple thing. Unavoidable,
in fact. A noodle would have seen it. I was referring"—and
his glance grew a trifle censorious—"to the fact that the
youngster had read of my experiments concerning the gamma-
ray sensitivity of *Siliconeus asteroidea*."

"Ah, yes," said Davenport. Of course, Dr. Urth was the
expert on siliconies. It was why Davenport had come to
consult him. He had only one question for the man, a simple
one, yet Dr. Urth had thrust out his full lips, shaken his
ponderous head, and asked to see all the documents in the
case.

Ordinarily that would have been out of the question, but

Dr. Urth had recently been of considerable use to the T.B.I. in that affair of the Singing Bells of Luna and the singular non-alibi shattered by Moon gravity, and the Inspector had yielded.

Dr. Urth finished the reading, laid the sheets down on his desk, yanked his shirttail out of the tight confines of his belt with a grunt and rubbed his glasses with it. He stared through the glasses at the light to see the effects of his cleaning, replaced them precariously on his nose, and clasped his hands on his paunch, stubby fingers interlacing.

"Your question again, Inspector?"

Davenport said patiently, "Is it true, in your opinion, that a silicony of the size and type described in the report could only have developed on a world rich in uranium—"

"Radioactive material," interrupted Dr. Urth. "Thorium, perhaps, though probably uranium."

"Is your answer yes, then?"

"Yes."

"How big would the world be?"

"A mile in diameter, perhaps," said the extraterrologist thoughtfully. "Perhaps even more."

"How many tons of uranium, or radioactive material, rather?"

"In the trillions. Minimum."

"Would you be willing to put all that in the form of a signed opinion in writing?"

"Of course."

"Very well then, Dr. Urth." Davenport got to his feet, reached for his hat with one hand and the file of reports with the other. "That is all we need."

But Dr. Urth's hand moved to the reports and rested heavily upon them. "Wait. How will you find the asteroid?"

"By looking. We'll assign a volume of space to every ship made available to us and—just look."

"The expense, the time, the effort! And you'll never find it."

"One chance in a thousand. We might."

"One chance in a million. You won't."

"We can't let the uranium go without some try. Your professional opinion makes the prize high enough."

"But there is a better way to find the asteroid. *I* can find it."

Davenport fixed the extraterrologist with a sudden, sharp glance. Despite appearances Dr. Urth was anything but a fool. He had personal experience of that. There was therefore just a bit of half-hope in his voice as he said, "How can you find it?"

"First," said Dr. Urth, "my price."

"Price?"

"Or fee, if you choose. When the government reaches the asteroid, there may be another large-size silicony on it. Siliconies are very valuable. The only form of life with solid silicone for tissues and liquid silicone as a circulating fluid. The answer to the question whether the asteroids were once part of a single planetary body may rest with them. Any number of other problems . . . Do you understand?"

"You mean you want a large silicony delivered to you?"

"Alive and well. And free of charge. Yes."

Davenport nodded. "I'm sure the government will agree. Now what have you on your mind?"

Dr. Urth said quietly, as though explaining everything, "The silicony's remark."

Davenport looked bewildered. "What remark?"

"The one in the report. Just before the silicony died. Vernadsky was asking it where the captain had written down the coordinates, and it said, 'On the asteroid.'"

A look of intense disappointment crossed Davenport's face. "Great space, Doctor, we know that, and we've gone into every angle of it. Every possible angle. It means nothing."

"Nothing at all, Inspector?"

"Nothing of importance. Read the report again. The silicony wasn't even listening to Vernadsky. He was feeling life depart and he was wondering about it. Twice, it asked, 'What after death?' Then, as Vernadsky kept questioning it, it said, 'On the asteroid.' Probably it never heard Vernadsky's question. It was answering its own question. It thought that after death it would return to its own asteroid; to its home, where it would be safe once more. That's all."

Dr. Urth shook his head. "You are too much a poet, you know. You imagine too much. Come, it is an interesting problem and let us see if you can't solve it for yourself. Suppose the silicony's remark *were* an answer to Vernadsky."

"Even so," said Davenport impatiently, "how would it help? *Which* asteroid? The uranium asteroid? We can't find it, so we can't find the coordinates. Some other asteroid which the *Robert Q.* had used as a home base? We can't find that either."

"How you avoid the obvious, Inspector. Why don't you ask yourself what the phrase 'on the asteroid' means to the silicony. Not to you or to me, but to the silicony."

Davenport frowned. "Pardon me, Doctor?"

"I'm speaking plainly. What did the word *asteroid* mean to the silicony?"

"The silicony learned about space out of an astronomy text that was read to it. I suppose the book explained what an asteroid was."

"Exactly," crowed Dr. Urth, putting a finger to the side of his snub nose. "And how would the definition go? An asteroid is a small body, smaller than the planets, moving about the sun in an orbit which, generally speaking, lies between those of Mars and Jupiter. Wouldn't you agree?"

"I suppose so."

"And what is the *Robert Q.?*"

"You mean the ship?"

"That's what *you* call it," said Dr. Urth. "The *ship*. But the astronomy book was an ancient one. It made no mention of ships in space. One of the crewmen said as much. He said it dated from before space flight. Then what is the *Robert Q.?* Isn't it a small body, smaller than the planets? And while the silicony was aboard, wasn't it moving about the sun in an orbit which, generally speaking, lay between those of Mars and Jupiter?"

"You mean the silicony considered the ship as just another asteroid, and when he said 'on the asteroid,' he meant 'on the ship'?"

"Exactly. I told you I would make you solve the problem for yourself."

No expression of joy or relief lightened the gloom on the Inspector's face. "That is no solution, Doctor."

But Dr. Urth blinked slowly at him and the bland look on his round face became, if anything, blander and more child-like in its uncomplicated pleasure. "Surely it is."

"Not at all. Dr. Urth, we didn't reason it out as you did. We dismissed the silicony's remark completely. But still, don't you suppose we searched the *Robert Q.?* We took it apart piece by piece, plate by plate. We just about unwelded the thing."

"And you found nothing?"

"Nothing."

"Perhaps you did not look in the right place."

"We looked in *every* place." He stood up, as though to go. "You understand, Dr. Urth? When we got through with the ship there was no possibility of those coordinates existing anywhere on it."

"Sit down, Inspector," said Dr. Urth calmly. "You are still not considering the silicony's statement properly. Now the silicony learned English by collecting a word here and a word there. It couldn't speak idiomatic English. Some of its statements, as quoted, show that. For instance, it said, 'the planet which is most far' instead of 'the farthest planet.' You see?"

"Well?"

"Someone who cannot speak a language idiomatically either uses the idioms of his own language translated word by word or else he simply uses foreign words according to their literal meaning. The silicony had no spoken language of its own so it could only make use of the second alternative. Let's be literal, then. He said, '*on* the asteroid,' Inspector. *On* it. He didn't mean on a piece of paper, he meant on the ship, literally."

"Dr. Urth," said Davenport sadly, "when the Bureau searches, it searches. There were no mysterious inscriptions *on* the ship either."

Dr. Urth looked disappointed. "Dear me, Inspector. I keep hoping you will see the answer. Really, you have had so many hints."

Davenport drew in a slow, firm breath. It went hard, but his voice was calm and even once more. "Will you tell me what you have in mind, Doctor?"

Dr. Urth patted his comfortable abdomen with one hand and replaced his glasses. "Don't you see, Inspector, that there is one place on board a spaceship where secret numbers are perfectly safe? Where, although in plain view, they would be perfectly safe from detection? Where though they were being stared at by a hundred eyes, they would be secure? Except from a seeker who is an astute thinker, of course."

"Where? Name the place!"

"Why, in those places where there happen to be numbers

already. Perfectly normal numbers. Legal numbers. Numbers that are supposed to be there."

"What are you talking about?"

"The ship's serial number, etched directly on the hull. *On* the hull, be it noted. The engine number, the field generator number. A few others. Each etched on integral portions of the ship. *On* the ship, as the silicony said. *On* the ship."

Davenport's heavy eyebrows rose with sudden comprehension. "You may be right—and if you are, I'm hoping we find you a silicony twice the size of the *Robert Q.*'s. One that not only talks, but whistles, 'Up, Asteroids, Forever!' " He hastily reached for the dossier, thumbed rapidly through it and extracted an official T.B.I. form. "Of course, we noted down all the identification numbers we found." He spread the form out. "If three of these resemble coordinates . . ."

"We should expect some small effort at disguise," Dr. Urth observed. "There will probably be certain letters and figures added to make the series appear more legitimate."

He reached for a scratch pad and shoved another toward the Inspector. For minutes the two men were silent, jotting down serial numbers, experimenting with crossing out obviously unrelated figures.

At last Davenport let out a sigh that mingled satisfaction and frustration. "I'm stuck," he admitted. "I think you're right; the numbers on the engine and the calculator are clearly disguised coordinates and dates. They don't run anywhere near the normal series, and it's easy to strike out the fake figures. That gives us two, but I'll take my oath the rest of these are absolutely legitimate serial numbers. What are your findings, Doctor?"

Dr. Urth nodded. "I agree. We now have two coordinates and we know where the third was inscribed."

"We know, do we? And how—" The Inspector broke off and uttered a sharp exclamation. "Of course! The number on the very ship itself, which isn't entered here—because it was on the precise spot on the hull where the meteor crashed through—I'm afraid there goes your silicony, Doctor." Then his craggy face brightened. "But I'm an idiot. The number's gone, but we can get it in a flash from Interplanetary Registry."

"I fear," said Dr. Urth, "that I must dispute at least the second part of your statement. Registry will have only the ship's original legitimate number, not the disguised coordinate to which the captain must have altered it."

"The exact spot on the hull," Davenport muttered. "And because of that chance shot the asteroid may be lost forever. What use to anybody are two coordinates without the third?"

"Well," said Dr. Urth precisely, "conceivably of very great use to a two-dimensional being. But creatures of our dimensions," he patted his paunch, "do require the third—which I fortunately happen to have right here."

"In the T.B.I. dossier? But we just checked the list of numbers—"

"*Your* list, Inspector. The file also includes young Vernadsky's original report. And of course the serial number listed there for the *Robert Q*. is the carefully faked one under which she was then sailing—no point in rousing the curiosity of a repair mechanic by letting him note a discrepancy."

Davenport reached for a scratch pad and the Vernadsky list. A moment's calculation and he grinned.

Dr. Urth lifted himself out of the chair with a pleased puff and trotted to the door. "It is always pleasant to see you, Inspector Davenport. Do come again. And remember the government can have the uranium, but I want the important thing: one giant silicony, alive and in good condition."

He was smiling.

"And preferably," said Davenport, "whistling."

Which he was doing himself as he walked out.

AFTERWORD

Of course, there is a catch about writing a mystery. You are apt to concentrate so hard on the mystery itself, on occasion, as to lose sight of important peripheral values.

After this story first appeared, I received quite a bit of mail expressing interest in the silicony and, in some cases, finding fault with me for allowing it to die in so cold-blooded a fashion.

As I reread the story, now I must admit the readers are right. I showed a lack of sensitivity to the silicony's rather pathetic death because I was concentrating on his mysterious last words. If I had to do it over again, I would certainly be warmer in my treatment of the poor thing.

I apologize.

This shows that even experienced writers don't always do the Right Thing, and can miss something that is bobbing up and down right at mustache level.

This next story is not, in the strictest sense of the word, a science fiction mystery, yet I include it. The reason is that science is closely and intimately involved with the mystery, and I hesitate to penalize it by non-inclusion merely because the science is of the present rather than of the future.

What's in a Name?

If you think it's hard to get hold of potassium cyanide, think again. I stood there with a pound bottle in my hand. Brown glass, a nice clear label saying "Potassium Cyanide CP" (the initials, I was told, meaning "chemically pure") with a small skull and crossbones underneath.

The fellow who owned the bottle polished his glasses and blinked at me. He was Associate Professor Helmuth Rodney of Carmody University. He was of middle height, stocky, with a soft chin, plump lips, a budding paunch, a shock of brown hair, and a look of complete indifference to the fact that I was holding in my hand enough poison to kill a regiment.

I said, "Do you mean to say this just stands on your shelf, Professor?"

He said in the kind of deliberate tone he probably used in lecturing his students, "Yes, it always has, Inspector. Along with the rest of the chemicals in alphabetic order."

I glanced about the cluttered room. Shelves lined the upper reaches of all the walls, and bottles, large and small, filled them all.

"This one," I pointed out, "is poison."

"A great many of them are," he said with composure.

"Do you keep track of what you've got?"

"In a general way." He rubbed his chin. "I know I have that bottle."

"But suppose someone came in here and helped himself to a spoonful of this stuff. Would you be able to tell?"

Professor Rodney shook his head. "I couldn't possibly."

"Well, then, who could get into this laboratory? Is it kept locked?"

He said, "It's locked when I leave in the evening, unless I forget. During the day, it isn't locked, and I'm in and out."

"In other words, Professor, anyone could come in here, even someone from the street, walk off with some of the cyanide, and no one would ever know."

"I'm afraid so."

"Tell me, Professor, why do you keep this much cyanide in the place anyway? To kill rats?"

"Good heavens, no." He seemed faintly repelled at the thought. "Cyanide is sometimes used in organic reactions to form necessary intermediates, to provide a proper basic medium, to catalyze—"

"I see. I see. Now in what other labs is cyanide available in this way?"

"In most of them," he answered at once. "Even in the student labs. After all, it's a common chemical, routinely used in syntheses."

"I wouldn't call its use today routine," I said.

He sighed and said, "No, I suppose not." He added thoughtfully, "They used to call them the 'Library Twins.'"

I nodded. I could see the reason for the nickname. The two girl librarians were very alike.

Not close up, of course. One had a small pointed chin on a round face, and the other had a square jaw and a long nose.

Still, bend them over a desk and both had honey-blond hair parted in the middle, with a similar wave. Look them quickly in the face and you would probably notice first wide-set eyes of about the same shade of blue. See them standing together at a moderate distance and you could see they were both of a height and both, probably, with the same brand and size up-lift brassière. Both had trim waists and neat legs. Today they had even dressed similarly. Both wore blue.

There was no confusing the two now, though. The one with the small chin and round face was full of cyanide, and quite dead.

The similarity was the first thing that struck me when I arrived with my partner, Ed Hathaway. There was one girl slumped in her chair and dead, her eyes open, one arm dangling straight down, with a broken teacup on the floor beneath like a period under an exclamation point. Her name, it turned out, was Louella-Marie Busch. There was a second girl, like the first one brought back to life, white and shaken, staring straight ahead and letting the police and their work flow about her without seeming to notice. Her name was Susan Morey.

The first question I asked was, "Relatives?"

They weren't. Not even second cousins.

I looked about the library. There were whole shelves of books in similar bindings, then other shelves with books in another set of bindings. They were volumes of different research journals. In another room were stacks of what I found later to be textbooks, monographs, and older books. In the back was a special alcove containing recent numbers of un-bound research periodicals in dull and closely printed paper covers. From wall to wall were long tables that might have seated a hundred people if all were fully occupied. Fortunately that wasn't the case.

We got the story out of Susan Morey in flat, toneless pieces.

Mrs. Nettler, the old Senior Librarian, had taken off for the afternoon and had left the two girls in charge. That, appar-ently, was not unusual.

At two o'clock, give or take five minutes, Louella-Marie took herself into the back room behind the library desk. There, in addition to new books that awaited cataloguing, stacks of periodicals that awaited binding, reserved books that awaited their reservers, there was also a small hot-plate, a small kettle, and the fixings for weak tea.

Two o'clock tea was apparently usual, too.

I said, "Did Louella-Marie prepare the tea every day?"

Susan looked at me out of her blank blue eyes. "Sometimes Mrs. Nettler does, but usually Lou—Louella-Marie did."

When the tea was ready, Louella-Marie emerged to say so and after a few moments the two retired.

"Both of you?" I asked sharply. "Who took care of the library?"

Susan shrugged as though this were a minor point to worry about, and said, "We can see out the door. If anyone came to the desk, one of us could have gone out."

"Did anyone come to the desk?"

"No one. It's intersession. Hardly anyone's around."

By intersession she meant that the spring semester was over and the summer sessions had not yet started. I learned quite a bit about college life that day.

What was left of the story was little enough. The tea bags were already out of the gently steaming cups and the sugar had been added.

I interrupted. "You both take sugar?"

Susan said slowly, "Yes. But mine didn't have any."

"No?"

"She never forgot before. She knows I take it. I just took a sip or two and I was going to reach for the sugar and tell her, you know, when—"

When Louella-Marie gave a queer strangled cry, dropped the cup, and was dead in a minute.

After that Susan screamed and eventually we came.

The routine passed smoothly enough. Photographs and fingerprints had been taken. The names and addresses of the men and women in the building were taken and they were sent home. Cause of death was obviously cyanide and the sugar bowl was the obvious villain. Samples were taken for official testing.

There had been six men in the library at the time of the murder. Five were students, who looked frightened, confused, or sick, depending, I suppose, on their personalities. The sixth was a middle-aged man, an outsider, who talked with a German accent and had no connection with the college at all. He looked frightened, confused, and sick, all three.

My sidekick, Hathaway, was leading them out of the library. The idea was to get them to the Co-educational Lounge and have them stay put till we could get to them in detail.

One of the students broke away and strode past me without a glance. Susan flew to meet him, clutching each sleeve above the elbow. "Pete. Pete."

Pete was built like a football player except that his profile looked as though he had never been within half a mile of the playing field. He was too good-looking for my taste, but then I get jealous easily.

Pete was looking past the girl, his face coming apart at the seams till its prettiness was drowned in uneasy horror. He said in a hoarse, choking way, "How did Lolly come to . . ."

Susan gasped, "I don't know. I don't know." She kept trying to meet his eye.

Pete pulled away. He never looked at Susan once, kept staring over her shoulder. Then he responded to Hathaway's grip on his elbow and let himself be led away.

I said, "Boy friend?"

Susan tore her eyes from the departing student. "What?"

"Is he your boy friend?"

She looked down at her twisting hands. "We've been out on dates."

"How serious?"

She whispered, "Pretty serious."

"Does he know the other girl, too? He called her Lolly?"

Susan shrugged. "Well . . ."

"Let's put it this way. Did he go out with her?"

"Sometimes."

"Seriously."

She snapped, "How should I know?"

"Come on, now. Was she jealous of you?"

"What's all this about?"

"Someone put the cyanide in the sugar and put the mixture in only one cup. Suppose Louella-Marie was jealous enough of you to try to poison you and leave herself a clear field with our friend Pete. And suppose she took the wrong teacup herself by mistake."

Susan said, "That's crazy. Louella-Marie wouldn't do such a thing."

But her lips were thin, her eyes sparkled, and I can tell hate in a voice when I hear it.

Professor Rodney came into the library. He was the first man I had met on entering the building and my feelings toward him had grown no warmer.

He had begun by informing me that as senior faculty member present, he was in charge.

I said, "I'm in charge now, Professor."

He said, "Of the investigation perhaps, Inspector, but it is I who am responsible to the Dean and I propose to fulfill my responsibilities."

And although he hadn't the figure of an aristocrat, more like a shopkeeper, if you follow me, he managed to look at me as though there were a microscope between us with himself on the large side.

Now he said, "Mrs. Nettler is in my office. She heard the news bulletin, apparently, and came at once. She is quite agitated. You will see her?" He made it sound like an order.

"Bring her in, Professor." I made it sound like permission.

Mrs. Nettler was in the usual quandary of the average old lady. She didn't know whether to be horrified or fascinated at the closeness with which death had struck. Horror won out after she looked into the inner office and noticed what was left of the tea things. The body was gone by then, of course.

She flopped into a chair and began crying. "I had tea here myself," she moaned. "It might have been . . ."

I said as quietly and soothingly as I could manage, "When did you drink tea here, Mrs. Nettler?"

She turned in her seat, looked up. "Why—why, just after one, I think. I offered Professor Rodney a cup, I remember. It was just after one, Professor Rodney, wasn't it?"

A trace of annoyance crossed Rodney's plump face. He said to me, "I was here a moment just after lunch to consult a reference. Mrs. Nettler did offer a cup. I was too busy, I'm afraid, to accept or to note the time exactly."

I grunted and turned back to the old lady. "Do you take sugar, Mrs. Nettler?"

"Yes, sir."

"*Did* you take sugar?"

She nodded and started crying again.

I waited a bit. Then, "Did you notice the condition of the sugar bowl?"

"It was—it was—" A sudden surprise at the question seemed to put her on her feet. "It was empty and I filled it myself. I used the two-pound box of granulated sugar and I remember saying to myself that whenever I wanted tea the sugar was gone and I wished the girls would—"

Maybe it was the mention of the girls in the plural. She broke out again.

I nodded to Hathaway to lead her away.

Between 1 and 2 P.M., obviously, someone had emptied the sugar bowl and then added just a bit of laced sugar—very neatly laced sugar.

Maybe it was Mrs. Nettler's appearance that pumped librarianship back into Susan, because when Hathaway came back and reached for one of his cigars—he already had the match lit—the girl said, "No smoking in the library, sir."

Hathaway was so surprised he blew the match out and replaced the cigar in his pocket.

Then the girl stepped briskly to one of the long tables and reached for a large volume that lay open on it.

Hathaway was ahead of her. "What are you going to do, Miss?"

Susan looked completely astonished. "I'm just going to put it back on the shelves."

"Why? What is it?" He looked down at the open page. I was there too, by then. I looked over his shoulder.

It was German. I can't read the language, but I can recognize it when I see it. The printing was small, and there were geometrical figures on the page with lines of letters attached at various places. I knew enough, too, to know those were chemical formulas.

I put my finger in the place, closed the book and looked at the backstrap. It said, "Beilstein—Organische Chemie—Band VI—System Nummer 499–608." I opened to the page again. It was 233 and the first words, just to give you an idea, were 4'-chlor-4-brom-2-nitrodiphenyläther-$C_{12}H_7O_3NC1Br$.

Hathaway was busy copying things down.

Professor Rodney was at the table too, which made four of us all gathered round the book.

The professor said in a cool voice, as though he were on a platform with a pointer in one hand and a piece of chalk in the other, "This is a volume of Beilstein." (He pronounced it Bile-shtine.) "It's a kind of encyclopedia of organic compounds. It lists hundreds of thousands of them."

"In this book?" demanded Hathaway.

"This book is only one of more than sixty volumes and supplementary volumes. It is a tremendous German work which is years out of date because, first, organic chemistry is progressing at an ever-increasing pace and, second, because of the interference of politics and war. Even so, there is nothing even faintly approaching its usefulness in English. For all research men in organic chemistry, these volumes are an absolute necessity."

The professor actually patted the book as he spoke, a fond pat. "Before dealing with any unfamiliar compound," he said, "it is good practice to look it up in Beilstein. It will give you methods of preparation, properties, references, and so on. It acts as a starting point. The various compounds are listed according to a logical system which is clear but not obvious. I myself give several lectures in my course on organic syntheses which deal entirely with methods for finding a particular compound somewhere in the sixty volumes."

I don't know how long he might have continued, but I wasn't there to learn organic syntheses and it was time to get down to cases. I said abruptly, "Professor, I want to speak to you in your laboratory."

I suppose I had some notion that cyanide was kept in a safe, that every bit of it was accounted for, that people had to sign out for it when they wanted some. I thought the question of opportunity to get some illicitly might supply what proof we needed.

And there I stood with a pound of it in my hand and the knowledge that anyone could have any amount for the asking, or without asking.

And he said thoughtfully, "They used to call them the 'Library Twins.'"

I nodded. "So?"

"Only that it proves how superficial the judgment of most

people is. There was nothing alike about them except the accident of hair and eyes. What happened in the library, Inspector?"

I told him Susan's story briefly and watched him.

He shook his head. "I suppose you think the dead girl planned murder."

My thoughts weren't for sale at the moment. I said, "Don't you?"

"No. She was incapable of it. Her attitude toward her duties was a pleasant and helpful one. Besides, why would she?"

"There's a student," I said. "Peter is his first name."

"Peter van Norden," he said at once. "A reasonably bright student, but, somehow, worthless."

"Girls look at these things differently, Professor. Both librarians were apparently interested. Susan may have been the more successful and Louella-Marie may have decided on direct measures."

"And then proceeded to take the wrong cup?"

I said, "People do queer things under tension."

"Not this queer," he said. "One cup was left unsugared, so the murderess wasn't taking chances. Presumably even if she had not carefully memorized which cup was which, she could count on the sweetness t give it away. She could easily have avoided a fatal dose."

I said dryly, "Both girls usually took sugar. The dead girl was used to sweet tea. In the excitement the accustomed sweetness didn't ring a bell."

"I don't believe it."

"What's the alternative, Professor? The sugar was ho-cused after Mrs. Nettler's tea at one o'clock. Did Mrs. Nettler do it?"

He looked up sharply. "What possible motive?"

I shrugged. "She might have been afraid the girls were going to be taking her job away."

"That's nonsense. She's retiring before the fall session begins."

"You were there, Professor," I said softly.

He took it in stride, to my surprise. "Motive?" he said.

I said, "You're not too old to have been interested in Louella-Marie, Professor. Suppose she had threatened to report some word or act of yours to the Dean."

The professor smiled bitterly. "How did I manage to make sure the right girl got the cyanide? Why should one cup remain unsugared? I may have hocused the sugar but I didn't prepare the tea."

I began to change my mind about Professor Rodney. He hadn't bothered to work up indignation or register shock. He simply pointed out the logical weakness and let it go at that. I liked that.

I said, "What do you think happened?"

He said, "The mirror-image. The reverse. I think the survivor told the truth inside out. Suppose it was Louella-Marie who was getting the boy and Susan who didn't like it, rather than the reverse. Suppose it was Susan who for once was preparing the tea and Louella-Marie who was at the front desk rather than the reverse. In that case, the girl who prepared the tea would have taken the right cup and remained safe. Everything would be logical instead of ridiculously improbable."

That did it. The man had come to the same conclusion I had and so I had to like him after all. I have a habit of feeling soft toward guys who agree with me. It comes of being Homo sapiens, I think.

I said, "We've got to prove that beyond reasonable doubt. How? I'd come up here, hoping to prove someone had had access to potassium cyanide and others had not. That's out. Everyone had access. Now what?"

The professor said, "Check on which girl was really at the desk at two o'clock when the tea was being prepared."

It was obvious to me that the professor read detective stories and had faith in witnesses. I didn't, but I got up anyway.

"All right, Professor. I'll do that."

The professor rose also. He said urgently, "May I be present?"

I considered. "Why? Your responsibilities to the Dean?"

"In a way. I would like to see a quick, clean end to this."

I said, "Come along, if you think that will help."

Ed Hathaway was waiting for me when I came down. He was sitting in an empty library. He said, "I got it."

"Got what?" I wanted to know.

"How it happened. I figured it out by deduction."

"Oh?"

He was paying no attention to Professor Rodney. "The cyanide had to be smuggled in. By whom? By the joker in the deck, the outsider, the guy with the accent—whatzisname."

He started scrabbling through a series of cards on which he had filed information on the various presumably innocent bystanders.

I knew who he meant so I said, "All right, never mind the name. What's in a name? Go on"—which shows that I can be as unbright as anyone.

"All right. The foreigner comes in with the cyanide in a little envelope. He tapes the envelope to a page in the German book, that organish whatzisname with all the volumes . . ."

The professor and I both nodded.

Hathaway went on. "He was German, so was the book. He was probably familiar with it. He put the envelope on a prearranged page according to a particular formula that had been picked out. The professor said there was a way to find any formula if you only knew how. Isn't that right, Professor?"

"That is right," said Rodney coldly.

"All right. The librarian knew the formula so she could find the page too. She picks up the cyanide and uses it for the tea. In the excitement, she forgets to close the book—"

I said, "Look, Hathaway. Why should that little guy be doing this? What's his excuse for being here?"

"He says he's a furrier reading up on moth repellents and insecticides. Now isn't that phony right off? Ever hear anything so phony?"

"Sure," I said, "your theory. Look, no one is going to hide an envelope with cyanide in a book. You don't have to find a particular formula or page with an envelope bulging a volume out of shape. Anyone who took the volume off the shelf would find that the book would fall open to the right page automatically. A hell of a hiding place."

Hathaway began to look foolish.

I drove on pitilessly, "Besides, cyanide doesn't have to be smuggled in from the outside. They've got tons of it here. They can use it to make snow-slides. Anyone who wants a pound or two can help himself."

"What?"

"Ask the professor."

Hathaway's eyes widened and then he fumbled in his jacket pocket and drew out an envelope. "Then what do I do with this?"

"What is it?"

He took out a printed page with German on it and said, "It's the page out of that German volume that—"

Professor Rodney grew suddenly scarlet. "You tore a page out of Beilstein?"

He shrieked it and surprised the hell out of me. I wouldn't have thought him capable of shrieking.

Hathaway said, "I thought we could test it for stickum from the scotch tape, or maybe for a little cyanide that leaked out."

"Give it to me!" yelled the professor. "You ignorant fool."

He smoothed out the sheet and looked at both sides as though to make sure that none of the print had been rubbed off.

"Vandal!" he said, and I'm sure that at the moment he could have killed Hathaway and laughed during the entire process.

Professor Rodney might be morally certain of Susan's guilt and so, for that matter, might I. Nevertheless, moral certainty cannot be taken before a jury. Evidence was needed.

So, lacking faith in witnesses, I attacked through the one weakness of any possibly guilty person—the possibly guilty person.

I brought her in to witness the new line of questioning, and if the questioning didn't pin her to her guilt, her own nerves might.

From her appearance I couldn't tell how good that "might" would be. Susan Morey sat at her desk, hands clasped before her, eyes cold, and the skin around her nostrils tight-looking.

The little German furrier was in first, looking sick with worry. "I did nothing," he babbled. "Please. I have business. How long must I stay?"

Hathaway had his name and vital statistics, so I skipped all that and got to the point.

"You came here a little before two o'clock. Right?"

"Yes. I wanted to know about moth repellents—"

"All right. When you came in you went to the desk. Right?"

"Yes. I told her my name, who I was, what I wanted—"

"Told whom?" That was the key question.

The little fellow stared at me. He had curly hair and a mouth that fell in as though he were toothless, but that was just appearance, for when he talked, small yellow teeth were plainly visible. He said, "Her. I told her. The girl sitting there."

"That's right," said Susan tonelessly. "He spoke to me."

Professor Rodney was gazing at her with a look of concentrated detestation. It occurred to me that his reason for wishing to see justice done quickly might be more personal than idealistic at that. However, that was none of my business.

I said to the furrier, "Are you *sure* this is the girl?"

He said, "Yes. I told her my name and my business, and she smiled. She told me where to find books on insecticides. Then, as I was stepping away, another girl came out from inside there."

"Good!" I said at once. "Now here's a photograph of another girl. Tell me, was it the girl at the desk you spoke to and the girl in the photograph who came out of the back room? Or was it the girl in the photograph you spoke to and the girl at the desk who came out of the back room?"

For a long minute, the furrier stared at the girl, then at the photograph, then at me. "They are alike."

I swore to myself. The faintest smile had passed over Susan's lips, hovering there a moment before vanishing. She must have counted on this. It was intersession. Hardly anyone would be in the library. None of them would pay much attention to the librarians who are fixtures like the bookshelves, and if any did, he could never swear which of the Library Twins he had seen.

I *knew* she was guilty now, but knowing meant nothing.

I said, "Well, which was it?"

He said, like one anxious to put an end to questioning, "I spoke to her, the girl right there at the desk."

"That's right," said Susan, perfectly calm.

My hope in her nerves hit bottom.

I said to the furrier, "Would you swear?"

He said at once, "No."

"All right. Hathaway, take him away. Send him home."

Professor Rodney leaned over to touch my elbow. He whispered, "Why did she smile at the fellow when he stated his business?"

I whispered back, "Why not?" but put the question to her anyway.

Her eyebrows went up a fraction of an inch. "I was just being pleasant. Is there anything wrong with that?"

She was almost enjoying herself. I could swear to that.

The professor shook his head slightly. He whispered to me again, "She's not the type to smile at a troublesome stranger. It had to be Louella-Marie at the desk."

I shrugged. I could see myself bringing that kind of evidence to the Commissioner.

Four of the students were a blank and took up little time. They were engaged in research, they knew what books they wanted, what shelves the books would be on. They went straight there without stopping at the desk. None could say whether Susan or Louella-Marie had been at the desk at any particular time. None had even looked up from their books, to hear them tell it, before the scream roused everything.

The fifth was Peter van Norden. He kept his eyes fixed firmly on his right thumb, which had a badly bitten nail. He did not look up at Susan as he was brought in.

I let him sit awhile and soften up.

Finally I said, "What are you doing here this time of year? I understand it's between sessions."

He muttered, "My Qualifyings are coming up next month. I'm studying. Qualifying examinations. If I pass, I can go on for my Ph.D., see?"

I said, "I suppose you stopped at the desk when you came in here?"

He mumbled.

I said, "What?"

He said in a low voice that was hardly an improvement, "I didn't. I don't think I stopped at the desk."

"You don't *think?*"

"I didn't."

I said, "Isn't that strange? I understand you're good friends of both Susan and Louella-Marie. Don't you say hello?"

"I was worried. I had this test in my mind. I had to study. I—"

"So you couldn't even take time out for a hello." I looked at Susan to see how this was going over. She seemed paler, but that might have been my imagination.

I said, "Isn't it true that you were practically engaged to one of them?"

He looked up with uneasy indignation. *"No!* I can't get engaged before I get my degree. Who told you I was engaged?"

"I said practically engaged."

"No! I had a few dates, maybe. So what! What's a date or two?"

I said smoothly, "Come on, Pete, which one was your girl?"

"I tell you it wasn't like that."

He was washing his hands of the whole matter so hard, he seemed buried and smothered in an invisible lather.

"How about it?" I asked suddenly, addressing Susan. "Did he stop at your desk?"

"He waved as he passed," she said.

"Did you, Pete?"

"I don't remember," he said sullenly. "Maybe I did. So what?"

"Nothing," I said. Inside me, I wished Susan joy of her bargain. If she had killed for the sake of this specimen, she had done it for nothing. To me it seemed a certainty that henceforward he would ignore her even if she fell off a two-story building and hit him on the head.

Susan must have realized that too. From the look she was giving Peter van Norden, I marked him down as a second candidate for cyanide—assuming she went free—and it certainly seemed as though she would.

I nodded to Hathaway to take him away. Hathaway rose to do that and said, "Say, you ever use those books?" and he pointed to the shelves where the sixty-odd volumes of the organic chemistry encyclopedia stretched from floor to ceiling.

The boy looked over his shoulder and said in honest astonishment. "Sure. I've got to. Lord, is something wrong with looking up compounds in Beilst—"

"It's all right," I assured him. "Come on, Ed."

Ed Hathaway scowled at me and led the boy out. He hates letting go of an exploded theory.

It was about six and I didn't see that anything more could be done. As it stood, it was Susan's word against no word. If she had been a hood with a record, we could have sweated out the truth in any of several effective, if tedious, ways. In this case, such a procedure was inadvisable.

I turned to the professor to say so, but he was staring at Hathaway's cards. At one of them, anyway, which he was holding in his hand. You know, people always talk about other people's hands shaking with excitement, but it's something you don't often see. Rodney's hand was shaking, though, shaking like the clapper of an old-fashioned alarm clock.

He cleared his throat. "Let me ask her something. Let me . . ."

I stared at him, then pushed my chair back. "Go ahead," I said. At this point, there was nothing to lose.

He looked at the girl, putting the card down on the desk, blank side up.

He said shakily, "Miss Morey?" He seemed to be deliberately avoiding the familiarity of her first name.

She stared at him. For a moment she had seemed nervous, but that passed and she was calm again. "Yes, Professor?"

The professor said, "Miss Morey, you smiled when the furrier told you his business here. Why was that?"

"I told you, Professor Rodney," she said, "I was being pleasant."

"Perhaps there was something peculiar about what he said? Something amusing?"

"I was just trying to be pleasant," she insisted.

"Perhaps you found his name amusing, Miss Morey?"

"Not particularly," she said indifferently.

"Well, no one has mentioned his name here. I didn't know it till I happened to look at this card." Then suddenly, tensely, he cried, "What *was* his name, Miss Morey?"

She paused before answering, "I don't remember."

"You *don't*? He gave it to you, didn't he?"

There was an edge to her voice now. "What if he did? It's just a name. After all that's happened, you can't expect me to remember some peculiar foreign name I happened to hear one time."

"It was *foreign*, then?"

She pulled up short, avoiding the trap. "I don't remember," she said. "I think it was a typically German name, but I don't remember. For all I know it was John Smith."

I had to admit I didn't see the professor's point. I said, "What are you trying to prove, Professor Rodney?"

"I'm trying to prove," he said tightly, "in fact I *am* proving, that it was Louella-Marie, the dead girl, who was at the desk when the furrier came in. He announced his name to Louella-Marie and she smiled in consequence. It was Miss Morey who was coming out of the inner office as he turned away. It was Miss Morey, *this* girl, who had just finished preparing and poisoning the tea."

"You're basing that on the fact I can't remember a man's name!" shrilled Susan Morey. "That's ridiculous."

"No, it isn't," said the professor. "If you had been the girl at the desk, you would remember his name. It would be *impossible* for you to forget it. *If* you were the girl at the desk." He was holding Hathaway's card up now. He said, "That furrier's first name is Ernest, but his last name is Beilstein. *His name is Beilstein!*"

The air went out of Susan as though she had been kicked in the stomach. She turned white as talcum powder.

The professor went on intensely, "No chemical librarian could possibly forget the name of anyone who came in and announced himself to be Beilstein. The sixty-volume encyclopedia we've mentioned half a dozen times today is referred to invariably by the name of its editor, Beilstein. The name is like Mother Goose to a chemical librarian, like George Washington, like Christopher Columbus. It is more second nature to her than any of them.

"If this girl claims to have forgotten the name, it is only because she never heard it. And she never heard it because she wasn't at the desk."

I rose and said grimly, "Well, Miss Morey"—I abandoned the first name too—"what about it?"

She was screaming in earsplitting hysteria. Half an hour later we had her confession.

Some years before this next story was written, two colleagues and I joined forces in writing a large and complicated textbook in biochemistry for medical students. We spent days—literally—on the galley proofs, and frequently we came across minor inconsistencies. We would spell a chemical one way here and another way there; here a hyphen and there no hyphen; here one phrase and yon an alternate.

We despaired of getting everything perfectly concordant and one of us finally said, "To quote Emerson: 'A foolish consistency is the hobgoblin of little minds.'"

We latched on to this with ebullient joy and thereafter, whenever the proofreader questioned a small inconsistency, we would write "Emerson!" in the margin and let it go.

Well, the following story revolves about the possible invention of mass transference, and in preparing these stories for inclusion in this volume, I noted that in "The Singing Bell"—an earlier story with the same background —mass transference was taken for granted as already existing.

I was about to make certain changes to eliminate that discrepancy, when I remembered. So if you don't mind, Gentle Reader, I cry "Emerson!" and pass on.

The Dying Night

It was almost a class reunion, and though it was marked by joylessness, there was no reason as yet to think it would be marred by tragedy.

Edward Talliaferro, fresh from the Moon and without his gravity legs yet, met the other two in Stanley Kaunas' room. Kaunas rose to greet him in a subdued manner. Battersley Ryger merely sat and nodded.

Talliaferro lowered his large body carefully to the couch, very aware of its unaccustomed weight. He grimaced a little, his plump lips twisting inside the rim of hair that surrounded them on lip, chin, and cheek.

They had seen one another earlier that day under more formal conditions. Now for the first time they were alone and Talliaferro said, "This is a kind of occasion. We're meeting for the first time in ten years. First time since graduation, in fact."

Ryger's nose twitched. It had been broken shortly before that same graduation and he had received his degree in astronomy with a bandage disfiguring his face. He said grumpily, "Anyone ordered champagne? Or something?"

Talliaferro said, "Come on! First big interplanetary astronomical convention in history is no place for glooming. And among friends, too!"

Kaunas said suddenly, "It's Earth. It doesn't feel right. I can't get used to it." He shook his head but his look of depression remained.

Talliaferro said, "I know. I'm so heavy. It takes all the energy out of me. At that, you're better off than I am, Kaunas. Mercurian gravity is 0.4 normal. On the Moon, it's only 0.16." He interrupted Ryger's beginning of a sound by saying, "And on Ceres they use pseudo-grav fields adjusted to 0.8. You have no problems at all, Ryger."

The Cerian astronomer looked annoyed. "It's the open air. Going outside without a suit gets me."

"Right," agreed Kaunas. "And letting the Sun beat down on you. Just letting it."

Talliaferro found himself insensibly drifting back in time. They had not changed much. Nor, he thought, had he himself. They were all ten years older, of course. Ryger had put on some weight and Kaunas' thin face had grown a bit leathery, but he would have recognized either if he had met him without warning.

He said, "I don't think it's Earth getting us. Let's face it."

Kaunas looked up sharply. He was a little fellow with quick, nervous movements of his hands and habitually wore clothes that looked a shade too large for him.

He said, "Villiers! I know. I think about him sometimes." Then, with an air of desperation, "I got a letter from him."

Ryger sat upright, his olive complexion darkening further, and said with energy, "You did? When?"

"A month ago."

Ryger turned to Talliaferro. "How about you?"

Talliaferro blinked placidly and nodded.

Ryger said, "He's gone crazy. He claims he's discovered a practical method of mass transference through space.—He told you two also?—That's it, then. He was always a little bent. Now he's broken."

He rubbed his nose fiercely and Talliaferro thought of the day Villiers had broken it.

For ten years Villiers had haunted them like the vague shadow of a guilt that wasn't really theirs. They had gone through their graduate work together, four picked and dedicated men being trained for a profession that had reached new heights in this age of interplanetary travel.

The observatories were opening on the other worlds, surrounded by vacuum, unblurred by air.

There was the Lunar Observatory, from which Earth and the inner planets could be studied; a silent world in whose sky the home planet hung suspended.

Mercury Observatory, closest to the Sun, perched at Mercury's north pole, where the terminator moved scarcely at all, and the Sun was fixed on the horizon and could be studied in the minutest detail.

Ceres Observatory, newest, most modern, with its range extending from Jupiter to the outermost galaxies.

There were disadvantages, of course. With interplanetary travel still difficult, leaves would be few, anything like normal life virtually impossible, but this was a lucky generation. Coming scientists would find the fields of knowledge well reaped and, until the invention of an interstellar drive, no new horizon as capacious as this one would be opened.

These lucky four, Talliaferro, Ryger, Kaunas, and Villiers, were to be in the position of a Galileo, who, by virtue of owning the first real telescope, could not point it anywhere in the sky without making a major discovery.

But then Romano Villiers had fallen sick and it was rheumatic fever. Whose fault was that? His heart had been left leaking and limping.

He was the most brilliant of the four, the most hopeful, the most intense—and he could not even finish his schooling and get his doctorate.

Worse than that, he could never leave Earth; the acceleration of a spaceship's takeoff would kill him.

Talliaferro was marked for the Moon, Ryger for Ceres, Kaunas for Mercury. Only Villiers stayed behind, a life prisoner of Earth.

They had tried telling their pity and Villiers had rejected it with something approaching hate. He had railed at them and cursed them. When Ryger lost his temper and lifted his fist, Villiers had sprung at him screaming and broken his nose.

Obviously Ryger hadn't forgotten that, as he caressed his nose gingerly with one finger.

Kaunas' forehead was an uncertain washboard of wrinkles. "He's at the Convention, you know. He's got a room in the hotel—405."

"*I* won't see him," said Ryger.

"He's coming up here. He said he wanted to see us. I thought he said nine. He'll be here any minute."

"In that case," said Ryger, "if you don't mind, I'm leaving."

Talliaferro said, "Oh, wait awhile. What's the harm in seeing him?"

"Because there's no point. He's insane."

"Even so. Let's not be petty about it. Are you afraid of him?"

"Afraid!" Ryger looked contemptuous.

"Nervous, then. What is there to be so nervous about?"

"I'm not nervous," said Ryger.

"Sure you are. We all feel guilty about him, and without real reason. Nothing that happened was our fault." But he was speaking defensively and he knew it.

And when, at that point, the door signal sounded, all three jumped and turned to stare uneasily at the barrier that stood between themselves and Villiers.

The door opened and Romano Villiers walked in. The others rose stiffly to greet him, then remained standing in embarrassment, without one hand being raised.

He stared them down sardonically.

He's changed, thought Talliaferro.

He had. He had shrunk in almost every dimension. A gathering stoop even made him seem shorter. The skin of his scalp glistened through thinning hair, the skin on the back of his hands was ridged crookedly with bluish veins. He looked ill. There seemed nothing to link him to the memory of the past except for his trick of shading his eyes with one hand when he stared intently and, when he spoke, the even, controlled baritone of his voice.

He said, "My friends! My space-trotting friends! We've lost touch."

Talliaferro said, "Hello, Villiers."

Villiers eyed him. "Are you well?"

"Well enough."

"And you two?"

Kaunas managed a weak smile and a murmur. Ryger snapped, "All right, Villiers. What's up?"

"Ryger, the angry man," said Villiers. "How's Ceres?"

"It was doing well when I left. How's Earth?"

"You can see for yourself," but Villiers tightened as he said that.

He went on, "I am hoping that the reason all three of you have come to the Convention is to hear my paper day after tomorrow."

"Your paper? What paper?" asked Talliaferro.

"I wrote you all about it. My method of mass transference."

Ryger smiled with one corner of his mouth. "Yes, you did. You didn't say anything about a paper, though, and I don't recall that you're listed as one of the speakers. I would have noticed it if you had been."

"You're right. I'm not listed. Nor have I prepared an abstract for publication."

Villiers had flushed and Talliaferro said soothingly, "Take it easy, Villiers. You don't look well."

Villiers whirled on him, lips contorted. "My heart's holding out, thank you."

Kaunas said, "Listen, Villiers, if you're not listed or abstracted—"

"*You* listen. I've waited ten years. You have the jobs in space and I have to teach school on Earth, but I'm a better man than any of you or all of you."

"Granted—" began Talliaferro.

"And I don't want your condescension, either. Mandel witnessed it. I suppose you've heard of Mandel. Well, he's chairman of the astronautics division at the Convention and I demonstrated mass transference for him. It was a crude device and it burned out after one use but— Are you listening?"

"We're listening," said Ryger coldly. "For what that counts."

"He'll let me talk about it my way. You bet he will. No warning. No advertisement. I'm going to spring it at them like a bombshell. When I give them the fundamental relationships involved it will break up the Convention. They'll scatter to their home labs to check on me and build devices. And they'll find it works. I made a live mouse disappear at one spot in my lab and appear in another. Mandel witnessed it."

He stared at them, glaring first at one face, then at another. He said, "You don't believe me, do you?"

Ryger said, "If you don't want advertisement, why do you tell us?"

"You're different. You're my friends, my classmates. You went out into space and left me behind."

"That wasn't a matter of choice," objected Kaunas in a thin, high voice.

Villiers ignored that. He said, "So I want you to know *now*. What will work for a mouse will work for a human. What will move something ten feet across a lab will move it a million miles across space. I'll be on the Moon, *and* on Mercury, *and* on Ceres and anywhere I want to go. I'll match every one of you and more. And I'll have done more for astronomy just teaching school and thinking than all of you with your observatories and telescopes and cameras and spaceships."

"Well," said Talliaferro, "I'm pleased. More power to you. May I see a copy of the paper?"

"Oh, no." Villiers' hands clenched close to his chest as though he were holding phantom sheets and shielding them from observation. "You wait like everyone else. There's only one copy and no one will see it till I'm ready. Not even Mandel."

"One copy!" cried Talliaferro. "If you misplace it—"

"I won't. And if I do, it's all in my head."

"If you—" Talliaferro almost finished that sentence with "die" but stopped himself. Instead, he went on after an almost imperceptible pause, "—have any sense, you'll scan it at least. For safety's sake."

"No," said Villiers shortly. "You'll hear me day after tomorrow. You'll see the human horizon expanded at one stroke as it never has been before."

Again he stared intently at each face. "Ten years," he said. "Good-bye."

"He's mad," said Ryger explosively, staring at the door as though Villiers were still standing before it.

"Is he?" said Talliaferro thoughtfully. "I suppose he is, in a way. He hates us for irrational reasons. And, then, not even to scan his paper as a precaution . . ."

Talliaferro fingered his own small scanner as he said that. It was just a neutrally colored, undistinguished cylinder, somewhat thicker and somewhat shorter than an ordinary pencil. In recent years it had become the hallmark of the scientist, much as the stethoscope was that of the physician and the microcomputer that of the statistician. The scanner was worn in a jacket pocket, or clipped to a sleeve, or slipped behind the ear or swung at the end of a string.

Talliaferro sometimes, in his more philosophical moments, wondered how it was in the days when research men had to make laborious notes of the literature or file away full-sized reprints. How unwieldy!

Now it was only necessary to scan anything printed or

written to have a micronegative which could be developed at leisure. Talliaferro had already recorded every abstract included in the program booklet of the Convention. The other two, he assumed with full confidence, had done likewise.

Talliaferro said, "Under the circumstances, refusal to scan is mad."

"Space!" said Ryger hotly. "There is no paper. There is no discovery. Scoring one on us would be worth any lie to him."

"But then what will he do day after tomorrow?" asked Kaunas.

"How do I know? He's a madman."

Talliaferro still played with his scanner and wondered idly if he ought to remove and develop some of the small slivers of film that lay stored away in its vitals. He decided against it. He said, "Don't underestimate Villiers. He's a brain."

"Ten years ago, maybe," said Ryger. "Now he's a nut. I propose we forget him."

He spoke loudly, as though to drive away Villiers and all that concerned him by the sheer force with which he discussed other things. He talked about Ceres and his work—the radio plotting of the Milky Way with new radioscopes capable of the resolution of single stars.

Kaunas listened and nodded, then chimed in with information concerning the radio emissions of sunspots and his own paper, in press, on the association of proton storms with the gigantic hydrogen flares on the Sun's surface.

Talliaferro contributed little. Lunar work was unglamorous in comparison. The latest information on long-scale weather forecasting through direct observation of terrestrial jet streams would not compare with radioscopes and proton storms.

More than that, his thoughts could not leave Villiers. Villiers *was* the brain. They all knew it. Even Ryger, for all his bluster, must feel that if mass transference were at all possible then Villiers was a logical discoverer.

The discussion of their own work amounted to no more than an uneasy admission that none of them had come to much. Talliaferro had followed the literature and knew. His own papers had been minor. The others had authored nothing of great importance.

None of them—face the fact—had developed into space shakers. The colossal dreams of schooldays had not come true and that was that. They were competent routine work-men. No more than that, they knew.

Villiers would have been more. They knew that, too. It was that knowledge, as well as guilt, which kept them in antago-nism.

Talliaferro felt uneasily that Villiers, despite everything, was yet to *be* more. The others must be thinking so too, and mediocrity could grow quickly unbearable. The mass trans-ference paper would come to pass and Villiers would be the great man after all, as he was always fated to be apparently, while his classmates, with all their advantages, would be forgotten. Their role would be no more than to applaud from the crowd.

He felt his own envy and chagrin and was ashamed of it, but felt it nonetheless.

Conversation died, and Kaunas said, his eyes turning away, "Listen, why don't we drop in on old Villiers?"

There was a false heartiness about it, a completely uncon-vincing effort at casualness. He added, "No use leaving bad feelings . . ."

Talliaferro thought. He wants to make sure about the mass transference. He's hoping it *is* only a madman's nightmare so he can sleep tonight.

But he was curious himself, so he made no objection, and even Ryger shrugged with ill grace and said, "Hell, why not?"

It was then a little before eleven.

Talliaferro was awakened by the insistent ringing of his door signal. He hitched himself to one elbow in the darkness and felt distinctly outraged. The soft glow of the ceiling in-dicator showed it to be not quite four in the morning.

He cried out, "Who is it?"

The ringing continued in spurts.

Growling, Talliaferro slipped into his bathrobe. He opened the door and blinked in the corridor light. He recognized the man who faced him from the trimensionals he had seen often enough.

Nevertheless the man said in an abrupt whisper, "My name is Hubert Mandel."

"Yes, sir," said Talliaferro. Mandel was one of the Names in astronomy, prominent enough to have an important execu-tive position with the World Astronomical Bureau, active enough to be Chairman of the astronautics section here at the Convention.

It suddenly struck Talliaferro that it was Mandel for whom Villiers claimed to have demonstrated mass transference. The thought of Villiers was somehow a sobering one.

Mandel said, "You are Dr. Edward Talliaferro?"

"Yes, sir."

"Then dress and come with me. It is very important. It concerns a common acquaintance."

"Dr. Villiers?"

Mandel's eyes flickered a bit. His brows and lashes were so fair as to give those eyes a naked, unfringed appearance. His hair was silky thin, his age about fifty.

He said, "Why Villiers?"

"He mentioned you last evening. I don't know any other common acquaintance."

Mandel nodded, waited for Talliaferro to finish slipping into his clothes, then turned and led the way. Ryger and Kaunas were waiting in a room one floor above Talliaferro's. Kaunas' eyes were red and troubled. Ryger was smoking a cigarette with impatient puffs.

Talliaferro said, "We're all here. Another reunion." It fell flat.

He took a seat and the three stared at one another. Ryger shrugged.

Mandel paced the floor, hands deep in his pockets. He said, "I apologize for any inconvenience, gentlemen, and I thank you for your cooperation. I would like more of it. Our friend Romano Villiers is dead. About an hour ago, his body was removed from the hotel. The medical judgment is heart failure."

There was a stunned silence. Ryger's cigarette hovered halfway to his lips, then sank slowly without completing its journey.

"Poor devil," said Talliaferro.

"Horrible," whispered Kaunas hoarsely. "He was . . ." His voice played out.

Ryger shook himself. "Well, he had a bad heart. There's nothing to be done."

"One little thing," corrected Mandel quietly. "Recovery."

"What does that mean?" asked Ryger sharply.

Mandel said, "When did you three see him last?"

Talliaferro spoke. "Last evening. It turned out to be a re-union. We all met for the first time in ten years. It wasn't a pleasant meeting, I'm sorry to say. Villiers felt he had cause for anger with us, and he was angry."

"That was—when?"

"About nine, the first time."

"The first time?"

"We saw him again later in the evening."

Kaunas looked troubled. "He had stormed off angrily. We couldn't leave it at that. We had to try. It wasn't as if we hadn't all been friends at one time. So we went to his room and—"

Mandel pounced on that. "You were all in his room?"

"Yes," said Kaunas, surprised.

"About when?"

"Eleven, I think." He looked at the others. Talliaferro nodded.

"And how long did you stay?"

"Two minutes," put in Ryger. "He ordered us out as though we were after his paper." He paused as if expecting Mandel to ask what paper, but Mandel said nothing. He went on, "I think he kept it under his pillow. At least he lay across the pillow as he yelled at us to leave."

"He may have been dying then," said Kaunas in a sick whisper.

"Not then," said Mandel shortly. "So you probably all left fingerprints."

"Probably," said Talliaferro. He was losing some of his automatic respect for Mandel and a sense of impatience was returning. It *was* four in the morning, Mandel or no. He said, "Now what's all this about?"

"Well, gentlemen," said Mandel, "there's more to Villiers' death than the fact of death. Villiers' paper, the only copy of it as far as I know, was stuffed into the flash-disposal unit and only scraps of it were left. I've never seen or read the paper, but I knew enough about the matter to be willing to swear in court if necessary that the remnants of unflashed paper in the disposal unit were of the paper he was planning to give at this Convention. You seem doubtful, Dr. Ryger."

Ryger smiled sourly. "Doubtful that he was going to give it. If you want my opinion, sir, he was mad. For ten years he was a prisoner of Earth and he fantasied mass transference as escape. It was all that kept him alive probably. He rigged up some sort of fraudulent demonstration. I don't say it was deliberate fraud. He was probably madly sincere, and sincerely mad. Last evening was the climax. He came to our rooms—he hated us for having escaped Earth—and triumphed over us. It was what he had lived for for ten years. It may have shocked him back to some form of sanity. He knew he couldn't actually give the paper; there was nothing to give. So he burned it and his heart gave out. It *is* too bad."

Mandel listened to the Cerian astronomer, wearing a look of sharp disapproval. He said, "Very glib, Dr. Ryger, but quite wrong. I am not so easily fooled by fraudulent demonstrations as you may believe. Now according to the registration data, which I have been forced to check rather hastily, you three were his classmates at college. Is that right?"

They nodded.

"Are there any other classmates of yours present at the Convention?"

"No," said Kaunas. "We were the only four qualifying for a doctorate in astronomy that year. At least he would have qualified except—"

"Yes, I understand," said Mandel. "Well, then, in that case one of you three visited Villiers in his room one last time at midnight."

There was a short silence. Then Ryger said coldly, "Not I." Kaunas, eyes wide, shook his head.

Talliaferro said, "What are you implying?"

"One of you came to him at midnight and insisted on seeing his paper. I don't know the motive. Conceivably it was with the deliberate intention of forcing him into heart failure. When Villiers collapsed, the criminal, if I may call him so, was ready. He snatched the paper, which, I might add, probably *was* kept under his pillow, and scanned it. Then he destroyed the paper itself in the flash-disposal, but he was in a hurry and destruction wasn't complete."

Ryger interrupted. "How do you know all this? Were you a witness?"

"Almost," said Mandel. "Villiers was not quite dead at the moment of his first collapse. When the criminal left, he managed to reach the phone and call my room. He choked out a few phrases, enough to outline what had occurred. Unfortunately I was not in my room; a late conference kept me away. However, my recording attachment taped it. I always play the recording tape back whenever I return to my room or office. Bureaucratic habit. I called back. He was dead."

"Well, then," said Ryger, "who did he say did it?"

"He didn't. Or if he did, it was unintelligible. But one word rang out clearly. It was *classmate*."

Talliaferro detached his scanner from its place in his inner jacket pocket and held it out toward Mandel. Quietly he said, "If you would like to develop the film in my scanner, you are welcome to do so. You will not find Villiers' paper there."

At once Kaunas did the same, and Ryger, with a scowl, joined.

Mandel took all three scanners and said dryly, "Presumably, whichever one of you has done this has already disposed of the piece of exposed film with the paper on it. However—"

Talliaferro raised his eyebrows. "You may search my person or my room."

But Ryger was still scowling. "Now wait a minute, wait one bloody minute. Are you the police?"

Mandel stared at him. "Do you *want* the police? Do you want a scandal and a murder charge? Do you want the Convention disrupted and the System press making a holiday out of astronomy and astronomers? Villiers' death might well have been accidental. He *did* have a bad heart. Whichever one of you was there may well have acted on impulse. It may not have been a premeditated crime. If whoever it is will return the negative, we can avoid a great deal of trouble."

"Even for the criminal?" asked Talliaferro.

Mandel shrugged. "There may be trouble for him. I will not promise immunity. But whatever the trouble, it won't be public disgrace and life imprisonment, as it might be if the police are called in."

Silence.

Mandel said, "It is one of you three."

Silence.

Mandel went on, "I think I can see the original reasoning of the guilty person. The paper would be destroyed. Only we four knew of the mass transference and only I had ever seen a demonstration. Moreover you had only his word, a madman's word perhaps, that I had seen it. With Villiers dead of heart failure and the paper gone, it would be easy to believe Dr.

Ryger's theory that there was no mass transference and never had been. A year or two might pass and our criminal, in possession of the mass transference data, could reveal it little by little, rig experiments, publish careful papers, and end as the apparent discoverer with all that would imply in terms of money and renown. Even his own classmates would suspect nothing. At most they would believe that the long-past affair with Villiers had inspired him to begin investigations in the field. No more."

Mandel looked sharply from one face to another. "But none of that will work now. Any of the three of you who comes through with mass transference is proclaiming himself the criminal. I've seen the demonstration; I know it is legitimate; I know that one of you possesses a record of the paper. The information is therefore useless to you. Give it up then."

Silence.

Mandel walked to the door and turned again. "I'd appreciate it if you would stay here till I return. I won't be long. I hope the guilty one will use the interval to consider. If he's afraid a confession will lose him his job, let him remember that a session with the police may lose him his liberty *and* cost him the psychoprobe." He hefted the three scanners, looked grim and somewhat in need of sleep. "I'll develop these."

Kaunas tried to smile. "What if we make a break for it while you're gone?"

"Only one of you has reason to try," said Mandel. "I think I can rely on the two innocent ones to control the third, if only out of self-protection."

He left.

It was five in the morning. Ryger looked at his watch indignantly. "A hell of a thing. I want to sleep."

"We can curl up here," said Talliaferro philosophically. "Is anyone planning a confession?"

Kaunas looked away and Ryger's lip lifted.

"I didn't think so." Talliaferro closed his eyes, leaned his large head back against the chair, and said in a tired voice, "Back on the Moon, they're in the slack season. We've got a two-week night and then it's busy, busy. Then there's two weeks of Sun and there's nothing but calculations, correlations, and bull sessions. That's the hard time. I hate it. If there were more women, if I could arrange something permanent . . ."

In a whisper, Kaunas talked about the fact that it was still impossible to get the entire Sun above the horizon and in view of the telescope on Mercury. But, with another two miles of track soon to be laid down for the observatory— move the whole thing, you know, tremendous forces involved, solar energy used directly—it might be managed. It *would* be managed.

Even Ryger consented to talk of Ceres after listening to the low murmur of the other voices. There was the problem there of the two-hour rotation period, which meant the stars whipped across the sky at an angular velocity twelve times that in Earth's sky. A net of three light scopes, three radioscopes, three of everything, caught the fields of study from one another as they whirled past.

"Could you use one of the poles?" asked Kaunas.

"You're thinking of Mercury and the Sun," said Ryger, impatiently. "Even at the poles the sky would still twist, and half of it would be forever hidden. Now if Ceres showed only one face to the Sun, the way Mercury does, we could have a permanent night sky with the stars rotating slowly once in three years."

The sky lightened and it dawned slowly.

Talliaferro was half-asleep, but he kept hold of halfconsciousness firmly. He would not fall asleep and leave the others awake. Each of the three, he thought, was wondering, "Who? Who?"

Except the guilty one, of course.

Talliaferro's eyes snapped open as Mandel entered again. The sky, as seen from the window, had grown blue. Talliaferro was glad the window was closed. The hotel was airconditioned, of course, but windows would be opened during the mild seasons of the year by those Earthmen who fancied the illusion of fresh air. Talliaferro, with Moon vacuum on his mind, shuddered at the thought with real discomfort.

Mandel said, "Have any of you anything to say?"

They looked at him steadily. Ryger shook his head.

Mandel said, "I have developed the film in your scanners,

gentlemen, and viewed the results." He tossed scanners and developed slivers of film on to the bed. "Nothing! You'll have trouble sorting out the film, I'm afraid. For that I'm sorry. And now there is still the question of the missing film."

"If any," said Ryger, and yawned prodigiously.

Mandel said, "I would suggest we come down to Villiers' room, gentlemen."

Kaunas looked startled. "Why?"

Talliaferro said, "Is this psychology? Bring the criminal to the scene of the crime and remorse will wring a confession from him?"

Mandel said, "A less melodramatic reason is that I would like to have the two of you who are innocent help me find the missing film of Villiers' paper."

"Do you think it's there?" asked Ryger challengingly.

"Possibly. It's a beginning. We can then search each of your rooms. The symposium on Astronautics doesn't start till tomorrow at 10 A.M. We have till then."

"And after that?"

"It may have to be the police."

They stepped gingerly into Villiers' room. Ryger was red, Kaunas pale. Talliaferro tried to remain calm.

Last night they had seen it under artificial lighting with a scowling, disheveled Villiers clutching his pillow, staring them down, ordering them away. Now there was the scentless odor of death about it.

Mandel fiddled with the window polarizer to let more light in and adjusted it too far, so that the eastern Sun slipped in.

Kaunas threw his arm up to shade his eyes and screamed, "The Sun!" so that all the others froze.

Kaunas' face had gone into a kind of terror, as though it were his Mercurian Sun that he had caught a blinding glimpse of.

Talliaferro thought of his own reaction to the possibility of open air and his teeth gritted. They were all bent crooked by their ten years away from Earth.

Kaunas ran to the window, fumbling for the polarizer, and then the breath came out of him in a huge gasp.

Mandel stepped to his side. "What's wrong?" and the other two joined them.

The city lay stretched below them and outward to the

horizon in broken stone and brick, bathed in the rising Sun, with the shadowed portions toward them. Talliaferro cast it all a furtive and uneasy glance.

Kaunas, his chest seemingly contracted past the point where he could cry out, stared at something much closer. There, on the outer window sill, one corner secured in a trifling imperfection, a crack in the cement, was an inch-long strip of milky-gray film, and on it were the early rays of the rising Sun.

Mandel, with an angry, incoherent cry, threw up the window and snatched it away. He shielded it in one cupped hand, staring out of hot and reddened eyes.

He said, "Wait here!"

There was nothing to say. When Mandel left, they sat down and stared stupidly at one another.

Mandel was back in twenty minutes. He said quietly—in a voice that gave the impression, somehow, that it was quiet only because its owner had passed far beyond the raving stage—"The corner in the crack wasn't overexposed. I could make out a few words. It is Villiers' paper. The rest is ruined; nothing can be salvaged. It's gone."

"What next?" said Talliaferro.

Mandel shrugged wearily. "Right now, I don't care. Mass transference is gone until someone as brilliant as Villiers works it out again. I shall work on it, but I have no illusions as to my own capacity. With it gone, I suppose you three don't matter, guilty or not. What's the difference?" His whole body seemed to have loosened and sunk into despair.

But Talliaferro's voice grew hard. "Now, hold on. In your eyes, any of the three of us might be guilty. I, for instance. You are a big man in the field and you will never have a good word to say for me. The general idea may arise that I am incompetent or worse. I will not be ruined by the shadow of guilt. Now let's solve this thing."

"I am no detective," said Mandel wearily.

"Then why don't you call in the police, damn it?"

Ryger said, "Wait awhile, Tal. Are you implying that I'm guilty?"

"I'm only saying that I'm innocent."

Kaunas raised his voice in fright. "It will mean the psychoprobe for each of us. There may be mental damage—"

Mandel raised both arms high in the air. "Gentlemen! Gentlemen! Please! There is one thing we might do short of the police; and you are right, Dr. Talliaferro, it would be unfair to the innocent to leave this matter here."

They turned to him in various stages of hostility. Ryger said, "What do you suggest?"

"I have a friend named Wendell Urth. You may have heard of him, or you may not, but perhaps I can arrange to see him tonight."

"What if we can?" demanded Talliaferro. "Where does that get us?"

"He's an odd man," said Mandel hesitantly. "Very odd. And very brilliant in his way. He has helped the police before this and he may be able to help us now."

Edward Talliaferro could not forbear staring at the room and its occupant with the greatest astonishment. It and he seemed to exist in isolation, and to be part of no recognizable world. The sounds of Earth were absent in this well-padded, windowless nest. The light and air of Earth had been blanked out in artificial illumination and conditioning.

It was a large room, dim and cluttered. They had picked their way across a littered floor to a couch from which book-films had been brusquely cleared and dumped to one side in an amorphous tangle.

The man who owned the room had a large round face on a stumpy round body. He moved quickly about on his short legs, jerking his head as he spoke until his thick glasses all but bounced off the thoroughly inconspicuous nubbin that served in the office of a nose. His thick-lidded, somewhat protuberant eyes gleamed in myopic good nature at them all, as he seated himself in his own chair-desk combination, lit directly by the one bright light in the room.

"So good of you to come, gentlemen. Pray excuse the condition of my room." He waved stubby fingers in a wide-sweeping gesture. "I am engaged in cataloguing the many objects of extraterrological interest I have accumulated. It is a tremendous job. For instance——"

He dodged out of his seat and burrowed in a heap of objects beside the desk till he came up with a smoky gray object, semitranslucent and roughly cylindrical. "This," he said, "is a Callistan object that may be a relic of intelligent nonhuman entities. It is not decided. No more than a dozen have been discovered and this is the most perfect single specimen I know of."

He tossed it to one side and Talliaferro jumped. The plump man stared in his direction and said, "It's not breakable." He sat down again, clasped his pudgy fingers tightly over his abdomen and let them pump slowly in and out as he breathed. "And now what can I do for you?"

Hubert Mandel had carried through the introductions and Talliaferro was considering deeply. Surely it was a man named Wendell Urth who had written a recent book entitled *Comparative Evolutionary Processes on Water-Oxygen Planets,* and surely this could not be the man.

He said, "Are you the author of *Comparative Evolutionary Processes,* Dr. Urth?"

A beatific smile spread across Urth's face. "You've read it?"

"Well, no, I haven't, but—"

Urth's expression grew instantly censorious. "Then you should. Right now. Here, I have a copy."

He bounced out of his chair again and Mandel cried, "Now wait, Urth, first things first. This is serious."

He virtually forced Urth back into his chair and began speaking rapidly as though to prevent any further side issues from erupting. He told the whole story with admirable word economy.

Urth reddened slowly as he listened. He seized his glasses and shoved them higher up on his nose. "Mass transference!" he cried.

"I saw it with my own eyes," said Mandel.

"And you never told me."

"I was sworn to secrecy. The man was . . . peculiar. I explained that."

Urth pounded the desk. "How could you allow such a discovery to remain the property of an eccentric, Mandel? The knowledge should have been forced from him by pschoprobe, if necessary."

"It would have killed him," protested Mandel.

But Urth was rocking back and forth with his hands clasped tightly to his cheeks. "Mass tranference. The only way a decent, civilized man could travel. The only possible way. The only conceivable way. If I had known. If I could have been there. But the hotel is nearly thirty miles away."

Ryger, who listened with an expression of annoyance on

his face, interposed, "I understand there's a flitter line direct to Convention Hall. It could have got you there in ten minutes."

Urth stiffened and looked at Ryger strangely. His cheeks bulged. He jumped to his feet and scurried out of the room.

Ryger said, "What the devil?"

Mandel muttered, "Damn it, I should have warned you."

"About what?"

"Dr. Urth doesn't travel on any sort of conveyance. It's a phobia. He moves about only on foot."

Kaunas blinked about in the dimness. "But he's an extraterrologist, isn't he? An expert on life forms of other planets?"

Talliaferro had risen and now stood before a Galactic Lens on a pedestal. He stared at the inner gleam of the star systems. He had never seen a Lens so large or so elaborate.

Mandel said, "He's an extraterrologist, yes, but he's never visited any of the planets on which he is expert and he never will. In thirty years, he's never been more than a few miles from this room."

Ryger laughed.

Mandel flushed angrily. "You may find it funny, but I'd appreciate your being careful what you say when Dr. Urth comes back."

Urth sidled in a moment later. "My apologies, gentlemen," he said in a whisper. "And now let us approach our problem. Perhaps one of you wishes to confess?"

Talliaferro's lips quirked sourly. This plump, self-imprisoned extra-terrologist was scarcely formidable enough to force a confession from anyone. Fortunately there would be no need of him.

Talliaferro said, "Dr. Urth, are you connected with the police?"

A certain smugness seemed to suffuse Urth's ruddy face. "I have no official connection, Dr. Talliaferro, but my unofficial relationships are very good indeed."

"In that case, I will give you some information which you can carry to the police."

Urth drew in his abdomen and hitched at his shirttail. It came free and slowly he polished his glasses with it. When he was quite through and had perched them precariously on his nose once more, he said, "And what is that?"

"I will tell you who was present when Villiers died and who scanned his paper."

"You have solved the mystery?"

"I've thought about it all day. I think I've solved it." Talliaferro rather enjoyed the sensation he was creating.

"Well, then?"

Talliaferro took a deep breath. This was not going to be easy to do, though he had been planning it for hours. "The guilty man," he said, "is obviously Dr. Hubert Mandel."

Mandel stared at Talliaferro in sudden, hard-breathing indignation. "Look here, Doctor," he began loudly, "if you have any basis—"

Urth's tenor voice soared above the interruption. "Let him talk, Hubert, let us hear him. You suspected him and there is no law that forbids him to suspect you."

Mandel fell angrily silent.

Talliaferro, not allowing his voice to falter, said, "It is more than just suspicion, Dr. Urth. The evidence is perfectly plain. Four of us knew about mass transference, but only one of us, Dr. Mandel, had actually seen a demonstration. He *knew* it to be a fact. He *knew* a paper on the subject existed. We three knew only that Villiers was more or less unbalanced. Oh, we might have thought there was just a chance. We visited him at eleven, I think, just to check on that, though none of us actually said so, but he only acted crazier than ever.

"Check special knowledge and motive then on Dr. Mandel's side. Now, Dr. Urth, picture something else. Whoever it was who confronted Villiers at midnight, saw him collapse, and scanned his paper (let's keep him anonymous for a moment) must have been terribly startled to see Villiers apparently come to life again and to hear him talking into the telephone. Our criminal, in the panic of the moment, realized one thing: he must get rid of the one piece of incriminating material evidence.

"He had to get rid of the undeveloped film of the paper and he had to do it in such a way that it would be safe from discovery so that he might pick it up once more if he remained unsuspected. The outer window sill was ideal. Quickly he threw up Villiers' window, placed the strip of film outside, and left. Now, even if Villiers survived or if his telephoning brought results, it would be merely Villiers' word against his

own and it would be easy to show that Villiers was unbalanced."

Talliaferro paused in something like triumph. This would be
irrefutable.

Wendell Urth blinked at him and wiggled the thumbs of his
clasped hands so that they slapped against his ample shirt
front. He said, "And the significance of all that?"

"The significance is that the window was thrown open and
the film placed in open air. Now Ryger has lived for ten years
on Ceres, Kaunas on Mercury, I on the Moon—barring short
leaves and not many of them. We commented to one another
several times yesterday on the difficulty of growing acclimated
to Earth.

"Our work worlds are each airless objects. We never go out
in the open without a suit. To expose ourselves to unenclosed
space is unthinkable. None of us could have opened the window without a severe inner struggle. Dr. Mandel, however,
has lived on Earth exclusively. Opening a window to him
is only a matter of a bit of muscular exertion. He could do it.
We couldn't. Ergo, he did it."

Talliaferro sat back and smiled a bit.

"Space, that's it!" cried Ryger with enthusiasm.

"That's not it at all," roared Mandel, half-rising as though
tempted to throw himself at Talliaferro. "I deny the whole
miserable fabrication. What about the record I have of
Villiers' phone call? He used the word *classmate*. The entire
tape makes it obvious—"

"He was a dying man," said Talliaferro. "Much of what he
said you admitted was incomprehensible. I ask you, Dr. Mandel, without having heard the tape, if it isn't true that Villiers'
voice is distorted past recognition?"

"Well—" said Mandel, confused.

"I'm sure it is. There is no reason to suppose, then, that you
might not have rigged up the tape in advance, complete with
the damning word *classmate*."

Mandel said, "Good Lord, how would I know there were
classmates at the Convention? How would I know they knew
about the mass transference?"

"Villiers might have told you. I presume he did."

"Now, look," said Mandel, "you three saw Villiers alive at
eleven. The medical examiner, seeing Villiers' body shortly

after 3 A.M., declared he had been dead at least two hours. That was certain. The time of death therefore, was between 11 P.M. and 1 A.M. I was at a late conference last night. I can prove my whereabouts, miles from the hotel, between ten and two, by a dozen witnesses, no one of whom anyone can possibly question. It that enough for you?"

Talliaferro paused a moment. Then he went on stubbornly, "Even so. Suppose you got back to the hotel by two-thirty. You went to Villiers' room to discuss his talk. You found the door open, or you had a duplicate key. Anyway, you found him dead. You seized the opportunity to scan the paper—"

"And if he were already dead, and couldn't make phone calls, why should I hide the film?"

"To remove suspicion. You may have a second copy of the film safe in your possession. For that matter, we have only your own word that the paper itself was destroyed."

"Enough. Enough!" cried Urth. "It is an interesting hypothesis, Dr. Talliaferro, but it falls to the ground of its own weight."

Talliaferro frowned. "That's your opinion, perhaps—"

"It would be anyone's opinion. Anyone, that is, with the power of human thought. Don't you see that Hubert Mandel did too much to be the criminal?"

"No," said Talliaferro.

Wendell Urth smiled benignly. "As a scientist, Dr. Talliaferro, you undoubtedly know better than to fall in love with your own theories to the exclusion of facts or reasoning. Do me the pleasure of behaving similarly as a detective.

"Consider that if Dr. Mandel had brought about the death of Villiers and faked an alibi, or if he had found Villiers dead and taken advantage of that, how little he would really have had to do! Why scan the paper or even pretend that anyone had done so? He could simply have taken the paper. Who else knew of its existence? Nobody, really. There was no reason to think Villiers told anyone else about it. Villiers was pathologically secretive. There would have been every reason to think that he told no one.

"No one knew Villers was giving a talk, except Dr. Mandel. It wasn't announced. No abstract was published. Dr. Mandel could have walked off with the paper in perfect confidence.

"Even if he had discovered that Villiers had talked to his

classmates about the matter, what of it? What evidence would his classmates have except the word of one whom they are themselves willing to consider a madman?

"By announcing instead that Villiers' paper had been destroyed, by declaring his death to be not entirely natural, by searching for a scanned copy of the film—in short by everything Dr. Mandel has done, he has aroused a suspicion that only he could possibly have aroused when he need only have remained quiet to have committed a perfect crime. If he were the criminal, he would be more stupid, more colossally obtuse than anyone I have ever known. And Dr. Mandel, after all, is none of that."

Talliaferro thought hard but found nothing to say.

Ryger said, "Then who did it?"

"One of you three. That's obvious."

"But which?"

"Oh, that's obvious too. I knew which of you was guilty the moment Dr. Mandel had completed his description of events."

Talliaferro stared at the plump extraterrologist with distaste. The bluff did not frighten him, but it was affecting the other two. Ryger's lips were thrust out and Kaunas' lower jaw had relaxed moronically. They looked like fish, both of them.

He said, "Which one, then? Tell us."

Urth blinked. "First, I want to make it perfectly plain that the important thing is mass transference. It can still be recovered."

Mandel, scowling still, said querulously, "What the devil are you talking about, Urth?"

"The man who scanned the paper probably looked at what he was scanning. I doubt that he had the time or the presence of mind to read it, and if he did, I doubt if he could remember it . . . consciously. However, there is the psychoprobe. If he so much as glanced at the paper, what impinged on his retina could be probed."

There was an uneasy stir.

Urth said at once, "No need to be afraid of the psychoprobe. Proper handling is safe, particularly if a man offers himself voluntarily. When damage is done, it is usually because of unnecessary resistance, a kind of mental tearing, you know. So if the guilty man will voluntarily confess, place himself in my hands—"

Talliaferro laughed. The sudden noise rang out sharply in the dim quiet of the room. The psychology was so transparent and artless.

Wendell Urth looked almost bewildered at the reaction and stared earnestly at Talliaferro over his glasses. He said, "I have enough influence with the police to keep the probing entirely confidential."

Ryger said savagely, "I didn't do it."

Kaunas shook his head.

Talliaferro disdained any answer.

Urth sighed. "Then I shall have to point out the guilty man. It will be traumatic. It will make things harder." He tightened the grip on his belly and his fingers twitched. "Dr. Talliaferro indicated that the film was hidden on the outer window sill so that it might remain safe from discovery and from harm. I agree with him."

"Thank you," said Talliaferro dryly.

"However, why should anyone think that an outer window sill is a particularly safe hiding place? The police would certainly look there.

"Even in the absence of the police it was discovered. Who would tend to consider anything outside a building as particularly safe? Obviously some person who has lived a long time on an airless world and has had it drilled into him that no one goes outside an enclosed place without detailed precautions.

"To someone on the Moon, for instance, anything hidden outside a Lunar Dome would be comparatively safe. Men venture out only rarely and then only on specific business. So he would overcome the hardship of opening a window and exposing himself to what he would subconsciously consider a vacuum for the sake of a safe hiding place. The reflex thought, *Outside an inhabited structure is safe,* would do the trick."

Talliaferro said between clenched teeth, "Why do you mention the Moon, Dr. Urth?"

Urth said blandly, "Only as an example. What I've said so far applies to all three of you. But now comes the crucial point, the matter of the dying night."

Talliaferro frowned. "You mean the night Villiers died?"

"I mean any night. See here, even granted that an outer window sill was a safe hiding place, which of you would be mad enough to consider it a safe hiding place *for a piece of unexposed film?* Scanner film isn't very sensitive, to be sure, and is made to be developed under all sorts of hit-and-miss conditions. Diffuse nighttime illumination wouldn't seriously affect it, but diffuse daylight would ruin it in a few minutes, and direct sunlight would ruin it at once. Everyone knows that."

Mandel said, "Go ahead, Urth. What is this leading to?"

"You're trying to rush me," said Urth, with a massive pout. "I want you to see this clearly. The criminal wanted, above all, to keep the film safe. It was his only record of something of supreme value to himself and to the world. Why would he put it where it would inevitably be ruined almost immediately by the morning Sun? Only because he did not expect the morning Sun ever to come. He thought the night, so to speak, was immortal.

"But nights *aren't* immortal. On Earth they die and give way to daytime. Even the six-month polar night is a dying night eventually. The nights on Ceres last only two hours; the nights on the Moon last two weeks. They are dying nights too, and Drs. Talliaferro and Ryger know that day must always come."

Kaunas rose. "But wait—"

Wendell Urth faced him full. "No longer any need to wait, Dr. Kaunas. Mercury is the only sizable object in the Solar System that turns only one face to the Sun. Even taking libration into account, fully three-eighths of its surface is true dark-side and never sees the Sun. The Polar Observatory is at the rim of that dark-side. For ten years you have grown used to the fact that nights are immortal, that a surface in darkness remains eternally in darkness, and so you entrusted unexposed film to Earth's night, forgetting in your excitement that nights must die—"

Kaunas came forward. "Wait—"

Urth was inexorable. "I am told that when Mandel adjusted the polarizer in Villiers' room, you screamed at the sunlight. Was that your ingrained fear of the Mercurian Sun, or your sudden realization of what sunlight meant to your plans? You rushed forward. Was that to adjust the polarizer, or to stare at the ruined film?"

Kaunas fell to his knees. "I didn't mean it. I wanted to speak to him, only to speak to him, and he screamed and collapsed. I thought he was dead and the paper was under his pillow and it all just followed. One thing led on to another and before I knew it I couldn't get out of it anymore. But I meant none of it. I swear it."

They had formed a semicircle about him and Wendell Urth stared at the moaning Kaunas with pity in his eyes.

An ambulance had come and gone. Talliaferro finally brought himself to say stiffly to Mandel, "I hope, sir, there will be no hard feelings for anything said here."

And Mandel had answered as stiffly, "I think we had all better forget as much as possible of what has happened during the last twenty-four hours."

They were standing in the doorway, ready to leave, and Wendell Urth ducked his smiling head and said, "There's the question of my fee, you know."

Mandel looked at him with a startled expression.

"Not money," said Urth at once. "But when the first mass transference setup for humans is established, I want a trip arranged for me right away."

Mandel continued to look anxious. "Now, wait. Trips through outer space are a long way off."

Urth shook his head rapidly. "Not outer space. Not at all. I would like to step across to Lower Falls, New Hampshire."

"All right. But why?"

Urth looked up. To Talliaferro's outright surprise, the extraterrologist's face wore an expression compounded equally of shyness and eagerness.

Urth said, "I once—quite a long time ago—knew a girl there. It's been many years—but I sometimes wonder . . ."

AFTERWORD

Some readers may realize that this story, first published in 1956, has been overtaken by events. In 1965, astronomers discovered that Mercury does not keep one side always to the Sun, but has a period of rotation of about fifty-four days, so that all parts of it are exposed to sunlight at one time or another.

Well, what can I do except say that I wish astronomers would get things right to begin with?

And I certainly refuse to change the story to suit their whims.

FOREWORD

This item is not strictly a mystery in the usual sense of the word, or even a story in the usual sense of the word. I don't know how to describe it, except perhaps as a good-natured satire on scientific research.

I received more mail after its publication than after any other item of comparable length. A particularly pleasant memory is that of receiving a telephone call from a man who spoke with a strong Central European accent. He said he was in Boston for a convention and wanted to thank me for the pleasure "Pâté de Foie Gras" had given him, since it so amusingly and effectively poked knowledgeable fun at science.

I tried to get his name, but he wouldn't give it to me. He was afraid, I suspect, that his reputation might suffer if it were found he read science fiction. If he is secretly reading this book and recognizes himself, I would like to assure him that he has plenty of company and can take off that plain wrapper.

Honest!

Pate de Foie Gras

I couldn't tell you my real name if I wanted to, and, under the circumstances, I don't want to.

I'm not much of a writer myself, so I'm having Isaac Asimov write this up for me. I've picked him for several reasons. First, he's a biochemist, so he understands what I tell him; some of it, anyway. Secondly, he can write; or at least he has published considerable fiction, which may not, of course, be the same thing.

I was not the first person to have the honor of meeting The Goose. That belongs to a Texas cotton farmer named Ian Angus MacGregor, who owned it before it became government property.

By summer of 1955 he had sent an even dozen of letters to the Department of Agriculture requesting information on the hatching of goose eggs. The department sent him all the booklets on hand that were anywhere near the subject, but his letters simply got more impassioned and freer in their references to his "friend," the local congressman.

My connection with this is that I am in the employ of the Department of Agriculture. Since I was attending a convention at San Antonio in July of 1955, my boss asked me to stop off at MacGregor's place and see what I could do to help him. We're servants of the public and besides we had finally received a letter from MacGregor's congressman.

On July 17, 1955, I met The Goose.

I met MacGregor first. He was in his fifties, a tall man with a lined face full of suspicion. I went over all the information he had been given, then asked politely if I might see his geese.

He said, "It's not geese, mister; it's one goose."

I said, "May I see the one goose?"

"Rather not."

"Well, then, I can't help you any further. If it's only one goose, then there's just something wrong with it. Why worry about one goose? Eat it."

I got up and reached for my hat.

He said, "Wait!" and I stood there while his lips tightened and his eyes wrinkled and he had a quiet fight with himself. "Come with me."

I went out with him to a pen near the house, surrounded by barbed wire, with a locked gate to it, and holding one goose—The Goose.

"That's The Goose," he said. The way he said it, I could hear the capitals.

I stared at it. It looked like any other goose, fat, self-satisfied and short-tempered.

MacGregor said, "And here's one of its eggs. It's been in the incubator. Nothing happens." He produced it from a capacious overall pocket. There was a queer strain about his manner of holding it.

I frowned. There was something wrong with the egg. It was smaller and more spherical than normal.

MacGregor said, "Take it."

I reached out and took it. Or tried to. I gave it the amount of heft an egg like that ought to deserve and it just sat where it was. I had to try harder and then up it came.

Now I knew what was queer about the way MacGregor held it. It weighed nearly two pounds.

I stared at it as it lay there, pressing down the palm of my hand, and MacGregor grinned sourly. "Drop it," he said.

I just looked at him, so he took it out of my hand and dropped it himself.

It hit soggy. It didn't smash. There was no spray of white and yolk. It just lay where it fell with the bottom caved in.

I picked it up again. The white eggshell had shattered where the egg had struck. Pieces of it had flaked away and what shone through was a dull yellow in color.

My hands trembled. It was all I could do to make my fingers work, but I got some of the rest of the shell flaked away, and stared at the yellow.

I didn't have to run any analyses. My heart told me.

I was face to face with The Goose!

The Goose That Laid The Golden Eggs! My first problem was to get MacGregor to give up that golden egg. I was almost hysterical about it.

I said, "I'll give you a receipt. I'll guarantee you payment. I'll do anything in reason."

"I don't want the government butting in," he said stubbornly.

But I was twice as stubborn and in the end I signed a receipt and he dogged me out to my car and stood in the road as I drove away, following me with his eyes.

The head of my section at the Department of Agriculture is Louis P. Bronstein. He and I are on good terms and I felt I could explain things without being placed under immediate observation. Even so, I took no chances. I had the egg with me and when I got to the tricky part, I just laid it on the desk between us.

I said, "It's a yellow metal and it could be brass only it isn't because it's inert to concentrated nitric acid."

Bronstein said, "It's some sort of hoax. It *must* be."

"A hoax that uses real gold? Remember, when I first saw this thing, it was covered completely with authentic unbroken eggshell. It's been easy to check a piece of the eggshell. Calcium carbonate."

Project Goose was started. That was July 20, 1955.

I was the responsible investigator to begin with and remained in titular charge throughout, though matters quickly got beyond me.

We began with the one egg. Its average radius was 35 millimeters (major axis, 72 millimeters; minor axis, 68 millimeters). The gold shell was 2.45 millimeters in thickness. Studying other eggs later on, we found this value to be rather high. The average thickness turned out to be 2.1 millimeters.

Inside *was* egg. It looked like egg and it smelled like egg.

Aliquots were analyzed and the organic constituents were reasonably normal. The white was 9.7 per cent albumin. The yolk had the normal complement of vitellin, cholesterol, phospholipid, and carotenoid. We lacked enough material to test for trace constituents, but later on with more eggs at our disposal we did and nothing unusual showed up as far as contents of vitamins, coenzymes, nucleotides, sulfhydryl groups, et cetera, et cetera were concerned.

One important gross abnormality that showed was the egg's behavior on heating. A small portion of the yolk, heated, "hard-boiled" almost at once. We fed a portion of the hard-boiled egg to a mouse. It survived.

I nibbled at another bit of it. Too small a quantity to taste, really, but it made me sick. Purely psychosomatic, I'm sure.

Boris W. Finley, of the Department of Biochemistry of Temple University—a department consultant—supervised these tests.

He said, referring to the hard-boiling, "The ease with which the egg proteins are heat-denatured indicates a partial denaturation to begin with and, considering the nature of the shell, the obvious guilt would lie at the door of heavy-metal contamination."

So a portion of the yolk was analyzed for inorganic constituents, and it was found to be high in chloraurate ion, which is a singly charged ion containing an atom of gold and four of chlorine, the symbol for which is $AuCl_4-$. (The "Au" symbol for gold comes from the fact that the Latin word for gold is "aurum.") When I say the chloraurate ion content was high, I mean it was 3.2 parts per thousand, or 0.32 per cent. That's high enough to form insoluble complexes of "gold protein" which would coagulate easily.

Finley said, "It's obvious this egg cannot hatch. Nor can any other such egg. It is heavy-metal poisoned. Gold may be more glamorous than lead but it is just as poisonous to proteins."

I agreed gloomily. "At least it's safe from decay, too."

"Quite right. No self-respecting bug would live in this chlorauriferous soup."

The final spectrographic analysis of the gold of the shell came in. Virtually pure. The only detectable impurity was iron which amounted to 0.23 per cent of the whole. The iron content of the egg yolk had been twice normal, also. At the moment, however, the matter of the iron was neglected.

One week after Project Goose was begun, an expedition was sent into Texas. Five biochemists went—the accent was still on biochemistry, you see—along with three truckloads of equipment, and a squadron of army personnel. I went along too, of course.

As soon as we arrived, we cut MacGregor's farm off from the world.

That was a lucky thing, you know—the security measures we took right from the start. The reasoning was wrong, at first, but the results were good.

The Department wanted Project Goose kept quiet at the start simply because there was always the thought that this might still be an elaborate hoax and we couldn't risk the bad publicity if it were. And if it weren't a hoax, we couldn't risk the newspaper hounding that would definitely result over any goose-and-golden-egg story.

It was only well after the start of Project Goose, well after our arrival at MacGregor's farm, that the real implications of the matter became clear.

Naturally MacGregor didn't like the men and equipment settling down all about him. He didn't like being told The Goose was government property. He didn't like having his eggs impounded.

He didn't like it but he agreed to it—if you can call it agreeing when negotiations are being carried on while a machine gun is being assembled in a man's barnyard and ten men, with bayonets fixed, are marching past while the arguing is going on.

He was compensated, of course. What's money to the government?

The Goose didn't like a few things, either—like having blood samples taken. We didn't dare anesthetize it for fear of doing anything to alter its metabolism, and it took two men to hold it each time. Ever try to hold an angry goose?

The Goose was put under a twenty-four-hour guard with the threat of summary court-martial to any man who let anything happen to it. If any of those soldiers read this article, they may get a sudden glimmer of what was going on. If so, they will probably have the sense to keep shut about it. At least, if they know what's good for them, they will.

The blood of The Goose was put through every test conceivable.

It carried 2 parts per hundred thousand (0.002 per cent) of chloraurate ion. Blood taken from the hepatic vein was richer than the rest, almost 4 parts per hundred thousand.

Finley grunted. "The liver," he said.

We took x rays. On the x-ray negative, the liver was a cloudy mass of light gray, lighter than the viscera in its neighborhood, because it stopped more of the x rays, because it contained more gold. The blood vessels showed up lighter than the liver proper and the ovaries were pure white. No x rays got through the ovaries at all.

It made sense, and in an early report Finley stated it as bluntly as possible. Paraphrasing the report, it went, in part:

"The chloraurate ion is secreted by the liver into the blood stream. The ovaries act as a trap for the ion, which is there reduced to metallic gold and deposited as a shell about the developing egg. Relatively high concentrations of unreduced chloraurate ion penetrate the contents of the developing egg.

"There is little doubt that The Goose finds this process useful as a means of getting rid of the gold atoms which, if allowed to accumulate, would undoubtedly poison it. Excretion by eggshell may be novel in the animal kingdom, even unique, but there is no denying that it is keeping The Goose alive.

"Unfortunately, however, the ovary is being locally poisoned to such an extent that few eggs are laid, probably not more than will suffice to get rid of the accumulating gold, and those few eggs are definitely unhatchable."

That was all he said in writing, but to the rest of us, he said, "That leaves one peculiarly embarrassing question."

I knew what it was. We all did.

Where was the gold coming from?

No answer to that for a while, except for some negative evidence. There was no perceptible gold in The Goose's feed, nor were there any gold-bearing pebbles about that it might have swallowed. There was no trace of gold anywhere in the soil of the area and a search of the house and grounds revealed nothing. There were no gold coins, gold jewelry, gold plate, gold watches, or gold anything. No one on the farm even had as much as gold fillings in his teeth.

There was Mrs. MacGregor's wedding ring, of course, but she had only had one in her life and she was wearing it.

So where was the gold coming from?

The beginnings of the answer came on August 16, 1955.

Albert Nevis, of Purdue, was forcing gastric tubes into The Goose—another procedure to which the bird objected strenuously—with the idea of testing the contents of its alimentary canal. It was one of our routine searches for exogenous gold.

Gold *was* found, but only in traces, and there was every reason to suppose those traces had accompanied the digestive secretions and were, therefore, endogenous—from within, that is—in origin.

However, something else showed up, or the lack of it, anyway.

I was there when Nevis came into Finley's office in the temporary building we had put up overnight—almost—near the goosepen.

Nevis said, "The Goose is low in bile pigment. Duodenal contents show about none."

Finley frowned and said, "Liver function is probably knocked loop-the-loop because of its gold concentration. It probably isn't secreting bile at all."

"It *is* secreting bile," said Nevis. "Bile acids are present in normal quantity. Near normal, anyway. It's just the bile pigments that are missing. I did a fecal analysis and that was confirmed. No bile pigments."

Let me explain something at this point. Bile acids are steroids secreted by the liver into the bile and via that are poured into the upper end of the small intestine. These bile acids are detergentlike molecules which help to emulsify the fat in our diet—or The Goose's—and distribute them in the form of tiny bubbles through the watery intestinal contents. This distribution, or homogenization, if you'd rather, makes it easier for the fat to be digested.

Bile pigments, the substances that were missing in The Goose, are something entirely different. The liver makes them out of hemoglobin, the red oxygen-carrying protein of the blood. Worn-out hemoglobin is broken up in the liver, the heme part being split away. The heme is made up of a squarish molecule—called a porphyrin—with an iron atom in the center. The liver takes the iron out and stores it for future use, then breaks the squarish molecule that is left. This broken porphyrin is bile pigment. It is colored brownish or greenish—depending on further chemical changes—and is secreted into the bile.

The bile pigments are of no use to the body. They are poured into the bile as waste products. They pass through the intestines and come out with the feces. In fact, the bile pigments are responsible for the color of the feces.

Finley's eyes began to glitter.

Nevis said, "It looks as though porphyrin catabolism isn't following the proper course in the liver. Doesn't it to you?"

It surely did. To me too.

There was tremendous excitement after that. This was the first metabolic abnormality, not directly involving gold, that had been found in The Goose!

We took a liver biopsy (which means we punched a cylindrical sliver out of The Goose reaching down into the liver). It hurt The Goose but didn't harm it. We took more blood samples, too.

This time we isolated hemoglobin from the blood and small quantities of the cytochromes from our liver samples. (The cytochromes are oxidizing enzymes that also contain heme.) We separated out the heme and in acid solution some of it precipitated in the form of a brilliant orange substance. By August 22, 1955, we had 5 micrograms of the compound.

The orange compound was similar to heme, but it was not heme. The iron in heme can be in the form of a doubly charged ferrous ion (Fe^{++}) or a triply charged ferric ion (Fe^{+++}), in which latter case, the compound is called hematin. (Ferrous and ferric, by the way, come from the Latin word for iron, which is "ferrum.")

The orange compound we had separated from heme had the porphyrin portion of the molecule all right, but the metal in the center was gold, to be specific, a triply charged auric ion (Au^{+++}). We called this compound "aureme," which is simply short for "auric heme."

Aureme was the first naturally occurring gold-containing organic compound ever discovered. Ordinarily it would rate headline news in the world of biochemistry. But now it was nothing; nothing at all in comparison to the further horizons its mere existence opened up.

The liver, it seemed, was not breaking up the heme to bile pigment. Instead it was converting it to aureme; it was replacing iron with gold. The aureme, in equilibrium with chloraurate ion, entered the blood stream and was carried to the ovaries, where the gold was separated out and the porphyrin portion of the molecule disposed of by some as yet unidentified mechanism.

Further analyses showed that 29 per cent of the gold in the blood of The Goose was carried in the plasma in the form of chloraurate ion. The remaining 71 per cent was carried in the red blood corpuscles in the form of "auremoglobin." An attempt was made to feed The Goose traces of radioactive gold so that we could pick up radioactivity in plasma and corpuscles and see how readily the auremoglobin molecules were handled in the ovaries. It seemed to us the auremoglobin should be much more slowly disposed of than the dissolved chloraurate ion in the plasma.

The experiment failed, however, since we detected no radioactivity. We put it down to inexperience since none of us were isotopes men, which was too bad since the failure was highly significant, really, and by not realizing it we lost several weeks.

The auremoglobin was, of course, useless as far as carrying oxygen was concerned, but it only made up about 0.1 per cent of the total hemoglobin of the red blood cells so there was no interference with the respiration of The Goose.

This still left us with the question of where the gold came from and it was Nevis who first made the crucial suggestion.

"Maybe," he said at a meeting of the group held on the evening of August 25, 1955, "The Goose doesn't replace the iron with gold. Maybe it *changes* the iron to gold."

Before I met Nevis personally that summer, I had known him through his publications—his field is bile chemistry and liver function—and had always considered him a cautious, clear-thinking person. Almost overcautious. One wouldn't consider him capable for a minute of making any such completely ridiculous statement.

It just shows the desperation and demoralization involved in Project Goose.

The desperation was the fact that there was nowhere, literally nowhere, that the gold could come from. The Goose was excreting gold at the rate of 38.9 grams a day and had been doing it over a period of months. That gold had to come from somewhere and, failing that—absolutely failing that—it had to be made from something.

The demoralization that led us to consider the second alternative was due to the mere fact that we were face to face with The Goose That Laid The Golden Eggs; the undeniable GOOSE. With that, everything became possible. All of us were living in a fairy-tale world and all of us reacted to it by losing all sense of reality.

Finley considered the possibility seriously. "Hemoglobin," he said, "enters the liver and a bit of auremoglobin comes out. The gold shell of the eggs has iron as its only impurity. The egg yolk is high in only two things; in gold, of course, and also, somewhat, in iron. It all makes a horrible kind of distorted sense. We're going to need help, men."

We did, and it meant a third stage of the investigation. The first stage had consisted of myself alone. The second was the biochemical task force. The third, the greatest, the most important of all, involved the invasion of the nuclear physicists.

On September 5, 1955, John L. Billings of the University of California arrived. He had some equipment with him and more arrived in the following weeks. More temporary structures were going up. I could see that within a year we would have a whole research institution built about The Goose.

Billings joined our conference the evening of the fifth.

Finley brought him up-to-date and said, "There are a great many serious problems involved in this iron-to-gold idea. For one thing, the total quantity of iron in The Goose can only be on the order of half a gram, yet nearly forty grams of gold a day are being manufactured."

Billings had a clear, high-pitched voice. He said, "There's a worse problem than that. Iron is about at the bottom of the packing fraction curve. Gold is much higher up. To convert a gram of iron to a gram of gold takes just about as much energy as is produced by the fissioning of one gram of U-235."

Finley shrugged. "I'll leave the problem to you."

Billings said, "Let me think about it."

He did more than think. One of the things done was to isolate fresh samples of heme from The Goose, ash it and send the iron oxide to Brookhaven for isotopic analysis. There was no particular reason to do that particular thing. It was just one of a number of individual investigations, but it was the one that brought results.

When the figures came back, Billings choked on them. He said, "There's no Fe^{56}."

"What about the other isotopes?" asked Finley at once.

"All present," said Billings, "in the appropriate relative ratios, but no detectable Fe^{56}."

I'll have to explain again: Iron, as it occurs naturally, is made up of four different isotopes. These isotopes are varieties of atoms that differ from one another in atomic weight. Iron atoms with an atomic weight of 56, or Fe^{56}, make up 91.6 per cent of all the atoms in iron. The other atoms have atomic weights of 54, 57, and 58.

The iron from the heme of The Goose was made up only of Fe^{54}, Fe^{57}, and Fe^{58}. The implication was obvious. Fe^{56} was disappearing while the other isotopes weren't and this meant a nuclear reaction was taking place. A nuclear reaction could take one isotope and leave others be. An ordinary chemical reaction, any chemical reaction at all, would have to dispose of all isotopes just about equally.

"But it's energically impossible," said Finley.

He was only saying that in mild sarcasm with Billings' initial remark in mind. As biochemists, we knew well enough that many reactions went on in the body which required an input of energy and that this was taken care of by coupling the energy-demanding reaction with an energy-producing reaction.

However, chemical reactions gave off or took up a few kilocalories per mole. Nuclear reactions gave off or took up millions. To supply energy for an energy-demanding nuclear reaction required, therefore, a second, and energy-producing, nuclear reaction.

We didn't see Billings for two days.

When he did come back, it was to say, "See here. The energy-producing reaction must produce just as much energy per nucleon involved as the energy-demanding reaction uses up. If it produces even slightly less, then the overall reaction won't go. If it produces even slightly more, then considering the astronomical number of nucleons involved, the excess energy produced would vaporize The Goose in a fraction of a second."

"So?" said Finley.

"So the number of reactions possible is very limited. I have been able to find only one plausible system. Oxygen-18, if converted to iron-56, will produce enough energy to drive the iron-56 on to gold-197. It's like going down one side of a roller coaster and then up the other. We'll have to test this."

"How?"

"First, suppose we check the isotopic composition of the oxygen in The Goose."

Oxygen is made up of three stable isotopes, almost all of it O^{16}. O^{18} makes up only one oxygen atom out of 250.

Another blood sample. The water content was distilled off in vacuum and some of it put through a mass spectrograph. There was O^{18} there but only one oxygen atom out of 1300. Fully 80 per cent of the O^{18} we expected wasn't there.

Billings said, "That's corroborative evidence. Oxygen-18 is being used up. It is being supplied constantly in the food and water fed to The Goose, but it is still being used up. Gold-197 is being produced. Iron-56 is one intermediate and since the reaction that uses up iron-56 is faster than the one that produces it, it has no chance to reach significant concentration and isotopic analysis shows its absence."

We weren't satisfied, so we tried again. We kept The Goose on water that had been enriched with O^{18} for a week. Gold production went up almost at once. At the end of a week it was producing 45.8 grams while the O^{18} content of its body water was no higher than before.

"There's no doubt about it," said Billings.

He snapped his pencil and stood up. "That Goose is a living nuclear reactor."

The Goose was obviously a mutation.

A mutation suggested radiation among other things and radiation brought up the thought of nuclear tests conducted in 1952 and 1953 several hundred miles away from the site of MacGregor's farm. (If it occurs to you that no nuclear tests have been conducted in Texas, it just shows two things; I'm not telling you everything and you don't know everything.)

I doubt that at any time in the history of the atomic era was background radiation so thoroughly analyzed and the radioactive content of the soil so rigidly sifted.

Back records were studied. It didn't matter how top-secret they were. By this time, Project Goose had the highest priority that had ever existed.

Even weather records were checked in order to follow the behavior of the winds at the time of the nuclear tests.

Two things turned up.

One: The background radiation at the farm was a bit

higher than normal. Nothing that could possibly do harm, I hasten to add. There were indications, however, that at the time of the birth of The Goose, the farm had been subjected to the drifting edge of at least two fallouts. Nothing really harmful, I again hasten to add.

Second: The Goose, alone of all geese on the farm, in fact, alone of all living creatures on the farm that could be tested, including the humans, showed no radioactivity at all. Look at it this way: *everything* shows traces of radioactivity; that's what is meant by background radiation. But The Goose showed none.

Finley sent one report on December 6, 1955, which I can paraphrase as follows:

"The Goose is a most extraordinary mutation, born of a high-level radioactivity environment which at once encouraged mutations in general and which made this particular mutation a beneficial one.

"The Goose has enzyme systems capable of catalyzing various nuclear reactions. Whether the enzyme system consists of one enzyme or more than one is not known. Nor is anything known of the nature of the enzymes in question. Nor can any theory be yet advanced as to how an enzyme can catalyze a nuclear reaction, since these involve particular interactions with forces five orders of magnitude higher than those involved in the ordinary chemical reactions commonly catalyzed by enzymes.

"The overall nuclear change is from oxygen-18 to gold-197. The oxygen-18 is plentiful in its environment, being present in significant amount in water and all organic foodstuffs. The gold-197 is excreted via the ovaries. One known intermediate is iron-56 and the fact that auremoglobin is formed in the process leads us to suspect that the enzyme or enzymes involved may have heme as a prosthetic group.

"There has been considerable thought devoted to the value this overall nuclear change might have to The Goose. The oxygen-18 does it no harm and the gold-197 is troublesome to be rid of, potentially poisonous, and a cause of its sterility. Its formation might possibly be a means of avoiding greater danger. This danger—"

But just reading it in the report, friend, makes it all seem so quiet, almost pensive. Actually, I never saw a man come closer to apoplexy and survive than Billings did when he found out about our own radioactive gold experiments which I told you about earlier—the ones in which we detected no radioactivity in the goose, so that we discarded the results as meaningless.

Many times over he asked how we could possibly consider it unimportant that we had lost radioactivity.

"You're like the cub reporter," he said, "who was sent to cover a society wedding and on returning said there was no story because the groom hadn't shown up.

"You fed The Goose radioactive gold and lost it. Not only that, you failed to detect any natural radioactivity about The Goose. Any carbon-14. Any potassium-40. And you called it failure."

We started feeding The Goose radioactive isotopes. Cautiously, at first, but before the end of January of 1956 we were shoveling it in.

The Goose remained nonradioactive.

"What it amounts to," said Billings, "is that this enzyme-catalyzed nuclear process of The Goose manages to convert any unstable isotope into a stable isotope."

"Useful," I said.

"Useful? It's a thing of beauty. It's the perfect defense against the atomic age. Listen, the conversion of oxygen-18 to gold-197 should liberate eight and a fraction positrons per oxygen atom. That means eight and a fraction gamma rays as soon as each positron combines with an electron. No gamma rays, either. The Goose must be able to absorb gamma rays harmlessly."

We irradiated The Goose with gamma rays. As the level rose, The Goose developed a slight fever and we quit in panic. It was just fever, though, not radiation sickness. A day passed, the fever subsided, and The Goose was as good as new.

"Do you see what we've got?" demanded Billings.

"A scientific marvel," said Finley.

"Man, don't you see the practical applications? If we could find out the mechanism and duplicate it in the test tube, we've got a perfect method of radioactive ash disposal. The most important drawback preventing us from going ahead with a full-scale atomic economy is the headache of what to do with the radioactive isotopes manufactured in the process. Sift them through an enzyme preparation in large vats and that would be it.

"Find out the mechanism, gentlemen, and you can stop worrying about fallouts. We would find a protection against radiation sickness.

"Alter the mechanism somehow and we can have Geese excreting any element needed. How about uranium-235 eggshells?

"The mechanism! The mechanism!"

We sat there, all of us, staring at The Goose.

If only the eggs would hatch. If only we could get a tribe of nuclear-reactor Geese.

"It must have happened before," said Finley. "The legends of such Geese must have started somehow."

"Do you want to wait?" asked Billings.

If we had a gaggle of such Geese, we could begin taking a few apart. We could study its ovaries. We could prepare tissue slices and tissue homogenates.

That might not do any good. The tissue of a liver biopsy did not react with oxygen-18 under any conditions we tried.

But then we might perfuse an intact liver. We might study intact embryos, watch for one to develop the mechanism.

But with only one Goose, we could do none of that.

We don't dare kill The Goose That Lays The Golden Eggs. The secret was in the liver of that fat Goose.

Liver of fat goose! *Pâté de foie gras!* No delicacy to us!

Nevis said thoughtfully, "We need an idea. Some radical departure. Some crucial thought."

"Saying it won't bring it," said Billings despondently.

And in a miserable attempt at a joke, I said, "We could advertise in the newspapers," and that gave *me* an idea.

"Science fiction!" I said.

"What?" said Finley.

"Look, science-fiction magazines print gag articles. The readers consider it fun. They're interested." I told them about the thiotimoline articles Asimov wrote and which I had once read.

The atmosphere was cold with disapproval.

"We won't even be breaking security regulations," I said, "because no one will believe it." I told them about the time in 1944 when Cleve Cartmill wrote a story describing the atom bomb one year early and the F.B.I. kept its temper.

"And science-fiction readers have ideas. Don't underrate them. Even if they think it's a gag article, they'll send their notions in to the editor. And since we have no ideas of our own, since we're up a dead-end street, what can we lose?"

They still didn't buy it.

So I said, "And you know . . . The Goose won't live forever."

That did it, somehow.

We had to convince Washington; then I got in touch with John Campbell, editor of the magazine, and he got in touch with Asimov.

Now the article is done. I've read it, I approve, and I urge you all not to believe it. Please don't.

Only—

Any ideas?

FOREWORD

Originally I had planned to make this another Wendell Urth story, but a new magazine was about to be published and I wanted to be represented in it with something that was not too clearly a holdover from another magazine. I adjusted matters accordingly. I am a little sorry now and I played with the thought of rewriting the story for this volume and restoring Dr. Urth, but inertia rose triumphant over all.

The Dust of Death

Like all men who worked under the great Llewes, Edmund Farley reached the point where he thought with longing of the pleasure it would give him to kill that same great Llewes.

No man who did not work for Llewes would quite understand the feeling. Llewes (men forgot his first name or grew, also unconsciously, to think it was Great, with a capital G) was Everyman's idea of the great prober into the unknown: both relentless and brilliant, neither giving up in the face of failure nor ever at a loss for a new and more ingenious attack.

Llewes was an organic chemist who had brought the Solar System to the service of his science. It was he who first used the Moon for large-scale reactions to be run in vacuum, at the temperature of boiling water or liquid air, depending on the time of month. Photochemistry became something new and wonderful when carefully designed apparatus was set floating freely in orbits about space stations.

But, truth to tell, Llewes was a credit stealer, a sin almost impossible to forgive. Some nameless student had first thought of setting up apparatus on the Lunar surface; a forgotten technician had designed the first self-contained space reactor. Somehow both achievements became associated with the name of Llewes.

And nothing could be done. An employee who resigned in anger would lose his recommendation and find it difficult to obtain another job. His unsupported word against that of Llewes would be worth nothing. On the other hand, those who remained with him, endured, and finally left with good grace and a recommendation were sure of future success.

But while they stayed, they at least enjoyed the dubious pleasure of voicing their hatred among themselves.

And Edmund Farley had full reason to join them. He had come from Titan, Saturn's largest satellite, where he had singlehandedly—aided by robots only—set up equipment to make full use of Titan's reducing atmosphere. The major planets had atmospheres composed largely of hydrogen and methane, but Jupiter and Saturn were too large to deal with, and Uranus and Neptune were still too expensively far. Titan, however, was Mars-size, small enough to operate upon and large enough and cold enough to retain a medium-thin hydrogen-methane atmosphere.

Large-scale reactions could proceed there easily in the hydrogen atmosphere, where on Earth those same reactions were kinetically troublesome. Farley had designed and redesigned and endured Titan for half a year and had come back with amazing data. Yet somehow, almost at once, Farley could see it fragment and begin to come together as a Llewes achievement.

The others sympathized, shrugged their shoulders, and bade him welcome to the fraternity. Farley tensed his acne-scarred face, brought his thin lips together, and listened to the others as they plotted violence.

Jim Gorham was the most outspoken. Farley rather despised him, for he was a "vacuum man" who had never left Earth.

Gorham said, "Llewes is an easy man to kill because of his regular habits, you see. You can rely on him. For instance, look at the way he insists on eating by himself. He closes his office at twelve sharp and opens it at one sharp. Right? No one goes into his office in that interval, so poison has plenty of time to work."

Belinsky said dubiously, "Poison?"

"Easy. Plenty of poison all over the place. You name it, we got it. Okay, then. Llewes eats one Swiss cheese on rye with a special kind of relish knee-deep in onions. We all know that, right? After all, we can smell him all afternoon and we all remember the miserable howl he raised when the lunchroom ran out of the relish once last spring. No one else in the place will ever touch the relish, so poison in it will hit only Llewes and no one else . . ."

It was all a kind of lunchtime make-believe, but not for Farley.

Grimly, and in earnest, he decided to murder Llewes.

It became an obsession with him. His blood tingled at the thought of Llewes dead, of himself able to take the credit that was rightfully his for those months of living in a small bubble of oxygen and tramping across frozen ammonia to remove products and set up new reactions in the thin, chill winds of hydrogen and methane.

But it would have to be something which couldn't possibly harm anyone but Llewes. That sharpened the matter and focused things on Llewes' atmosphere room. It was a long, low room, isolated from the rest of the laboratories by cement blocks and fireproof doors. No one but Llewes ever entered, except in Llewes' presence and with his permission. Not that the room was ever actually locked. The effective tyranny Llewe had established made the faded slip of paper on the laboratory door, reading "Do Not Enter" and signed with his initials, more of a barrier than any lock . . . except where the desire for murder superseded all else.

Then what about the atmosphere room? Llewes' routine of testing, his almost infinite caution, left nothing to chance. Any tampering with the equipment itself, unless it were unusually subtle, would certainly be detected.

Fire then? The atmosphere room contained inflammable materials and to spare, but Llewes didn't smoke and was perfectly aware of the danger of fires. No one took greater precautions against one.

Farley thought impatiently of the man on whom it seemed so difficult to wreak a just vengeance; the thief playing with his little tanks of methane and hydrogen where Farley had used it by the cubic mile. Llewes for the little tanks and fame; Farley for the cubic miles and oblivion.

All those little tanks of gas; each its own color; each a synthetic atmosphere. Hydrogen gas in red cylinders and methane in striped red and white, a mixture of the two representing the atmosphere of the outer planets. Nitrogen in brown cylinders and carbon dioxide in silver for the atmosphere of Venus. The yellow cylinders of compressed air and the green cylinders of oxygen, where Earthly chemistry was good enough. A parade of the rainbow, each color dating back through centuries of convention.

Then he had the thought. It was not born painfully, but came all at once. In one moment it had all crystallized in Farley's mind and he knew what he had to do.

Farley waited a painful month for the eighteenth of September, which was Space Day. It was the anniversary of man's first successful space flight and no one would be working that night. Space Day was, of all holidays, the one most meaningful to the scientist in particular and even the dedicated Llewes would be making merry then.

Farley entered Central Organic Laboratories—to use its official title—that night, certain he was unobserved. The labs weren't banks or museums. They were not subject to thievery and such nightwatchmen as there were had a generally easygoing attitude toward their jobs.

Farley closed the main door carefully behind him and moved slowly down the darkened corridors toward the atmosphere room. His equipment consisted of a flashlight, a small vial of black powder, and a thin brush he had bought in an art-supply store at the other end of town three weeks before. He wore gloves.

His greatest difficulty came in actually entering the atmosphere room. Its "forbiddenness" hampered him more than the general forbiddenness of murder. Once in, however, once past the mental hazard, the rest was easy.

He cupped the flashlight and found the cylinder without hesitation. His heart was beating so as almost to deafen him, while his breath came quickly and his hand trembled.

He tucked the flash under his arm, then dipped the tip of the artist's brush into the black dust. Grains of it adhered to the brush and Farley pointed it into the nozzle of the gauge attached to the cylinder. It took eons-long seconds for that trembling tip to enter the nozzle.

Farley moved it about delicately, dipped it into the black dust again, and inserted it once more in the nozzle. He repeated it over and over, almost hypnotized by the intensity of his own concentration. Finally, using a bit of facial tissue dampened with saliva, he began to wipe off the outer rim of the nozzle, enormously relieved that the job was done and he'd soon be out.

It was then his hand froze, and the sick uncertainty of fear surged through him. The flashlight dropped clattering to the floor.

Fool! Incredible and miserable fool! He hadn't been *thinking!*

Under the stress of his emotion and anxiety, he had ended at the wrong cylinder!

He snatched up the flash, put it out, and, his heart thumping alarmingly, listened for any noise.

In the continuing dead silence, he regained a portion of his self-control, and screwed himself to the realization that what could be done once could be done again. If the wrong cylinder had been tampered with, then the right one would take two minutes more.

Once again, the brush and the black dust came into play. At least, he had not dropped the vial of dust; the deadly, burning dust. This time, the cylinder was the right one.

He finished, wiping the nozzle again, with a badly trembling hand. His flash then played about quickly and rested upon a reagent bottle of toluene. That would do. He unscrewed the plastic cap, splashed some of the toluene on the floor, and left the bottle open.

He then stumbled out of the building as in a dream, made his way to his rooming house and the safety of his own room. As nearly as he could tell, he was unobserved throughout.

He disposed of the facial tissue he had used to wipe the nozzles of the gas cylinders by cramming it into the flash-disposal unit. It vanished into molecular dispersion. So did the artist's brush that followed.

The vial of dust could not be so gotten rid of without adjustments to the disposal unit he did not think it safe to make. He would walk to work, as he often did, and toss it off the Grand Street bridge . . .

Farley blinked at himself in the mirror the next morning and wondered if he dared go to work. It was an idle thought; he didn't dare *not* to go to work. He must do nothing that would attract attention to him on this day of all days.

With grayish desperation, he worked to reproduce normal acts of nothingness that made up so much of the day. It was a fine, warm morning and he walked to work. It was only a flicking motion of the wrist that was necessary to get rid of the vial. It made a tiny splash in the river, filled with water, and sank.

He sat at his desk, later that morning, staring at his hand computer. Now that it had all been done, would it work? Llewes might ignore the smell of toluene. Why not? The odor was unpleasant, but not disgusting. Organic chemists were used to it.

Then, if Llewes were still hot on the trail of the hydrogenation procedures Farley had brought back from Titan, the gas cylinder would be put into use at once. It would have to be. With a day of holiday behind him, Llewes would be more than usually anxious to get back to work.

Then, as soon as the gauge cock was turned, a bit of gas would spurt out and turn into a sheet of flame. If there were the proper quantity of toluene in the air, it would turn as quickly into an explosion—

So intent was Farley in his reverie that he accepted the dull boom in the distance as the creation of his own mind, a counterpoint to his own thoughts, until footsteps thudded by.

Farley looked up, and out of a dry throat, cried, "What— what—"

"Dunno," yelled back the other. "Something wrong in the atmosphere room. Explosion. Hell of a mess."

The extinguishers were on and men beat out the flames and snatched the burned and battered Llewes out of the wreckage. He had the barest flicker of life left in him and died before a doctor had time to predict that he would.

On the outskirts of the group that hovered about the scene in grim and grisly curiosity stood Edmund Farley. His pallor and the glisten of perspiration on his face did not, at that moment, mark him as different from the rest. He tottered back to his desk. He could be sick now. No one would remark on it.

But somehow he wasn't. He finished out the day and in the evening the load began to lighten. Accident was accident, wasn't it? There were occupational risks all chemists ran, especially those working with inflammable compounds. No one would question the matter.

And if anyone did, how could they possibly trace anything back to Edmund Farley? He had only to go about his life as though nothing had happened.

Nothing? Good Lord, the credit for Titan would now be his. He would be a great man.

The load lightened indeed and that night he slept.

Jim Gorham had faded a bit in twenty-four hours. His yellow hair was stringy and only the light color of his stubble masked the fact that he needed a shave badly.

"We all talked murder," he said.

H. Seton Davenport of the Terrestrial Bureau of Investigation tapped one finger against the desktop methodically, and so lightly that it could not be heard. He was a stocky man with a firm face and black hair, a thin, prominent nose made for utility rather than beauty, and a star-shaped scar on one cheek.

"Seriously?" he asked.

"No," said Gorham, shaking his head violently. "At least, I didn't think it was serious. The schemes were wild: poisoned sandwich spreads and acid on the helicopter, you know. Still, someone must have taken the matter seriously after all . . . The madman! For what reason?"

Davenport said, "From what you've said, I judge because the dead man appropriated other people's work."

"So what?" cried Gorham. "It was the price he charged for what he did. He held the entire team together. He was its muscles and guts. Llewes was the one who dealt with Congress and got the grants. He was the one who got permission to set up projects in space and send men to the Moon or wherever. He talked spaceship lines and industrialists into doing millions of dollars of work for us. He *organized* Central Organic."

"Have you realized all this overnight?"

"Not really. I've always known this, but what could I do? I've chickened out of space travel, found excuses to avoid it. I was a vacuum man, who never even visited the Moon. The truth was, I was afraid, and even more afraid to have the others think I was afraid." He virtually spat self-contempt.

"And now you want to find someone to punish?" said Davenport. "You want to make up to the dead Llewes your crime against the live one?"

"No! Leave psychiatry out of this. I tell you it *is* murder. It's *got* to be. You didn't know Llewes. The man was a monomaniac on safety. No explosion could possibly have happened anywhere near him unless it were carefully arranged."

Davenport shrugged. "What exploded, Dr. Gorham?"

"It could have been almost anything. He handled organic compounds of all sorts—benzene, ether, pyridine—all of them inflammable."

"I studied chemistry once, Dr. Gorham, and none of those liquids is explosive at room temperature as I remember. There has to be some sort of heat, a spark, a flame."

"There was fire all right."

"How did that happen?"

"I can't imagine. There were no burners in the place and no matches. Electrical equipment of all sorts was heavily shielded. Even little ordinary things like clamps were specially manufactured out of beryllium copper or other nonsparking alloys. Llewes didn't smoke and would have fired on the spot anyone who approached within a hundred feet of the room with a lighted cigarette."

"What was the last thing he handled, then?"

"Hard to tell. The place was a shambles."

"I suppose it has been straightened out by now, though."

The chemist said with instant eagerness, "No, it hasn't. I took care of that. I said we had to investigate the cause of the accident to prove it wasn't neglect. You know, to avoid bad publicity. So the room hasn't been touched."

Davenport nodded. "All right. Let's take a look at it."

In the blackened, disheveled room, Davenport said, "What's the most dangerous piece of equipment in the place?"

Gorham looked about. "The compressed oxygen tanks," he said, pointing.

Davenport looked at the variously colored cylinders standing against the wall cradled in a binding chain. Some leaned heavily against the chain, tipped by the force of the explosion.

Davenport said, "How about this one?" He toed a red cylinder which lay flat on the ground in the middle of the room. It was heavy and didn't budge.

"That one's hydrogen," said Gorham.

"Hydrogen is explosive, isn't it?"

"That's right—when heated."

Davenport said, "Then why do you say the compressed oxygen is the most dangerous? Oxygen doesn't explode, does it?"

"No. It doesn't even burn, but it supports combustion, see. Things burn in it."

"So?"

"Well, look here." A certain vivacity entered Gorham's voice; he was the scientist explaining something simple to the intelligent layman. "Sometimes a person might accidentally put some lubricant on the valve before tightening it onto the cylinder, to make a tighter seal, you know. Or he might get something inflammable smeared on it by mistake. When he opens the valve then, the oxygen rushes out, and whatever goo is on the valve explodes, wrenching off the valve. Then the rest of the oxygen blows out of the cylinder, which would then take off like a miniature jet and go through a wall; the heat of the explosion would fire other inflammable liquids nearby."

"Are the oxygen tanks in this place intact?"

"Yes, they are."

Davenport kicked the hydrogen cylinder at his feet. "The gauge on this cylinder reads zero. I suppose that means it was in use at the time of explosion and has emptied itself since then."

Gorham nodded. "I suppose so."

"Could you explode hydrogen by smearing oil on the gauge?"

"Definitely not."

Davenport rubbed his chin. "Is there anything that would make hydrogen burst into flame outside of a spark of some sort?"

Gorham muttered, "A catalyst, I suppose. Platinum black is the best. That's powdered platinum."

Davenport looked astonished. "Do you have such a thing?"

"Of course. It's expensive, but there's nothing better for catalyzing hydrogenations." He fell silent and stared down at the hydrogen cylinder for a long moment. "Platinum black," he finally whispered. "I wonder—"

Davenport said, "Platinum black would make hydrogen burn, then?"

"Oh, yes. It brings about the combination of hydrogen and oxygen at room temperature. No heat necessary. The explosion would be just as though it were caused by heat, just the same."

Excitement was building up in Gorham's voice and he fell to his knees beside the hydrogen cylinder. He passed his finger over the blackened tip. It might be just soot and it might be—"

He got to his feet, "Sir, that must be the way it was done. I'm going to get every speck of foreign material off that nozzle and run a spectrographic analysis."

"How long will it take?"

"Give me fifteen minutes."

Gorham came back in twenty. Davenport had made a meticulous round of the burned-out laboratory. He looked up. "Well?"

Gorham said triumphantly, "It's there. Not much, but there."

He held up a strip of photographic negative against which there were short white parallel lines, irregularly spaced and of different degrees of brightness. "Mostly extraneous material, but you see those lines . . ."

Davenport peered closely. "*Very* faint. Would you swear in court that platinum was present?"

"Yes," said Gorham at once.

"Would any other chemist? If this photo were shown a chemist hired by the defense, could he claim the lines were too faint to be certain evidence?"

Gorham was silent.

Davenport shrugged.

The chemist cried, "But it *is* there. The stream of gas and the explosion would have blown most of it out. You wouldn't expect much to be left. You see that, don't you?"

Davenport looked about thoughtfully. "I do. I admit there's a reasonable chance this is murder. So now we look for more and better evidence. Do you suppose this is the only cylinder that might have been tampered with?"

"I don't know."

"Then the first thing we do is check every other cylinder in the place. Everything else, too. If there is a murderer, he might conceivably have set other booby traps in the place. It's got to be checked."

"I'll get started—" began Gorham eagerly.

"Uh—not you," said Davenport. "I'll have a man from our labs do it."

The next morning, Gorham was in Davenport's office again. This time he had been summoned.

Davenport said, "It's murder, all right. A second cylinder had been tampered with."

"You see!"

"An oxygen cylinder. There was platinum black inside the tip of the nozzle. Quite a bit of it."

"Platinum black? On the *oxygen* cylinder?"

Davenport nodded. "Right. Now why do you suppose that would be?"

Gorham shook his head. "Oxygen won't burn and nothing will make it burn. Not even platinum black."

"So the murderer must have put it on the oxygen cylinder by mistake in the tension of the moment. Presumably he corrected himself and tampered with the right cylinder, but meanwhile he left final evidence that this is murder and not accident."

"Yes. Now it's only a matter of finding the person."

The scar on Davenport's cheek crinkled alarmingly as he smiled. "*Only*, Dr. Gorham? How do we do that? Our quarry left no calling card. There are a number of people in the laboratories with motive; a greater number with the chemical knowledge required to commit the crime and with the opportunity to do so. Is there any way we can trace the platinum black?"

"No," said Gorham hesitantly. "Any of twenty people

could have gotten into the special supply room without trouble. What about alibis?"

"For what time?"

"For the night before."

Davenport leaned across his desk. "When was the last time, previous to the fatal moment, that Dr. Llewes used that hydrogen cylinder?"

"I—I don't know. He worked alone. Very secretly. It was part of his way of making sure he had sole credit."

"Yes, I know. We've been making our own inquiries. So the platinum black might have been put on the cylinder a week before for all we know."

Gorham whispered disconsolately, "Then what do we do?"

Davenport said, "The only point of attack, it seems to me, is the platinum black on the oxygen cylinder. It's an irrational point and the explanation may hold the solution. But I'm no chemist and you are, so if the answer is anywhere it's inside you. Could it have been a mistake—could the murderer have confused the oxygen with the hydrogen?"

Gorham shook his head at once. "No. You know about the colors. A green tank is oxygen; a red tank is hydrogen."

"What if he were color blind?" asked Davenport.

This time Gorham took more time. Finally he said, "No. Color-blind people don't generally go in for chemistry. Detection of color in chemical reactions is too important. And if anybody in this organization were color blind, he'd have enough trouble with one thing or another so that the rest of us would know about it."

Davenport nodded. He fingered the scar on his cheek absently. "All right. If the oxygen cylinder wasn't smeared by ignorance or accident, could it have been done on purpose? Deliberately?"

"I don't understand you."

"Perhaps the murderer had a logical plan in mind when he smeared the oxygen cylinder, then changed his mind. Are there any conditions where platinum black would be dangerous in the presence of oxygen? Any conditions at all? You're the chemist, Dr. Gorham."

There was a puzzled frown on the chemist's face. He shook his head. "No, none. There can't be. Unless—"

"Unless?"

"Well, this is ridiculous, but if you stuck the oxygen jet into a container of hydrogen gas, platinum black on the gas cylinder could be dangerous. Naturally you'd need a big container to make a satisfactory explosion."

"Suppose," said Davenport, "our murderer had counted on filling the room with hydrogen and then having the oxygen tank turned on."

Gorham said, with a half-smile, "But why bother with the hydrogen atmosphere when—" The half-smile vanished completely while a complete pallor took its place. He cried, "Farley! Edmund Farley!"

"What's that?"

"Farley just returned from six months on Titan," said Gorham in gathering excitement. "Titan has a hydrogen-methane atmosphere. He is the only man here to have had experience in such an atmosphere, and it all makes sense now. On Titan a jet of oxygen will combine with the surrounding hydrogen if heated, or treated with platinum black. A jet of hydrogen won't. The situation is exactly the reverse of what it is here on Earth. It *must* have been Farley. When he entered Llewes' lab to arrange an explosion, he put the platinum black on the oxygen, out of recent habit. By the time he recalled that the situation was the other way round on Earth, the damage was done."

Davenport nodded in grim satisfaction. "That does it, I think." His hand reached out to an intercom and he said to the unseen recipient at the other end, "Send out a man to pick up Dr. Edmund Farley at Central Organic."

A Loint of Paw

There was no question that Montie Stein had, through clever fraud, stolen better than $100,000. There was also no question that he was apprehended one day after the statute of limitations had expired.

It was his manner of avoiding arrest during that interval that brought on the epoch-making case of the State of New York *vs.* Montgomery Harlow Stein, with all its consequences. It introduced law to the fourth dimension.

For, you see, after having committed the fraud and possessed himself of the hundred grand plus, Stein had calmly entered a time machine, of which he was in illegal possession, and set the controls for seven years and one day in the future.

Stein's lawyer put it simply. Hiding in time was not fundamentally different from hiding in space. If the forces of law had not uncovered Stein in the seven-year interval that was their hard luck.

The District Attorney pointed out that the statute of limitations was not intended to be a game between the law and the criminal. It was a merciful measure designed to protect a culprit from indefinitely prolonged fear of arrest. For certain crimes, a defined period of apprehension of apprehension— so to speak—was considered punishment enough. But Stein, the D.A. insisted, had not experienced any period of apprehension at all.

Stein's lawyer remained unmoved. The law said nothing about measuring the extent of a culprit's fear and anguish. It simply set a time limit.

The D.A. said that Stein had not lived through the limit.

Defense stated that Stein was seven years older now than at the time of the crime and had therefore lived through the limit.

The D.A. challenged the statement and the defense produced Stein's birth certificate. He was born in 2973. At the time of the crime, 3004, he was thirty-one. Now, in 3011, he was thirty-eight.

The D.A. shouted that Stein was not physiologically thirty-eight, but thirty-one.

Defense pointed out freezingly that the law, once the individual was granted to be mentally competent, recognized solely chronological age, which could be obtained only by subtracting the date of birth from the date of now.

The D.A., growing impassioned, swore that if Stein were allowed to go free, half the laws on the books would be useless.

Then change the laws, said Defense, to take time travel into account; but until the laws are changed, let them be enforced as written.

Judge Neville Preston took a week to consider and then handed down his decision. It was a turning point in the history of law. It is almost a pity, then, that some people suspect Judge Preston to have been swayed in his way of thinking by the irresistible impulse to phrase his decision as he did.

For that decision, in full, was:

"A niche in time saves Stein."

AFTERWORD

If you expect me to apologize for this, you little know your man. I consider a play on words the noblest form of wit, so there!

FOREWORD

This is a James Bond type of story, written before I had ever heard of James Bond.

Actually, those who know my writing know that I never introduce naughty motifs into my stories. You can tell that from the other stories in this volume.

However, an editor—I won't mention his name—once told me he suspected that I never had love scenes in my stories because I was incapable of writing them. Naturally I repudiated that suggestion with the scorn and contumely it deserved and said with heat that it was merely my natural purity and wholesomeness that kept me from doing so.

Since the expression on his face was one of obvious disbelief, I said, "I'll show you. I'll write a science-fiction love story, but not for publication."

But it turned out also to be a mystery, and I was so pleased with it I let it be published.

Anyway, it shows I can do it if I want to. It's just that I don't want to, ordinarily.

I'm in Marsport Without Hilda

It worked itself out, to begin with, like a dream. I didn't have to make any arrangements. I didn't have to touch it. I just watched things work out. Maybe right then's when I should have smelled catastrophe.

It began with my usual month's layoff between assignments. A month on and a month off is the right and proper routine for the Galactic Service. I reached Marsport for the usual three-day layover before the short hop to Earth.

Ordinarily, Hilda, God bless her, as sweet a wife as any man ever had, would be there waiting for me and we'd have a nice sedate time of it—a nice little interlude for the two of us. The only trouble with that is that Marsport is the rowdiest hellhole in the system, and a nice little interlude isn't exactly what fits in. Only, how do I explain that to Hilda, hey?

Well, *this* time my mother-in-law—God *bless* her, for a change—got sick just two days before I reached Marsport; and the night before landing, I got a spacegram from Hilda saying she would stay on Earth with her mother and wouldn't meet me this one time.

I grammed back my loving regrets and my feverish anxiety concerning her mother; and when I landed, there I was:

I was in Marsport without Hilda!

That was still nothing, you understand. It was the frame of the picture, the bones of the woman. Now there was the matter of the lines and coloring inside the frame; the skin and flesh outside the bones.

So I called up Flora—Flora of certain rare episodes in the past—and for the purpose I used a video booth. Damn the expense, full speed ahead.

I was giving myself ten to one odds she'd be out, she'd be busy with her videophone disconnected, she'd be dead, even.

But she was in, with her videophone connected and she was anything but dead.

She looked better than ever. Age cannot wither nor custom stale, as somebody or other once said, her infinite variety. And the robe she wore—or, rather, almost didn't wear—helped a lot.

Was she glad to see me? She squealed, "Max! It's been years."

"I know, Flora, but this is it, if you're available. Because guess what! I'm in Marsport without Hilda."

She squealed again. "Isn't that *nice!* Then come on over."

I goggled a bit. This was too much. "You mean you *are* available?" You have to understand that Flora was never available without plenty of notice. Well, she was that kind of knockout.

She said, "Oh, I've got some quibbling little arrangement, Max, but I'll take care of that. You come on over."

"I'll come," I said happily.

Flora was the kind of girl—Well, I tell you, she had her rooms under Martian gravity, 0.4 Earth-normal. The gadget to free her of Marsport's pseudo-gray field was expensive, of course, but I'll tell you just in passing that it was worth it, and she had no trouble paying it off. If you've ever held a girl in your arms at 0.4 gees, you need no explanation. If you haven't, explanations will do no good. I'm also sorry for you.

Talk about floating on clouds . . .

And mind you, the girl has to know how to handle low gravity. Flora did. I won't talk about myself, you understand, but Flora didn't howl for me to come over and start breaking previous engagements just because she was at loose ends. Her ends were never loose.

I closed connections, and only the prospect of seeing it all in the flesh—such flesh!—could have made me wipe out the image with such alacrity. I stepped out of the booth.

And at that point, that precise point, that very split instant of time, the first whiff of catastrophe nudged itself up to me.

That first whiff was the bald head of that lousy Rog Crinton of the Mars offices, gleaming over a headful of pale blue eyes, pale yellow complexion, and pale brown mustache. He was the same Rog Crinton, with some Slavic strain in his ancestry, that half the people out on field work thought had a middle name that went sunnuvabich.

I didn't bother getting on all fours and beating my forehead against the ground because my vacation had started the minute I had gotten off the ship.

I said with only normal politeness, "What the hell do you want and I'm in a hurry. I've got an appointment."

He said, "You've got an appointment with me. I've got a little job for you."

I laughed and told him in all necessary anatomical detail where he could put the little job, and offered to get him a mallet to help. I said, "It's my month off, friend."

He said, "Red emergency alert, friend."

Which meant, no vacation, just like that. I couldn't believe it. I said, "Nuts, Rog. Have a heart. I got an emergency alert of my own."

"Nothing like this."

"Rog," I pleaded, "can't you get someone else? Anyone else?"

"You're the only Class A agent on Mars."

"Send to Earth, then. They stack agents like micropile units at Headquarters."

"This has got to be done before 11 P.M. What's the matter? You haven't got three hours?"

I grabbed my head. The boy just didn't *know*. I said, "Let me make a call, will you?"

I stepped back in the booth, glared at him, and said, "Private!"

Flora shone on the screen again, like a mirage on an asteroid. She said, "Something wrong, Max? Don't say something's wrong. I canceled my other engagement."

I said, "Flora, baby, I'll be there. I'll *be* there. But something's come up."

She asked the natural question in a hurt tone of voice and I said, "*No*. Not another girl. With you in the same town they don't make any other girls. Females, maybe. Not girls. Baby! Honey! It's business. Just hold on. It won't take long."

She said, "All right," but she said it kind of like it was just enough *not* all right so that I got the shivers.

I stepped out of the booth and said, "All right, Rog Sunnuvabich, what kind of mess have you cooked up for me?"

We went into the spaceport bar and got us an insulated

booth. He said, "The *Antares Giant* is coming in from Sirius in exactly half an hour, at 8 P.M. local time."

"Okay."

"Three men will get out, among others, and will wait for the *Space Eater* coming in from Earth at 11 P.M. and leaving for Capella some time thereafter. The three men will get on the *Space Eater* and will then be out of our jurisdiction."

"So."

"So between eight and eleven, they will be in a special waiting room and you will be with them. I have a trimensional image of each for you so you'll know who they are and which is which. You have between eight and eleven to decide which one is carrying contraband."

"What kind of contraband?"

"The worst kind. Altered Spaceoline."

"*Altered* Spaceoline?"

He had thrown me. I knew what Spaceoline was. If you've been on a space hop you know too. And in case you're Earthbound yourself the bare fact is that everyone needs it on the first space trip; almost everybody needs it for the first dozen trips; lots need it every trip. Without it, there is vertigo associated with free fall, screaming terrors, semipermanent psychoses. With it, there is nothing; you don't mind a thing. And it isn't habit-forming; it has no adverse side effects. Spaceoline is ideal, essential, unsubstitutable. When in doubt take Spaceoline.

Rog said, "That's right, altered Spaceoline. It can be changed chemically, by a simple reaction that can be conducted in anyone's basement, into a drug that will give one giant-size charge and become your baby-blue habit the first time. It is on a par with the most dangerous alkaloids we know."

"And we just found out about it?"

"No. The Serivce has known about it for years, and we've kept others from knowing by squashing every discovery flat. Now, however, the discovery has gone too far."

"In what way?"

"One of the men who will be stopping over at this spaceport is carrying some of the altered Spaceoline on his person. Chemists in the Capellan system, which is outside the Federation, will analyze it and set up ways of synthesizing more.

After that, it's either fight the worst drug menace we've ever seen or suppress the matter by suppressing the source."

"You mean Spaceoline."

"Right. And if we suppress Spaceoline, we suppress space travel."

I decided to put my finger on the point. "Which one of the three has it?"

Rog smiled nastily. "If we knew, would we need you? You're to find out which of the three."

"You're calling on me for a lousy frisk job?"

"Touch the wrong one at the risk of a haircut down to the larynx. Every one of the three is a big man on his own planet. One is Edward Harponaster; one is Joaquin Lipsky; and one is Andiamo Ferrucci. Well?"

He was right. I'd heard of every one of them. Chances are you have too. *Important,* very important people, and not one was touchable without proof in advance. I said, "Would one of them touch a dirty deal like—"

"There are trillions involved," said Rog, "which means any one of the three would. And one of them *has,* because Jack Hawk got that far before he was killed—"

"Jack Hawk's *dead?"*

"Right, and one of those guys arranged the killing. Now you find out which. You put the finger on the right one before eleven and there's a promotion, a raise in pay, a pay-back for poor Jack Hawk, and a rescue of the Galaxy. You put the finger on the wrong one and there'll be a nasty interstellar situation and you'll be out on your ear and also on every blacklist from here to Antares and back."

I said, "Suppose I don't finger anybody?"

"That would be like fingering the wrong one as far as the Service is concerned."

"I've got to finger someone, but only the right one, or my head's handed to me?"

"In thin slices. You're beginning to understand me, Max."

In a long lifetime of looking ugly, Rog Crinton had never looked uglier. The only comfort I got out of staring at him was the realization that he was married too, and that he lived with his wife at Marsport all year round. And does he deserve that! Maybe I'm hard on him, but he *deserves* it.

I put in a quick call to Flora, as soon as Rog was out of sight.

She said, "Well?" The magnetic seams on her robe were opened just right and her voice sounded as thrillingly soft as she looked.

I said, "Baby, honey, it's something I can't talk about, but I've got to do it, see? Now you hang on, I'll get it over with if I have to swim the Grand Canal to the icecap in my underwear, see? If I have to claw Phobos out of the sky. If I have to cut myself in pieces and mail myself parcel post."

"Gee," she said, "if I thought I was going to have to wait . . ."

I winced. She just wasn't the type to respond to poetry. Actually, she was a simple creature of action . . . but after all, if I were going to be drifting through low gravity in a sea of jasmine perfume with Flora, poetry response is not the type of qualification I would consider most indispensable.

I said urgently, "Just hold on, Flora. I won't be any time at all. I'll make it up to you."

I was annoyed, sure, but I wasn't worried as yet. Rog hadn't more than left me when I figured out exactly how I was going to tell the guilty man from the others.

It was easy. I should have called Rog back and told him, but there's no law against wanting egg in your beer and oxygen in your air. It would take me five minutes and then off I would go to Flora; a little late, maybe, but with a promotion, a raise, and a slobbering kiss from the Service on each cheek.

You see, it's like this. Big industrialists don't go space hopping much; they use transvideo reception. When they do go to some ultra-high interstellar conference, as these three were probably going, they took Spaceoline. For one thing, they didn't have enough hops under their belt to risk doing without. For another, Spaceoline was the expensive way of doing it and industrialists did things the expensive way. I know their psychology.

Now that would hold for two of them. The one who carried contraband, however, couldn't risk Spaceoline—even at the price of risking space sickness. Under Spaceoline influence, he could throw the drug away, or give it away, or talk gibberish about it. He would *have* to stay in control of himself.

It was as simple as that.

The *Antares Giant* was on time. They brought in Lipsky first. He had thick, ruddy lips, rounded jowls, very dark eyebrows, and hair just beginning to show gray. He just looked at me and sat down. Nothing. He was under Spaceoline.

I said, "Good evening, sir."

He said, in a dreamy voice, "Surrealismus of Panamy hearts in three-quarter time for a cup of coffeedom of speech."

That was Spaceoline all the way. The buttons in the human mind were set free-swinging. Each syllable suggests the next in free association.

Andiamo Ferrucci came in next. Black mustache, long and waxed, olive complexion, pock-marked face. He sat down.

I said, "Nice trip?"

He said, "Trip the light fantastic tock the clock is crowings on the bird."

Lipsky said, "Bird to the wise guyed book to all places everybody."

I grinned. That left Harponaster. I had my needle gun neatly palmed and out of sight and the magnetic coil ready to grip him.

And then Harponaster came in. He was thin, leathery, and, though near-bald, considerably younger than he seemed in his trimensional image. And he was Spaceolined to the gills.

I said, "Damn!"

Harponaster said, "Damyankee note speech to his last time I saw wood you say so."

Ferrucci said, "Sow the seed the territory under dispute do well to come along long road tonightingale."

Lipsky said, "Gay lords hopping pong balls."

I stared from one to the other as the nonsense ran down in shorter and shorter spurts and then silence.

I got the picture, all right. One of them was faking. He had thought ahead and realized that omitting the Spaceoline would be a giveaway. He might have bribed an official into injecting saline or dodged it some other way.

One of them was faking. It wasn't hard to fake the thing. Comedians on sub-etheric had a Spaceoline skit regularly. It was amazing the liberties they could take with the moral code in that way. *You*'ve heard them.

I stared at them and got the first prickle at the base of my skull that said: What if you *don't* finger the right one?

It was eight-thirty and there was my job, my reputation, my head growing rickety upon my neck to be considered. I saved it all for later and thought of Flora. She wasn't going to wait for me forever. For that matter, chances were she wouldn't wait for half an hour.

I wondered. Could the faker keep up free association if nudged gently onto dangerous territory?

I said, "The floor's covered with a nice solid rug" and ran the last two words together to make it "soli drug."

Lipsky: "Drug from underneath the dough re mi fa sol to be saved."

Ferrucci said, "Saved and a haircut above the common herd something about younicorny as Kansas high as my knee."

Harponaster said, "Kneether wind nor snow use trying to by four ever and effervescence and sensibilityter totter."

Lipsky said, "Totters and rags."

Ferrucci said, "Agsactly."

Harponaster said, "Actlymation."

A few grunts and they ran down.

I tried again and I didn't forget to be careful. They would remember everything I said afterward and what I said had to be harmless. I said, "This is a darned good space-line."

Ferrucci said, "Lines and tigers and elephanthills on the prairie dogs do bark of the boughwough—"

I interrupted, looking at Harponaster, "A darned good space-line."

"Line the bed and rest a little black sheepishion of wrong way to ring the clothes of a perfect day."

I interrupted again, glaring at Lipsky, "Good space-line."

"Liron is hot-chacolit ain't gonna be the same on you vee and double the stakes and potato and heel."

Someone else said, "Heel the sicknecessaryd and write will wincetance."

"Tance with mealtime."

"I'm comingle."

"Inglish."

"Ishter seals."

"Eels."

I tried a few more times and got nowhere. The faker, whichever he was, had practiced or had natural talents at talking free association. He was disconnecting his brain and letting the words come out any old way. And he must be inspired by knowing exactly what I was after. If "drug" hadn't given it away, "space-line" three times repeated must have. I was safe with the other two, but *he* would know.

And he was having fun with me. All three were saying phrases that might have pointed to a deep inner guilt—"sol to be saved," "little black sheepishion of wrong,"—"drug from underneath," and so on. Two were saying such things helplessly, randomly. The third was amusing himself.

So how did I find the third? I was in a feverish thrill of hatred against him and my fingers twitched. The bastard was subverting the Galaxy. More than that, he was keeping me from Flora.

I could go up to each of them and start searching. The two who were really under Spaceoline would make no move to stop me. They could feel no emotion, no fear, no anxiety, no hate, no passion, no desire for self-defense. And if one made the slightest gesture of resistance I would have my man.

But the innocent ones would remember afterward.

I sighed. If I tried it, I would get the criminal all right, but later I would be the nearest thing to chopped liver any man had ever been. There would be a shakeup in the Service, a big stink the width of the Galaxy, and in the excitement and disorganization, the secret of altered Spaceoline would get out anyway and so what the hell.

Of course, the one I wanted might be the first one I touched. One chance out of three. I'd have one out and only God can make a three.

Damn it, something had started them going while I was muttering to myself and Spaceoline is contagioust a gigolo my, oh—

I stared desperately at my watch and my line of sight focused on nine-fifteen.

Where the devil was the time going to?

Oh, my; oh, nuts; oh, Flora!

I had no choice. I made my way to the booth for another quick call to Flora. Just a quick one, you understand, to keep things alive, assuming they weren't dead already.

I kept saying to myself: She won't answer.

I tried to prepare myself for that. There were other girls, there were other—

Hell, there were no other girls.

If Hilda had been in Marsport, I would never have had

Flora on my mind in the first place and it wouldn't have mattered. But I was in Marsport *without* Hilda and I had made a date with Flora; Flora and a body that had been made up out of heaping handfuls of all that was soft and fragrant and firm; Flora and a low-gravity room and a way about her that made it seem like free fall through a warm, breathable ocean of champagne-flavored meringue—

The signal was signaling and signaling and I didn't dare break off.

Answer! Answer!

She answered. She said, "It's *you!*"

"Of course, sweetheart, who else would it be?"

"Lots of people. Someone who would *come.*"

"There's just this little detail of business, honey."

"What business? Plastons for who?"

I almost corrected her grammar, but I was wondering what this plastons kick was.

Then I remembered. I told her once I was a plaston salesman. That was the time I brought her a plaston nightgown that was a honey. Just thinking of it made me ache where I needed no more ache.

I said, "Look. Just give me another half-hour . . ."

Her eyes grew moist. "I'm sitting here all by myself."

"I'll make it up to you." To show you how desperate I was getting, I was definitely beginning to think along paths that could lead only to jewelry, even though a sizable dent in the bankbook would show up to Hilda's piercing eye like the Horsehead Nebula interrupting the Milky Way.

She said, "I had a perfectly good date and I broke it off."

I protested, "You said it was a quibbling little arrangement."

That was a mistake. I knew it the minute I said it.

She shrieked, "*Quibbling little arrangement!*" It was what she had said. But having the truth on your side just makes it worse in arguing with a woman. Don't I know? "You call a man who's promised me an estate on Earth—"

She went on and on about that estate on Earth. There wasn't a gal in Marsport who wasn't wangling for an estate on Earth and you could count the number who got one on the sixth finger of either hand. But hope springs eternal in the human breast, and Flora had plenty of room for it to spring in.

I tried to stop her. I threw in honeys and babies until you

would have thought that every bee on the planet Earth was pregnant.

No use.

She finally said, "And here I am all alone, with *nobody,* and what do you think *that* will do to my reputation?" and broke off contact.

Well, she was right. I felt like the lowest heel in the Galaxy. If the word did get around that she had been stood up, the word would also get around that she was standuppable, that she was losing the old touch. A thing like that can ruin a girl.

I went back into the reception room. A flunky outside the door saluted me in.

I stared at the three industrialists and speculated on the order in which I would slowly choke each to death if I could but receive choking orders. Harponaster first, maybe. He had a thin, stringy neck that the fingers could go around neatly and a sharp Adam's apple against which the thumbs could find purchase.

It cheered me up infinitesimally, to the point where I muttered, "Boy!" just out of sheer longing.

It started them off at once. Ferrucci said, "Boyl the watern the spout you go in the snow to sneeze—"

Harponaster of the scrawny neck added, "Nies and nephew don't like orporalley cat."

Lipsky said, "Cattle for shipmentering the home stretchings are good bait and drank drunk."

"Drunkle aunterior passagewayt a while."

"While beasts oh pray."

"Rayls to Chicago."

"Go way."

"Waiter."

"Terble."

"Ble."

Then nothing.

They stared at me. I stared at them. They were empty of emotion—or two were—and I was empty of ideas. And time passed.

I stared at them some more and thought about Flora. It occurred to me that I had nothing to lose that I had not already lost. I might as well talk about her.

I said, "Gentlemen, there is a girl in this town whose name

I will not mention for fear of compromising her. Let me describe her to you, gentlemen."

And I did. If I say so myself, the last two hours had honed me to such a fine force-field edge that the description of Flora took on a kind of poetry that seemed to be coming from some wellspring of masculine force deep in the subbasement of my unconscious.

And they sat frozen, almost as though they were listening, and hardly ever interrupting. People under Spaceoline have a kind of politeness about them. They won't speak when someone else is speaking. That's why they take turns.

Occasionally, of course, I paused a bit because the poignancy of the subject matter made me want to linger and then one of them might put in a few words before I could gather myself together and continue.

"Pinknic of champagnes and aches and bittern of the century box."

"Round that and/or thisandy beaches."

"Assault and peppert girlieping leopard."

I drowned them out and kept talking. "This young lady, gentlemen," I said, "has an apartment fitted out for low gravity. Now you might ask of what use is low gravity? I intend to tell you, gentlemen, for if you have never had occasion to spend a quiet evening with a Marsport prima donna in privacy, you cannot imagine—"

But I tried to make it unnecessary for them to imagine— the way I told it they were *there*. They would remember all this afterward but I doubted mightily that either of the two innocents would object to it in hindsight. Chances were they would look me up to ask a phone number.

I kept it up, with loving, careful detail and a kind of heartfelt sadness in my voice, until the loudspeaker announced the arrival of the *Space Eater*.

That was that. I said in a loud voice, "Rise, gentlemen."

They got up in unison, faced the door, started walking, and as Ferrucci passed me, I tapped him on the shoulder and said, "Not you, you murdering louse," and my magnetic coil was on his wrist before he could breathe twice.

Ferrucci fought like a demon. *He* was under no Spaceoline influence. They found the altered Spaceoline in thin flesh-colored plastic pads hugging the inner surface of his thighs, with hairs affixed to it in the normal pattern. You couldn't see it at all; you could only feel it, and even then it took a knife to make sure.

Afterward, Rog Crinton, grinning and half-insane with relief, held me by the lapel with a death grip. "How did you do it? What gave it away?"

I said, trying to pull loose, "One of them was faking a Spaceoline jag. I was sure of it. So I told them—" I grew cautious. None of the bum's business as to the details, you know. "—uh, ribald stories, see, and two of them never reacted, so they were Spaceolined. But Ferrucci's breathing speeded up and the beads of sweat came out on his forehead. I gave a pretty dramatic rendition, and he reacted, so he was under no Spaceoline. And when they all stood up to head out for the ship, I was sure of my man and stopped him. Now will you let me go?"

He let go and I almost fell over backward.

I was set to take off. My feet were pawing at the ground without any instructions for me, but I turned back.

"Hey, Rog," I said, "can you sign me a chit for a thousand credits without its going on the record—for services rendered to the Service?"

That's when I realized he was half-insane with relief and very temporary gratitude, because he said, "Sure, Max, sure. Ten thousand credits if you want it."

"I *want*," I said. "I want. I want."

He filled out an official Service chit for ten thousand credits, good as cash anywhere in half the Galaxy. He was actually grinning as he gave it to me and you can bet I was grinning as I took it.

How *he* intended accounting for it was his affair. The point was that I wouldn't have to account for it to Hilda.

I stood in the booth, one last time, signaling Flora. I didn't dare let matters go till I reached her place. The additional half-hour might just give her time to get someone else, if she hadn't already.

Make her answer. Make her answer. Make her—

She answered, but she was in formal clothes. She was going out and I had obviously caught her by two minutes.

"I am going out," she announced. "*Some* men can be decent. And I do not wish to see you in the henceforward. I do not wish ever to find my eyes upon you. You will do me a great favor, Mister Whoeveryouare, if you will unhand my signal combination and never pollute it with—"

I wasn't saying anything. I was just standing there holding my breath and also holding the chit up where she could see it. Just standing there. Just holding.

Sure enough, at the word "pollute" she came in for a closer look. She wasn't much on education, that girl, but she could read "ten thousand credits" faster than any college graduate in the Solar System.

She said, "Max! For me?"

"All for you, baby," I said. "I told you I had a little business to do. I wanted to surprise you."

"Oh, Max, that's sweet of you. I didn't really mind. I was joking. Now you come right here to me." She took off her coat, which with Flora is a *very* interesting action to watch.

"What about your date?" I said.

"I *said* I was joking," she said. She dropped her coat gently to the floor, and toyed with a brooch that seemed to hold together what there was of her dress.

"I'm coming," I said faintly.

"With every single one of those credits now," she said roguishly.

"With every single one," I said.

I broke contact, stepped out of the booth, and now, finally, I was set, really set.

I heard my name called.

"Max! Max!" Someone was running toward me. "Rog Crinton said I would find you here. Mama's all right after all, so I got special passage on the *Space Eater* and what's this about ten thousand credits?"

I didn't turn. I said, "Hello, Hilda."

I stood rock steady.

And then I turned and did the hardest thing I ever succeeded in doing in all my goddam, good-for-nothing, space-hopping life.

I smiled.

FOREWORD

This requires a little explanation. "Marooned Off Vesta," the first of this connected pair of stories, is not a mystery in any way. It does, however, happen to be the first story I ever published. When the twentieth anniversary of that first publication approached, the editors of the magazine in which it had appeared asked me if I would write a story to mark the anniversary. I did, and with predictable corniness this second story, "Anniversary," dealt with the meeting of the characters of the first story on the twentieth anniversary of the events in that first story. And the pair of stories, taken together, make a mystery.

I think it only fair to tell the Gentle Reader that very little of that first-published story has been changed. If my inexperience shows—I was in my teens when it was published—forgive me. What's more, to meet the suspicions of some readers who never read the story in its first appearance—not having been born at the time—I did not change one word of the first story in order to make it easier to plot the mystery in the second.

It is a sobering thought that when this book appears the thirtieth anniversary of that first publication will be only a year away.

Marooned Off Vesta

"Will you please stop walking up and down like that?" said Warren Moore from the couch. "It won't do any of us any good. Think of our blessings; we're airtight, aren't we?"

Mark Brandon whirled and ground his teeth at him. "I'm glad you feel happy about that," he spat out viciously. "Of course, you don't know that our air supply will last only three days." He resumed his interrupted stride with a defiant air.

Moore yawned and stretched, assumed a more comfortable position, and replied, "Expending all that energy will only use it up faster. Why don't you take a hint from Mike here? He's taking it easy."

"Mike" was Michael Shea, late a member of the crew of the *Silver Queen*. His short, squat body was resting on the only chair in the room and his feet were on the only table. He looked up as his name was mentioned, his mouth widening in a twisted grin.

"You've got to expect things like this to happen sometimes," he said. "Bucking the asteroids is risky business. We should've taken the hop. It takes longer, but it's the only safe way. But no, the captain wanted to make the schedule; he *would* go through"—Mike spat disgustedly—"and here we are."

"What's the 'hop'?" asked Brandon.

"Oh, I take it that friend Mike means that we should have avoided the asteroid belt by plotting a course outside the plane of the ecliptic," answered Moore. "That's it, isn't it, Mike?"

Mike hesitated and then replied cautiously, "Yeah—I guess that's it."

Moore smiled blankly and continued, "Well, I wouldn't blame Captain Crane too much. The replusion screen must have failed five minutes before that chunk of granite barged into us. That's not his fault, though of course we ought to have steered clear instead of relying on the screen." He shook his head meditatively. "The *Silver Queen* just went to pieces. It's really miraculously lucky that this part of the ship remained intact, and what's more, airtight."

"You've got a funny idea of luck, Warren," said Brandon. "Always have, for as long as I've known you. Here we are in a tenth part of a spaceship, comprising only three *whole* rooms, with air for three days, and no prospect of being alive after that, and you have the infernal gall to prate about luck."

"Compared to the others who died instantly when the asteroid struck, yes," was Moore's answer.

"You think so, eh? Well, let me tell you that instant death isn't so bad compared with what we're going to have to go through. Suffocation is a damned unpleasant way of dying."

"We may find a way out," Moore suggested hopefully.

"Why not face facts!" Brandon's face was flushed and his voice trembled. "We're done, I tell you! Through!"

Mike glanced from one to the other doubtfully and then coughed to attract their attention. "Well, gents, seeing that we're all in the same fix, I guess there's no use hogging things." He drew a small bottle out of his pocket that was filled with greenish liquid. "Grade A Jabra this is. I ain't too proud to share and share alike."

Brandon exhibited the first signs of pleasure for over a day. "Martian Jabra water. Why didn't you say so before?"

But as he reached for it, a firm hand clamped down upon his wrist. He looked up into the calm blue eyes of Warren Moore.

"Don't be a fool," said Moore, "there isn't enough to keep us drunk for three days. What do you want to do? Go on a tear now and then die cold sober? Let's save this for the last six hours when the air gets stuffy and breathing hurts—then we'll finish the bottle among us and never *know* when the end comes, or *care*."

Brandon's hand fell away reluctantly. "Damn it, Warren, you'd bleed ice if you were cut. How can you think straight at a time like this?" He motioned to Mike and the bottle was once more stowed away. Brandon walked to the porthole and gazed out.

Moore approached and placed a kindly arm over the shoulders of the younger man. "Why take it so hard, man?" he asked. "You can't last at this rate. Inside of twenty-four hours you'll be a madman if you keep this up."

There was no answer. Brandon stared bitterly at the globe that filled almost the entire porthole, so Moore continued, "Watching Vesta won't do you any good either."

Mike Shea lumbered up to the porthole. "We'd be safe if we were only down there on Vesta. There're people there. How far away are we?"

"Not more than three or four hundred miles judging from its apparent size," answered Moore. "You must remember that it is only two hundred miles in diameter."

"Three hundred miles from salvation," murmured Brandon, "and we might as well be a million. If there were only a way to get ourselves out of the orbit this rotten fragment adopted. You know, manage to give ourselves a push so as to start falling. There'd be no danger of crashing if we did, because that midget hasn't got enough gravity to crush a cream puff."

"It has enough to keep us in the orbit," retorted Brandon. "It must have picked us up while we were lying unconscious after the crash. Wish it had come closer; we might have been able to land on it."

"Funny place, Vesta," observed Mike Shea. "I was down there two-three times. What a dump! It's all covered with some stuff like snow, only it ain't snow. I forget what they call it."

"Frozen carbon dioxide?" prompted Moore.

"Yeah, dry ice, that carbon stuff, that's it. They say that's what makes Vesta so shiny."

"Of course! That would give it a high albedo."

Mike cocked a suspicious eye at Moore and decided to let it pass. "It's hard to see anything down there on account of the snow, but if you look close"—he pointed—"you can see a sort of gray smudge. I think that's Bennett's dome. That's where they keep the observatory. And there is Calorn's dome up there. That's a fuel station, that is. There're plenty more, too, only I don't see them."

He hesitated and then turned to Moore. "Listen, boss, I've been thinking. Wouldn't they be looking for us as soon as they hear about the crash? And wouldn't we be easy to find from Vesta, seeing we're so close?"

Moore shook his head, "No, Mike, they won't be looking for us. No one's going to find out about the crash until the

Silver Queen fails to turn up on schedule. You see, when the asteroid hit, we didn't have time to send out an SOS"—he sighed—"and they won't find us down there at Vesta, either. We're so small that even at our distance they couldn't see us unless they knew what they were looking for, and exactly where to look."

"Hmm." Mike's forehead was corrugated in deep thought. "Then we've got to get to Vesta before three days are up."

"You've got the gist of the matter, Mike. Now, if we only knew how to go about it, eh?"

Brandon suddenly exploded, "Will you two stop this infernal chitter-chatter and do something? For God's sake, do something."

Moore shrugged his shoulders and without answer returned to the couch. He lounged at ease, apparently carefree, but there was the tiniest crease between his eyes which bespoke concentration.

There was no doubt about it; they *were* in a bad spot. He reviewed the events of the preceding day for perhaps the twentieth time.

After the asteroid had struck, tearing the ship apart, he'd gone out like a light; for how long he didn't know, his own watch being broken and no other timepiece available. When he came to, he found himself, along with Mark Brandon, who shared his room, and Mike Shea, a member of the crew, sole occupants of all that was left of the *Silver Queen*.

This remnant was now careening in an orbit about Vesta. At present, things were fairly comfortable. There was a food supply that would last a week. Likewise there was a regional Gravitator under the room that kept them at normal weight and would continue to do so for an indefinite time, certainly for longer than the air would last. The lighting system was less satisfactory but had held on so far.

There was no doubt, however, where the joker in the pack lay. Three days' air! Not that there weren't other disheartening features. There was no heating system—though it would take a long time for the ship to radiate enough heat into the vacuum of space to render them too uncomfortable. Far more important was the fact that their part of the ship had neither a means of communication nor a propulsive mechanism. Moore sighed. One fuel jet in working order would fix everything, for one blast in the right direction would send them safely to Vesta.

The crease between his eyes deepened. What was to be done? They had but one spacesuit among them, one heat ray, and one detonator. That was the sum total of space appliances after a thorough search of the accessible parts of the ship. A pretty hopeless mess, that.

Moore shrugged, rose, and drew himself a glass of water. He swallowed it mechanically, still deep in thought, when an idea struck him. He glanced curiously at the empty cup in his hand.

"Say, Mike," he said, "what kind of water supply have we? Funny that I never thought of that before."

Mike's eyes opened to their fullest extent in an expression of ludicrous surprise. "Didn't you know, boss?"

"Know *what*?" asked Moore impatiently.

"We've got all the water there was." He waved his hand in an all-inclusive gesture. He paused, but as Moore's expression showed nothing but total mystification, he elaborated, "Don't you see? We've got the main tank, the place where all the water for the whole ship was stored." He pointed to one of the walls.

"Do you mean to say that there's a tank full of water adjoining us?"

Mike nodded vigorously, "Yep! Cubic vat a hundred feet each way. And she's three-quarters full."

Moore was astonished. "Seven hundred and fifty thousand cubic feet of water." Then suddenly: "Why hasn't it run out through the broken pipes?"

"It only has one main outlet, which runs down the corridor just outside this room. I was fixing that main when the asteroid hit and had to shut it off. After I came to I opened the pipe leading to our faucet, but that's the only outlet open now."

"Oh." Moore had a curious feeling way down deep inside. An idea had half-formed in his brain, but for the life of him he could not drag it into the light of day. He knew only that there was something in what he had just heard that had some important meaning but he just could not place his finger on it.

Brandon, meanwhile, had been listening to Shea in silence, and now he emitted a short, humorless laugh. "Fate seems to be having its fill of fun with us, I see. First, it puts us within

arm's reach of a place of safety and then sees to it that we
have no way of getting there.

"Then she provides us with a week's food, three days' air,
and *a year's supply of water*. A year's supply, do you hear me?
Enough water to drink and to gargle and to wash and to take
baths in and—and to do anything else we want. Water—damn
the water!"

"Oh, take a less serious view, Mark," said Moore in an
attempt to break the younger man's melancholy. "Pretend
we're a satellite of Vesta—which we are. We have our own
period of revolution and of rotation. We have an equator and
an axis. Our 'north pole' is located somewhere toward the top
of the porthole, pointing toward Vesta, and our 'south' sticks
out away from Vesta through the water tank somewhere.
Well, as a satellite, we have an atmosphere, and now, you see,
we have a newly discovered ocean.

"And seriously, we're not so badly off. For the three days
our atmosphere will last, we can eat double rations and drink
ourselves soggy. Hell, we have water enough to throw
away—"

The idea which had been half-formed before suddenly
sprang to maturity and was nailed. The careless gesture with
which he had accompanied the last remark was frozen in mid-
air. His mouth closed with a snap and his head came up with
a jerk.

But Brandon, immersed in his own thoughts, noticed nothing of Moore's strange actions. "Why don't you complete the
analogy to a satellite," he sneered, "or do you, as a Professional Optimist, ignore any and all disagreeable facts? If *I*
were you, I'd continue this way." Here he imitated Moore's
voice: "The satellite is at present habitable and inhabited but,
due to the approaching depletion of its atmosphere in three
days, is expected to become a dead world.

"Well, why don't you answer? Why do you persist in
making a joke out of this? Can't you see— *What's the
matter?*"

The last was a surprised exclamation and certainly
Moore's actions did merit surprise. He had risen suddenly
and, after giving himself a smart rap on the forehead, remained stiff and silent, staring into the far distance with
gradually narrowing eyelids. Brandon and Mike Shea
watched him in speechless astonishment.

Suddenly Moore burst out, "Ha! I've got it. Why didn't I think of it before?" His exclamations degenerated into the unintelligible.

Mike drew out the Jabra bottle with a significant look, but Moore waved it away impatiently. Whereupon Brandon, without any warning, lashed out with his right, catching the surprised Moore flush on the jaw and toppling him.

Moore groaned and rubbed his chin. Somewhat indignant, he asked, "What was the reason for that?"

"Stand up and I'll do it again," shouted Brandon, "I can't stand it anymore. I'm sick and tired of being preached at, and having to listen to your Pollyanna talk. *You're* the one that's going daffy."

"Daffy, nothing! Just a little overexcited, that's all. Listen, for God's sake. I think I know a way—"

Brandon glared at him balefully. "Oh, you do, do you? Raise our hopes with some silly scheme and then find it doesn't work. I won't take it, do you hear? I'll find a real use for the water—drown you—and save some of the air besides."

Moore lost his temper. "Listen, Mark, you're out of this. I'm going through alone. I don't need your help and I don't want it. If you're that sure of dying and that afraid, why not have the agony over? We've got one heat ray and one detonator, both reliable weapons. Take your choice and kill yourself. Shea and I won't interfere." Brandon's lip curled in a last weak gesture of defiance and then suddenly he capitulated, completely and abjectly. "All right, Warren, I'm with you. I—I guess I didn't quite know what I was doing. I don't feel well, Warren. I—I—"

"Aw, that's all right, boy." Moore was genuinely sorry for him. "Take it easy. I know how you feel. It's got me too. But you mustn't give in to it. Fight it, or you'll go stark, raving mad. Now you just try and get some sleep and leave everything to me. Things will turn out right yet."

Brandon, pressing a hand to an aching forehead, stumbled to the couch and tumbled down. Silent sobs shook his frame while Moore and Shea remained in embarrassed silence nearby.

At last Moore nudged Mike. "Come on," he whispered, "let's get busy. We're going places. Airlock five is at the end of the corridor, isn't it?" Shea nodded and Moore continued, "Is it airtight?"

"Well," said Shea after some thought, "the inner door is, of course, but I don't know anything about the outer one. For all I know it may be a sieve. You see, when I tested the wall for airtightness, I didn't dare open the inner door, because if there was anything wrong with the outer one—blooey!" The accompanying gesture was very expressive.

"Then it's up to us to find out about that outer door right now. I've got to get outside some way and we'll just have to take chances. Where's the spacesuit?"

He grabbed the lone suit from its place in the cupboard, threw it over his shoulder and led the way into the long corridor that ran down the side of the room. He passed closed doors behind whose airtight barriers were what once had been passenger quarters but which were now merely cavities, open to space. At the end of the corridor was the tight-fitting door of Airlock 5.

Moore stopped ond surveyed it appraisingly. "Looks all right," he observed, "but of course you can't tell what's outside. God, I hope it'll work." He frowned. "Of course we could use the entire corridor as an airlock, with the door to our room as the inner door and this as the outer door, but that would mean the loss of half our air supply. We can't afford that—yet."

He turned to Shea. "All right, now. The indicator shows that the lock was last used for entrance, so it should be full of air. Open the door the tiniest crack, and if there's a hissing noise, shut it quick."

"Here goes," and the lever moved one notch. The mechanism had been severely shaken up during the shock of the crash and its former noiseless workings had given way to a harsh, rasping sound, but it was still in commission. A thin black line appeared on the left-hand side of the lock, marking where the door had slid a fraction of an inch on the runners.

There was no hiss! Moore's look of anxiety faded somewhat. He took a small pasteboard from his pocket and held it against the crack. If air were leaking, that card should have held there, pushed by the escaping gas. It fell to the floor.

Mike Shea stuck a forefinger in his mouth and then put it

against the crack. "Thank the Lord," he breathed, "not a sign of a draft."

"Good, good. Open it wider. Go ahead."

Another notch and the crack opened farther. And still no draft. Slowly, ever so slowly, notch by notch, it creaked its way wider and wider. The two men held their breaths, afraid that while not actually punctured, the outer door might have been so weakened as to give way any moment. But it held! Moore was jubilant as he wormed into the spacesuit.

"Things are going fine so far, Mike," he said. "You sit down right here and wait for me. I don't know how long I'll take, but I'll be back. Where's the heat ray? Have you got it?"

Shea held out the ray and asked, "But what are you going to do? I'd sort of like to know."

Moore paused as he was about to buckle on the helmet. "Did you hear me say inside that we had water enough to throw away? Well, I've been thinking it over and that's not such a bad idea. I'm going to throw it away." With no other explanation, he stepped into the lock, leaving behind him a very puzzled Mike Shea.

It was with a pounding heart that Moore waited for the outer door to open. His plan was an extraordinarily simple one, but it might not be easy to carry out.

There was a sound of creaking gears and scraping ratchets. Air sighed away to nothingness. The door before him slid open a few inches and stuck. Moore's heart sank as for a moment he thought it would not open at all, but after a few preliminary jerks and rattles the barrier slid the rest of the way.

He clicked on the magnetic grapple and very cautiously put a foot out into space. Clumsily he groped his way out to the side of the ship. He had never been outside a ship in open space before and a vast dread overtook him as he clung there, flylike, to his precarious perch. For a moment dizziness overcame him.

He closed his eyes and for five minutes hung there, clutching the smooth sides of what had once been the *Silver Queen*. The magnetic grapple held him firm and when he opened his eyes once more he found his self-confidence in a measure returned.

He gazed about him. For the first time since the crash he saw the stars instead of the vision of Vesta which their porthole afforded. Eagerly he searched the skies for the little blue-white speck that was Earth. It had often amused him that Earth should always be the first object sought by space travelers when star-gazing, but the humor of the situation did not strike him now. However, his search was in vain. From where he lay, Earth was invisible. It, as well as the Sun, must be hidden behind Vesta.

Still, there was much else that he could not help but note. Jupiter was off to the left, a brilliant globe the size of a small pea to the naked eye. Moore observed two of its attendant satellites. Saturn was visible too, as a brilliant planet of some negative magnitude, rivaling Venus as seen from Earth.

Moore had expected that a goodly number of asteroids world be visible—marooned as they were in the asteroid belt—but space seemed surprisingly empty. Once he thought he could see a hurtling body pass within a few miles, but so fast had the impression come and gone that he could not swear that it was not fancy.

And then, of course, there was Vesta. Almost directly below him it loomed like a balloon filling a quarter of the sky. It floated steadily, snowy white, and Moore gazed at it with earnest longing. A good hard kick against the side of the ship, he thought, might start him falling toward Vesta. He *might* land safely and get help for the others. But the chance was too great that he would merely take on a new orbit about Vesta. No, it would have to be better than that.

This reminded him that he had no time to lose. He scanned the side of the ship, looking for the water tank, but all he could see was a jungle of jutting walls, jagged, crumbling, and pointed. He hesitated. Evidently the only thing to do was to make for the lighted porthole to their room and proceed to the tank from there.

Carefully he dragged himself along the wall of the ship. Not five yards from the lock the smoothness stopped abruptly. There was a yawning cavity which Moore recognized as having once been the room adjoining the corridor at the far end. He shuddered. Suppose he were to come across a bloated dead body in one of those rooms. He had known most of the passengers, many of them personally. But he overcame his squeamishness and forced himself to continue his precarious journey toward its goal.

And here he encountered his first practical difficulty. The room itself was made of non-ferrous material in many parts. The magnetic grapple was intended for use only on outer hulls and was useless throughout much of the ship's interior. Moore had forgotten this when suddenly he found himself floating down an incline, his grapple out of use. He gasped and clutched at a nearby projection. Slowly he pulled himself back to safety.

He lay for a moment, almost breathless. Theoretically he should be weightless out here in space—Vesta's influence being negligible—but the regional Gravitator under his room was working. Without the balance of the other Gravitators, it tended to place him under variable and suddenly shifting stresses as he kept changing his position. For his magnetic grapple to let go suddenly might mean being jerked away from the ship altogether. And then what?

Evidently this was going to be even more difficult than he had thought.

He inched forward in a crawl, testing each spot to see if the grapple would hold. Sometimes he had to make long, circuitous journeys to gain a few feet's headway and at other times he was forced to scramble and slip across small patches of non-ferrous material. And always there was that tiring pull of the Gravitator, continually changing directions as he progressed, setting horizontal floors and vertical walls at queer and almost haphazard angles.

Carefully he investigated all objects that he came across. But it was a barren search. Loose articles, chairs, tables had been jerked away at the first shock, probably, and now were independent bodies of the Solar System. He did manage, however, to pick up a small field glass and fountain pen. These he placed in his pocket. They were valueless under present conditions, but somehow they seemed to make more real this macabre trip across the sides of a dead ship.

For fifteen minutes, twenty, half an hour, he labored slowly toward where he thought the porthole should be. Sweat poured down into his eyes and rendered his hair a matted mass. His muscles were beginning to ache under the unaccustomed strain. His mind, already strained by the ordeal of the previous day, was beginning to waver, to play him tricks.

The crawl began to seem eternal, something that had always existed and would exist forever. The object of the journey, that for which he was striving, seemed unimportant; he only knew that it was necessary to move. The time, one hour back, when he had been with Brandon and Shea, seemed hazy and lost in the far past. That more normal time, two days ago, wholly forgotten.

Only the jagged walls before him, only the vital necessity of getting at some uncertain destination existed in his spinning brain. Grasping, straining, pulling. Feeling for the iron alloy. Up and into gaping holes that were rooms and then out again. Feel and pull—feel and pull—and—a light.

Moore stopped. Had he not been glued to the wall he would have fallen. Somehow that light seemed to clear things. It was the porthole; not the many dark, staring ones he had passed, but alive and alight. Behind it was Brandon. A deep breath and he felt better, his mind cleared.

And now his way lay plain before him. Toward that spark of life he crept. Nearer, and nearer, and nearer until he could touch it. He was there!

His eyes drank in the familiar room. God knows that it hadn't any happy associations in his mind, but it was something real, something almost natural. Brandon slept on the couch. His face was worn and lined but a smile passed over it now and then.

Moore raised his fist to knock. He felt the urgent desire to talk with someone, if only by sign language; yet at the last instant he refrained. Perhaps the kid was dreaming of home. He was young and sensitive and had suffered much. Let him sleep. Time enough to wake him when—and if—his idea had been carried through.

He located the wall within the room behind which lay the water tank and then tried to spot it from the outside. Now it was not difficult; its rear wall stood out prominently. Moore marveled, for it seemed a miracle that it had escaped puncture. Perhaps the Fates had not been so ironic after all.

Passage to it was easy though it was on the other side of the fragment. What was once a corridor led almost directly to it. Once when the *Silver Queen* had been whole, that corridor had been level and horizontal, but now, under the unbalanced pull of the regional gravitator, it seemed more of a steep incline than anything else. And yet it made the path simple. Since it was of uniform beryl-steel, Moore found no trouble holding on as he wormed up the twenty-odd feet to the water supply.

And now the crisis—the last stage—had been reached. He felt that he ought to rest first, but his excitement grew rapidly in intensity. It was either now or bust. He pulled himself out to the bottom-center of the tank. There, resting on the small ledge formed by the floor of the corridor that had once extended on that side of the tank, he began operations.

"It's a pity that the main pipe is pointing in the wrong direction," he muttered. "It would have saved me a lot of trouble had it been right. As it is . . ." He sighed and bent to his work. The heat ray was adjusted to maximum concentration and the invisible emanations focused at a spot perhaps a foot above the floor of the tank.

Gradually the effect of the excitatory beam upon the molecules of the wall became noticeable. A spot the size of a dime began shining faintly at the point of focus of the ray gun. It wavered uncertainly, now dimming, now brightening, as Moore strove to steady his tired arm. He propped it on the ledge and achieved better results as the tiny circle of radiation brightened.

Slowly the color ascended the spectrum. The dark, angry red that had first appeared lightened to a cherry color. As the heat continued pouring in, the brightness seemed to ripple out in widening areas, like a target made of successively deepening tints of red. The wall for a distance of some feet from the focal point was becoming uncomfortably hot even though it did not glow and Moore found it necessary to refrain from touching it with the metal of his suit.

Moore cursed steadily, for the ledge itself was also growing hot. It seemed that only imprecations could soothe him. And as the melting wall began to radiate heat in its own right, the chief objects of his maledictions were the spacesuit manufacturers. Why didn't they build a suit that could keep heat *out* as well as keep it *in*?

But what Brandon called Professional Optimism crept up. With the salt tang of perspiration in his mouth, he kept consoling himself, "It could be worse, I suppose. At least, the two inches of wall here don't present too much of a barrier. Suppose the tank had been built flush against the outer hull. Whew! Imagine trying to melt through a foot of this." He gritted his teeth and kept on.

The spot of brightness was now flickering into the orange-yellow and Moore knew that the melting point of the beryl-steel alloy would soon be reached. He found himself forced to watch the spot only at widely spaced intervals and then only for fleeting moments.

Evidently it would have to be done quickly if it were to be done at all. The heat ray had not been fully loaded in the first place, and, pouring out energy at maximum as it had been doing for almost ten minutes now, must be approaching exhaustion. Yet the wall was just barely passing the plastic stage. In a fever of impatience, Moore jammed the muzzle of the gun directly at the center of the spot, drawing it back speedily.

A deep depression formed in the soft metal, but a puncture had not been formed. However, Moore was satisfied. He was almost there now. Had there been air between himself and the wall, he would undoubtedly have heard the gurgling and the hissing of the steaming water within. The pressure was building up. How long would the weakened wall endure?

Then, so suddenly that Moore did not realize it for a few moments, he was through. A tiny fissure formed at the bottom of that little pit made by the ray gun and in less time than it takes to imagine, the churning water within had its way.

The soft, liquid metal at that spot puffed out, sticking out raggedly around a pea-sized hole. And from that hole there came a hissing and a roaring. A cloud of steam emerged and enveloped Moore.

Through the mist he could see the steam condense almost immediately to ice droplets and saw these icy pellets shrink rapidly into nothingness.

For fifteen minutes he watched the steam shoot out.

Then he became aware of a gentle pressure pushing him away from the ship. A savage joy welled up within him as he realized that this was the effect of acceleration on the ship's part. His own inertia was holding him back.

That meant his work had been finished—and successfully. That stream of water was substituting for the rocket blast.

He started back.

If the horrors and dangers of the journey to the tank had been great, those of the way back should have been greater. He was infinitely more tired, his aching eyes were all but blind, and added to the crazy pull of the Gravitator was the force induced by the varying acceleration of the ship. But whatever his labors to return, they did not bother him. In later time, he never even remembered the heartbreaking trip.

How he managed to negotiate the distance in safety he did not know. Most of the time he was lost in a haze of happiness, scarcely realizing the actualities of the situation. His mind was filled with one thought only—to get back quickly, to tell the happy news of their escape.

Suddenly he found himself before the airlock. He hardly grasped the fact that it *was* the airlock. He almost did not understand why he pressed the signal button. Some instinct told him it was the thing to do.

Mike Shea was waiting. There was a creak and a rumble and the outer door started opening, caught, and stopped at the same place as before, but once again it managed to slide the rest of the way. It closed behind Moore, then the inner door opened and he stumbled into Shea's arms.

As in a dream he felt himself half-pulled, half-carried down the corridor to the room. His suit was ripped off. A hot, burning liquid stung his throat. Moore gagged, swallowed, and felt better. Shea pocketed the Jabra bottle once more.

The blurred, shifting images of Brandon and Shea before him steadied and became solid. Moore wiped the perspiration from his face with a trembling hand and essayed a weak smile.

"Wait," protested Brandon, "don't say anything. You look half-dead. Rest, will you!"

But Moore shook his head. In a hoarse, cracked voice he narrated as well as he could the events of the past two hours. The tale was incoherent, scarcely intelligible but marvelously impressive. The two listeners scarcely breathed during the recital.

"You mean," stammered Brandon, "that the water spout is pushing us toward Vesta, like a rocket exhaust?"

"Exactly—same thing as—rocket exhaust," panted Moore. "Action and reaction. Is located—on side opposite Vesta— hence pushing us toward Vesta."

Shea was dancing before the porthole. "He's right, Brandon, me boy. You can make out Bennett's dome as clear as day. We're getting there, we're getting there."

Moore felt himself recovering. "We're approaching in spiral path on account of original orbit. We'll land in five or six hours probably. The water will last for quite a long while and the pressure is still great, since the water issues as steam."

"Steam—at the low temperature of space?" Brandon was surprised.

"Steam—at the low pressure of space!" corrected Moore. "The boiling point of water falls with the pressure. It is very low indeed in a vacuum. Even ice has a vapor pressure sufficient to sublime."

He smiled. "As a matter of fact, it freezes and boils at the same time. I watched it." A short pause, then, "Well, how do you feel now, Brandon? Much better, eh?"

Brandon reddened and his face fell. He groped vainly for words for a few moments. Finally he said in a half-whisper, "You know, I must have acted like a damn fool and a coward at first. I—I guess I don't deserve all this after going to pieces and letting the burden of our escape rest on your shoulders.

"I wish you'd beat me up, or something, for punching you before. It'd make me feel better. I mean it." And he really did seem to mean it.

Moore gave him an affectionate push. "Forget it. You'll never know how near I came to breaking down myself." He raised his voice in order to drown out any further apologies on Brandon's part. "Hey, Mike, stop staring out of that porthole and bring over that Jabra bottle."

Mike obeyed with alacrity, bringing with him three Plexatron units to be used as makeshift cups. Moore filled each precisely to the brim. He was going to be drunk with a vengeance.

"Gentlemen," he said solemnly, "a toast." The three raised the mugs in unison, "Gentlemen, I give you the year's supply of good old H_2O *we used to have.*"

Anniversary

The annual ritual was all set.

It was the turn of Moore's house this year, of course, and Mrs. Moore and the children had resignedly gone to her mother's for the evening.

Warren Moore surveyed the room with a faint smile. Only Mark Brandon's enthusiasm kept it going at the first, but he himself had come to like this mild remembrance. It came with age, he supposed; twenty additional years of it. He had grown paunchy, thin-haired, soft-jowled, and—worst of all—sentimental.

So all the windows were polarized into complete darkness and the drapes were drawn. Only occasional stipples of wall were illuminated, thus celebrating the poor lighting and the terrible isolation of that day of wreckage long ago.

There were spaceship rations in sticks and tubes on the table and, of course, in the center an unopened bottle of sparkling green Jabra water, the potent brew that only the chemical activity of Martian fungi could supply.

Moore looked at his watch. Brandon would be here soon; he was never late for this occasion. The only thing that disturbed him was the memory of Brandon's voice on the tube: "Warren, I have a surprise for you this time. Wait and see. Wait and see."

Brandon, it always seemed to Moore, aged little. The younger man had kept his slimness, and the intensity with which he greeted all in life, to the verge of his fortieth birthday. He retained the ability to be in high excitement over the good and in deep despair over the bad. His hair was going gray, but except for that, when Brandon walked up and down, talking rapidly at the top of his voice about anything at all,

Moore didn't even have to close his eyes to see the panicked youngster on the wreck of the *Silver Queen*.

The door signal sounded and Moore kicked the release without turning round. "Come, Mark."

It was a strange voice that answered, though; softly, tentatively, "Mr. Moore?"

Moore turned quickly. Brandon was there, to be sure, but only in the background, grinning with excitement. Someone else was standing before him; short, squat, quite bald, nutbrown and with the feel of space about him.

Moore said wonderingly, "Mike Shea—*Mike Shea*, by all space."

They pounded hands together, laughing.

Brandon said, "He got in touch with me through the office. He remembered I was with Atomic Products—"

"It's been *years*," said Moore. "Let's see, you were on Earth twelve years ago—"

"He's never been here on an anniversary," said Brandon. "How about that? He's retiring now. Getting out of space to a place he's buying in Arizona. He came to say hello before he left—stopped off at the city just for that—and I was sure he came for the anniversary. 'What anniversary?' says the old jerk."

Shea nodded, grinning. "He said you made a kind of celebration out of it every year."

"You bet," said Brandon enthusiastically, "and this will be the first one with all three of us here, the first *real* anniversary. It's twenty years, Mike; twenty years since Warren scrambled over what was left of the wreck and brought us down to Vesta."

Shea looked about. "Space ration, eh? That's old home week to me. And Jabra. Oh, sure, I remember . . . twenty years. I never give it a thought and now, all of a sudden, it's yesterday. Remember when we got back to Earth finally?"

"Do I!" said Brandon. "The parades, the speeches. Warren was the only real hero of the occasion and we kept saying so, and they kept paying no attention. Remember?"

"Oh, well," said Moore. "We were the first three men ever to survive a spaceship crash. We were unusual and anything unusual is worth a celebration. These things are irrational."

"Hey," said Shea, "any of you remember the songs they

wrote? The marching one? 'You can sing of routes through Space and the weary maddened pace of the—' "

Brandon joined in with his clear tenor and even Moore added his voice to the chorus so that the last line was loud enough to shake the drapes. "On the *wreck* of the *Silver* Que-e-en," they roared out, and ended laughing wildly.

Brandon said, "Let's open the Jabra for the first little sip. This one bottle has to last all of us all night."

Moore said, "Mark insists on complete authenticity. I'm surprised he doesn't expect me to climb out the window and human-fly my way around the building."

"Well, now, that's an idea," said Brandon.

"Remember the last toast we made?" Shea held his empty glass before him and intoned, " 'Gentlemen, I give you the year's supply of good old H_2O *we used to have.*' Three drunken bums when we landed. Well, we were kids. I was thirty and I thought I was old. And now," his voice was suddenly wistful, "they've retired me."

"Drink!" said Brandon. "Today you're thirty again, and we remember the day on the *Silver Queen* even if no one else does. Dirty, fickle public."

Moore laughed. "What do you expect? A national holiday every year with space ration and Jabra the ritual food and drink?"

"Listen, we're still the only men ever to survive a spaceship crash and now look at us. We're in oblivion."

"It's pretty good oblivion. We had a good time to begin with and the publicity gave us a healthy boost up the ladder. We are doing well, Mark. And so would Mike Shea be if he hadn't wanted to return to space."

Shea grinned and shrugged his shoulder. "That's where I like to be. I'm not sorry, either. What with the insurance compensation I got, I have a nice piece of cash now to retire on."

Brandon said reminiscently, "The wreck set back Transspace Insurance a real packet. Just the same, there's still something missing. You say 'Silver Queen' to anyone these days and he can only think of Quentin, if he can think of anyone."

"Who?" said Shea.

"Quentin. Dr. Horace Quentin. He was one of the nonsurvivors on the ship. You say to anyone, 'What about the

three men who survived?' and they'll just stare at you. 'Huh?'
they'll say."

Moore said calmly, "Come, Mark, face it. Dr. Quentin
was one of the world's great scientists and we three are
just three of the world's nothings."

"We survived. We're still the only men on record to
survive."

"So? Look, John Hester was on the ship, and he was an
important scientist too. Not in Quentin's league, but important. As a matter of fact, I was next to him at the last
dinner before the rock hit us. Well, just because Quentin
died in the same wreck, Hester's death was drowned out.
No one ever remembers Hester died on the *Silver Queen*.
They only remember Quentin. We may be forgotten too,
but at least we're alive."

"I tell you what," said Brandon after a period of silence
during which Moore's rationale had obviously failed to take,
"we're marooned again. Twenty years ago today, we were
marooned off Vesta. Today, we're marooned in oblivion.
Now here are the three of us back together again at last,
and what happened before can happen again. Twenty years
ago, Warren pulled us down to Vesta. Now let's solve
this new problem."

"Wipe out the oblivion, you mean?" said Moore. "Make
ourselves famous?"

"Sure. Why not? Do you know of any better way of
celebrating a twentieth anniversary?"

"No, but I'd be interested to know where you expect to
start. I don't think people remember the *Silver Queen* at all,
except for Quentin, so you'll have to think of some way of
bringing the wreck back to mind. That's just to begin with."

Shea stirred uneasily and a thoughtful expression crossed
his blunt countenance. "Some people remember the *Silver
Queen*. The insurance company does, and you know that's
a funny thing, now that you bring up the matter. I was on
Vesta about ten-eleven years ago, and I asked if the piece
of the wreck we brought down was still there and they said
sure, who would cart it away? So I thought I'd take a look
at it and shot over by reaction motor strapped to my back.
With Vestan gravity, you know, a reaction motor is all you
need. Anyway, I didn't get to see it except from a distance.
It was circled off by force field."

Brandon's eyebrows went sky-high. "Our *Silver Queen?* For what reason?"

"I went back and asked how come? They didn't tell me and they said they didn't know I was going there. They said it belonged to the insurance company."

Moore nodded. "Surely. They took over when they paid off. I signed a release, giving up my salvage rights when I accepted the compensation check. You did too, I'm sure."

Brandon said, "But why the force field? Why all the privacy?"

"I don't know."

"The wreck isn't worth anything even as scrap metal. It would cost too much to transport it."

Shea said, "That's right. Funny thing, though; they were bringing pieces back from space. There was a pile of it there. I could see it and it looked like just junk, twisted pieces of frame, you know. I asked about it and they said ships were always landing and unloading more scrap, and the insurance company had a standard price for any piece of the *Silver Queen* brought back, so ships in the neighborhood of Vesta were always looking. Then, on my last voyage in, I went to see the *Silver Queen* again and that pile was a lot bigger."

"You mean they're still looking?" Brandon's eyes glittered.

"I don't know. Maybe they've stopped. But the pile was bigger than it was ten-eleven years ago so they were still looking then."

Brandon leaned back in his chair and crossed his legs. "Well, now, that's very queer. A hard-headed insurance company is spending all kinds of money, sweeping space near Vesta, trying to find pieces of a twenty-year-old wreck."

"Maybe they're trying to prove sabotage," said Moore.

"After twenty years? They won't get their money back even if they do. It's a dead issue."

"They may have quit looking years ago."

Brandon stood up with decision. "Let's ask. There's something funny here and I'm just Jabrified enough and anniversaried enough to want to find out."

"Sure," said Shea, "but ask who?"

"Ask Multivac," said Brandon.

Shea's eyes opened wide. "Multivac! Say, Mr. Moore, do you have a Multivac outlet here?"

"Yes."

"I've never seen one, and I've always wanted to."

"It's nothing to look at, Mike. It looks just like a typewriter. Don't confuse a Multivac outlet with Multivac itself. I don't know anyone who's seen Multivac."

Moore smiled at the thought. He doubted if ever in his life he would meet any of the handful of technicians who spent most of their working days in a hidden spot in the bowels of Earth tending a mile-long super-computer that was the repository of all the facts known to man, that guided man's economy, directed his scientific research, helped make his political decisions, and had millions of circuits left over to answer individual questions that did not violate the ethics of privacy.

Brandon said as they moved up the power ramp to the second floor, "I've been thinking of installing a Multivac, Jr., outlet for the kids. Homework and things, you know. And yet I don't want to make it just a fancy and expensive crutch for them. How do you work it, Warren?"

Moore said tersely, "They show me the questions first. If I don't pass them, Multivac does not see them."

The Multivac outlet was indeed a simple typewriter arrangement and little more.

Moore set up the co-ordinates that opened his portion of the planet-wide network of circuits and said, "Now listen. For the record, I'm against this and I'm only going along because it's the anniversary and because I'm just jackass enough to be curious. Now how ought I to phrase the question?"

Brandon said, "Just ask: Are pieces of the wreck of the *Silver Queen* still being searched for in the neighborhood of Vesta by Trans-space Insurance? It only requires a simple yes or no."

Moore shrugged and tapped it out, while Shea watched with awe.

The spaceman said, "How does it answer? Does it talk?"

Moore laughed gently, "Oh, no. I don't spend *that* kind of money. This model just prints the answer on a slip of tape that comes out that slot."

A short strip of tape did come out as he spoke. Moore removed it and, after a glance, said, "Well, Multivac says yes."

"Hah!" cried Brandon. "Told you. Now ask why."

"Now that's silly. A question like that would obviously be against privacy. You'll just get a yellow state-your-reason."

"Ask and find out. They haven't made the search for the pieces secret. Maybe they're not making the reason secret."

Moore shrugged. He tapped out: Why is Trans-space Insurance conducting its *Silver Queen* search-project to which reference was made in the previous question?

A yellow slip clicked out almost at once: *State Your Reason For Requiring The Information Requested.*

"All right," said Brandon unabashed. "You tell it we're the three survivors and have a right to know. Go ahead. Tell it."

Moore tapped that out in unemotional phrasing and another yellow slip was pushed out at them: *Your Reason Is Insufficient. No Answer Can Be Given.*

Brandon said, "I don't see they have a right to keep that secret."

"That's up to Multivac," said Moore. "It judges the reasons given it and if it decides the ethics of privacy is against answering, that's it. The government itself couldn't break those ethics without a court order, and the courts don't go against Multivac once in ten years. So what are you going to do?"

Brandon jumped to his feet and began the rapid walk up and down the room that was so characteristic of him. "All right, then let's figure it out for ourselves. It's something important to justify all their trouble. We're agreed they're not trying to find evidence of sabotage, not after twenty years. But Trans-space must be looking for *something*, something so valuable that it's worth looking for all this time. Now what could be that valuable?"

"Mark, you're a dreamer," said Moore.

Brandon obviously didn't hear him. "It can't be jewels or money or securities. There just couldn't be enough to pay them back for what the search has already cost them. Not if the *Silver Queen* were pure gold. What would be more valuable?"

"You can't judge value, Mark," said Moore. "A letter might be worth a hundredth of a cent as wastepaper and yet make a difference of a hundred million dollars to a corporation, depending on what's in the letter."

Brandon nodded his head vigorously. "Right. Documents.

Valuable papers. Now who would be most likely to have papers worth billions in his possession on that trip?"

"How could anyone possibly say?"

"How about Dr. Horace Quentin? How about that, Warren? He's the one people remember because he was so important. What about the papers he might have had with him? Details of a new discovery, maybe. Damn it, if I had only seen him on that trip, he might have told me something, just in casual conversation, you know. Did *you* ever see him, Warren?"

"Not that I recall. Not to talk to. So casual conversation with me is out too. Of course, I might have passed him at some time without knowing it."

"No, you wouldn't have," said Shea, suddenly thoughtful. "I think I remember something. There was one passenger who never left his cabin. The steward was talking about it. He wouldn't even come out for meals."

"And that was Quentin?" said Brandon, stopping his pacing and staring at the spaceman eagerly.

"It might have been, Mr. Brandon. It might have been him. I don't know that anyone *said* it was. I don't remember. But it must have been a big shot, because on a spaceship you don't fool around bringing meals to a man's cabin unless he *is* a big shot."

"And Quentin was *the* big shot on the trip," said Brandon, with satisfaction. "So he had something in his cabin. Something very important. Something he was concealing."

"He might just have been space sick," said Moore, "except that—" He frowned and fell silent.

"Go ahead," said Brandon urgently. "You remember something too?"

"Maybe. I told you I was sitting next to Dr. Hester at the last dinner. He was saying something about hoping to meet Dr. Quentin on the trip and not having any luck."

"Sure," cried Brandon, "because Quentin wouldn't come out of his cabin."

"He didn't *say* that. We got to talking about Quentin, though. Now what was it he said?" Moore put his hands to his temples as though trying to squeeze out the memory of twenty years ago by main force. "I can't give you the exact words, of course, but it was something about Quentin being very theatrical or a slave of drama or something like that, and they were heading out to some scientific conference on Ganymede and Quentin wouldn't even announce the title of his paper."

"It all fits." Brandon resumed his rapid pacing. "He had a new, great discovery, which he was keeping absolutely secret, because he was going to spring it on the Ganymede conference and get maximum drama out of it. He wouldn't come out of his cabin because he probably thought Hester would pump him—and Hester would, I'll bet. And then the ship hit the rock and Quentin was killed. Trans-space Insurance investigated, got rumors of this new discovery and figured that if they gained control of it they could make back their losses and plenty more. So they took ownership of the ship and have been hunting for Quentin's papers among the pieces ever since."

Moore smiled, in absolute affection for the other man. "Mark, that's a beautiful theory. The whole evening is worth it, just watching you make something out of nothing."

"Oh, yeah? Something out of nothing? Let's ask Multivac again. I'll pay the bill for it this month."

"It's all right. Be my guest. If you don't mind, though, I'm going to bring up the bottle of Jabra. I want one more little shot to catch up with you."

"Me, too," said Shea.

Brandon took his seat at the typewriter. His fingers trembled with eagerness as he tapped out: What was the nature of Dr. Horace Quentin's final investigations?

Moore had returned with the bottle and glasses, when the answer came back, on white paper this time. The answer was long and the print was fine, consisting for the most part of references to scientific papers in journals twenty years old.

Moore went over it. "I'm no physicist, but it looks to me as though he was interested in optics."

Brandon shook his head impatiently. "But all that is published. We want something he had not published yet."

"We'll never find out anything about that."

"The insurance company did."

"That's just your theory."

Brandon was kneading his chin with an unsteady hand. "Let me ask Multivac one more question."

He sat down again and tapped out: Give me the name and tube number of the surviving colleagues of Dr. Horace Quentin from among those associated with him at the University on whose faculty he served.

"How do you know he was on a University faculty?" asked Moore.

"If not, Multivac will tell us."

A slip popped out. It contained only one name.

Moore said, "Are you planning to call the man?"

"I sure am," said Brandon. "Otis Fitzsimmons, with a Detroit tube number. Warren, may I—"

"Be my guest, Mark. It's still part of the game."

Brandon set up the combination on Moore's tube keyboard. A woman's voice answered. Brandon asked for Dr. Fitzsimmons and there was a short wait.

Then a thin voice said, "Hello." It sounded old.

Brandon said, "Dr. Fitzsimmons, I'm representing Transspace Insurance in the matter of the late Dr. Horace Quentin—"

"For heaven's sake, Mark," whispered Moore, but Brandon held up a sharply restraining hand.

There was a pause so long that a tube breakdown began to seem possible and then the old voice said, "After all these years? Again?"

Brandon snapped his fingers in an irrepressible gesture of triumph. But he said smoothly, almost glibly, "We're still trying to find out, Doctor, if you have remembered further details about what Dr. Quentin might have had with him on that last trip that would pertain to his last unpublished discovery."

"Well"—there was an impatient clicking of the tongue—"I've told you, I don't know. I don't want to be bothered with this again. I don't know that there was *anything*. The man hinted, but he was always hinting about some gadget or other."

"What gadget, sir?"

"I tell you I don't know. He used a name once and I told you about that. I don't think it's significant."

"We don't have the name in our records, sir."

"Well, you should have. Uh, what was that name? An optikon, that's it."

"With a K?"

"C or K. I don't know or care. Now, please, I do not

wish to be disturbed again about this. Good-bye." He was still mumbling querulously when the line went dead.

Brandon was pleased.

Moore said, "Mark, that was the stupidest thing you could have done. Claiming a fraudulent identity on the tube is illegal. If he wants to make trouble for you—"

"Why should he? He's forgotten about it already. But don't you see, Warren? Trans-space has been asking him about this. He kept saying he'd explained all this before."

"All right. But you'd assumed that much. What else do you know?"

"We also know," said Brandon, "that Quentin's gadget was called an optikon."

"Fitzsimmons didn't sound certain about that. And even so, since we already know he was specializing in optics toward the end, a name like optikon does not push us any further forward."

"And Trans-space Insurance is looking either for the optikon or for papers concerning it. Maybe Quentin kept the details in his hat and just had a model of the instrument. After all, Shea said they were picking up metal objects. Right?"

"There was a bunch of metal junk in the pile," agreed Shea.

"They'd leave that in space if it were papers they were after. So that's what we want, an instrument that might be called an optikon."

"Even if all your theories were correct, Mark, and we're looking for an optikon, the search is absolutely hopeless now," said Moore flatly. "I doubt that more than ten per cent of the debris would remain in orbit about Vesta. Vesta's escape velocity is practically nothing. It was just a lucky thrust in a lucky direction and at a lucky velocity that put our section of the wreck in orbit. The rest is gone, scattered all over the Solar System in any conceivable orbit about the Sun."

"They've been picking up pieces," said Brandon.

"Yes, the ten per cent that managed to make a Vestan orbit out of it. That's all."

Brandon wasn't giving up. He said thoughtfully, "Suppose it *were* there and they hadn't found it. Could someone have beat them to it?"

Mike Shea laughed. "We were right there, but we sure

didn't walk off with anything but our skins, and glad to do that much. Who else?"

"That's right," agreed Moore, "and if anyone else picked it up, why are they keeping it a secret?"

"Maybe they don't know what it is."

"Then how do we go about—" Moore broke off and turned to Shea, "What did you say?"

Shea looked blank. "Who, me?"

"Just now, about us being there." Moore's eyes narrowed. He shook his head as though to clear it, then whispered, "Great Galaxy!"

"What is it?" asked Brandon tensely. "What's the matter, Warren?"

"I'm not sure. You're driving me mad with your theories; so mad, I'm beginning to take them seriously, I think. You know, we *did* take some things out of the wreck with us. I mean besides our clothes and what personal belongings we still had. Or at least I did."

"What?"

"It was when I was making my way across the outside of the wreckage—space, I seem to be there now, I see it so clearly—I picked up some items and put them in the pocket of my spacesuit. I don't know why; I wasn't myself, really. I did it without thinking. And then, well, I held on to them. Souvenirs, I suppose. I brought them back to Earth."

"Where are they?"

"I don't know. We haven't stayed in one place, you know."

"You didn't throw them out, did you?"

"No, but things do get lost when you move."

"If you didn't throw them out, they must be somewhere in this house."

"If they didn't get lost. I swear I don't recall seeing them in fifteen years."

"What were they?"

Warren Moore said, "One was a fountain pen, as I recall; a real antique, the kind that used an ink-spray cartridge. What gets me, though, is that the other was a small field glass, not more than about six inches long. You see what I mean? A field glass?"

"An optikon," shouted Brandon. "Sure!"

"It's just a coincidence," said Moore, trying to remain levelheaded. "Just a curious coincidence."

But Brandon wasn't having it. "A coincidence, nuts! Transspace couldn't find the optikon on the wreck and they couldn't find it in space because you had it all along."

"You're crazy."

"Come on, we've got to find the thing now."

Moore blew out his breath. "Well, I'll look, if that's what you want, but I doubt that I'll find it. Okay, let's start with the storage level. That's the logical place."

Shea chuckled. "The logical place is usually the worst place to look." But they all headed for the power ramp once more and the additional flight upward.

The storage level had a musty, unused odor to it. Moore turned on the precipitron. "I don't think we've precipitated the dust in two years. That shows you how often I'm up here. Now, let's see—if it's anywhere at all, it would be in with the bachelor collection. I mean the junk I've been hanging on to since bachelor days. We can start here."

Moore started leafing through the contents of plastic collapsibles while Brandon kept peering anxiously over his shoulder.

Moore said, "What do you know? My college yearbook. I was a sonist in those days; a real bug on it. In fact, I managed to get a voice recording with the picture of every senior in this book." He tapped its cover fondly. "You could swear there was nothing there but the usual trimensional photos, but each one has an imprisoned—"

He grew aware of Brandon's frown and said, "Okay, I'll keep looking."

He gave up on the collapsibles and opened a trunk of heavy, old-fashioned woodite. He separated the contents of the various compartments.

Brandon said, "Hey, is that it?"

He pointed to a small cylinder that rolled out on the floor with a small clunk.

Moore said, "I don't— Yes! That's the pen. There it is. And here's the field glass. Neither one works, of course. They're both broken. At least, I suppose the pen's broken. Something's loose and rattles in it. Hear? I wouldn't have the slightest idea about how to fill it so I can check whether it really works. They haven't even made ink-spray cartridges in years."

Brandon held it under the light. "It has initials on it."

"Oh? I don't remember noticing any."

"It's pretty worn down. It looks like. J.K.Q."

"Q.?"

"Right, and that's an unusual letter with which to start a last name. This pen might have belonged to Quentin. An heirloom he kept for luck or sentiment. It might have belonged to a great-grandfather in the days when they used pens like this; a great-grandfather called Jason Knight Quentin or Judah Kent Quentin or something like that. We can check the names of Quentin's ancestors through Multivac."

Moore nodded. "I think maybe we should. See, you've got me as crazy as you are."

"And if this is so, it proves you picked it up in Quentin's room. So you picked up the field glass there too."

"Now hold it. I don't remember that I picked them both up in the same place. I don't remember the scrounging over the outside of the wreck that well."

Brandon turned the small field glass over and over under the light. "No initials here."

"Did you expect any?"

"I don't see anything, in fact, except this narrow joining mark here." He ran his thumbnail into the fine groove that circled the glass near its thicker end. He tried to twist it unsuccessfully. "One piece." He put it to his eye. "This thing doesn't work."

"I told you it was broken. No lenses—"

Shea broke in. "You've got to expect a little damage when a spaceship hits a good-sized meteor and goes to pieces."

"So even if this were it," said Moore, pessimistic again, "if this were the optikon, it would not do us any good."

He took the field glass from Brandon and felt along the empty rims. "You can't even tell where the lenses belonged. There's no groove I can feel into which they might have been seated. It's as if there never— *Hey!*" He exploded the syllable violently.

"Hey what?" said Brandon.

"The name! The name of the thing!"

"Optikon, you mean?"

"Optikon, I don't mean! Fitzsimmons, on the tube, called it an optikon and we thought he said 'an optikon.'"

"Well, he did," said Brandon.

"Sure," said Shea. "I heard him."

"You just thought you heard him. He said 'anoptikon.' Don't you get it? Not 'an optikon,' two words, 'anoptikon,' one word."

"Oh," said Brandon blankly. "And what's the difference?"

"A hell of a difference. 'An optikon' would mean an instrument with lenses, but 'anoptikon,' one word, has the Greek prefix 'an-' which means 'no.' Words of Greek derivation use it for 'no.' Anarchy means 'no government,' anemia means 'no blood,' anonymous means 'no name,' and anoptikon means—"

"No lenses," cried Brandon.

"Right! Quentin must have been working on an optical device without lenses and this may be it and it may not be broken."

Shea said, "But you don't see anything when you look through it."

"It must be set to neutral," said Moore. "There must be some way of adjusting it." Like Brandon, he placed it in both hands and tried to twist it about that circumscribing groove. He placed pressure on it, grunting.

"Don't break it," said Brandon.

"It's giving. Either it's supposed to be stiff or else it's corroded shut." He stopped, looked at the instrument impatiently, and put it to his eye again. He whirled, unpolarized a window and looked out at the lights of the city.

"I'll be dumped in space," he breathed.

Brandon said, "What? What?"

Moore handed the instrument to Brandon wordlessly. Brandon put it to his eyes and cried out sharply, "It's a telescope."

Shea said at once, "Let me see."

They spent nearly an hour with it, converting it into a telescope with turns in one direction, a microscope with turns in the other.

"How does it work?" Brandon kept asking.

"I don't know," Moore kept saying. In the end he said, "I'm sure it involves concentrated force fields. We are turning against considerable field resistance. With larger instruments, power adjustment will be required."

"It's a pretty cute trick," said Shea.

"It's more than that," said Moore. "I'll bet it represents a completely new turn in theoretical physics. It focuses light without lenses, and it can be adjusted to gather light over a wider and wider area without any change in focal length. I'll bet we could duplicate the five-hundred-inch Ceres telescope in one direction and an electron microscope in the other. What's more, I don't see any chromatic aberration, so it must bend light of all wavelengths equally. Maybe it bends radio waves and gamma rays also. Maybe it distorts gravity, if gravity is some kind of radiation. Maybe—"

"Worth money?" asked Shea, breaking in dryly.

"All kinds if someone can figure out how it works."

"Then we don't go to Trans-space Insurance with this. We go to a lawyer first. Did we sign these things away with our salvage rights or didn't we? You had them already in your possession before signing the paper. For that matter, is the paper any good if we didn't know what we were signing away? Maybe it might be considered fraud."

"As a matter of fact," said Moore, "with something like this, I don't know if any private company ought to own it. We ought to check with some government agency. If there's money in it—"

But Brandon was pounding both fists on his knees. "To *hell* with the money, Warren. I mean, I'll take any money that comes my way but that's not the important thing. We're going to be famous, man, famous! Imagine the story. A fabulous treasure lost in space. A giant corporation combing space for twenty years to find it and all the time we, the forgotten ones, have it in our possession. Then, on the twentieth anniversary of the original loss, we find it again. If this thing works, if anoptics becomes a great new scientific technique, they'll *never* forget us."

Moore grinned, then started laughing. "That's right. You did it, Mark. You did just what you set out to do. You've rescued us from being marooned in oblivion."

"We all did it," said Brandon. "Mike Shea started us off with the necessary basic information. I worked out the theory, and you had the instrument."

"Okay. It's late, and the wife will be back soon, so let's get the ball rolling right away. Multivac will tell us which agency would be appropriate and who—"

"No, no," said Brandon. "Ritual first. The closing toast of

the anniversary, please, and with the appropriate change. Won't you oblige, Warren?" He passed over the still half-full bottle of Jabra water.

Carefully, Moore filled each small glass precisely to the brim. "Gentlemen," he said solemnly, "a toast." The three raised the glasses in unison. "Gentlemen, I give you the *Silver Queen* souvenirs *we used to have*."

I am ashamed to say that the idea for this story occurred to me when I read the obituary of a fellow science fiction writer in the New York Times *and began to wonder whether my own obituary, when it came, would be as long. From that to this story was but a tiny little step.*

Obituary

My husband, Lancelot, always reads the paper at breakfast. What I see of him when he first appears is his lean, abstracted face, carrying its perpetual look of angry and slightly puzzled frustration. He doesn't greet me, and the newspaper, carefully unfolded in readiness for him, goes up before his face.

Thereafter, there is only his arm, emerging from behind the paper for a second cup of coffee into which I have carefully placed the necessary level teaspoonful of sugar—neither heaping nor deficient under pain of a stinging glare.

I am no longer sorry for this. It makes for a quiet meal, at least.

However, on this morning the quiet was broken when

Lancelot barked out abruptly, "Good Lord! That fool Paul Farber is dead. Stroke!"

I just barely recognized the name. Lancelot had mentioned him on occasion, so I knew him as a colleague, as another theoretical physicist. From my husband's exasperated epithet, I felt reasonably sure he was a moderately famous one who had achieved the success that had eluded Lancelot.

He put down the paper and stared at me angrily. "Why do they fill obituaries with such lying trash?" he demanded. "They make him out to be a second Einstein for no better reason than that he died of a stroke."

If there was one subject I had learned to avoid, it was that of obituaries. I dared not even nod agreement.

He threw down the paper and walked away and out of the room, leaving his eggs half-finished and his second cup of coffee untouched.

I sighed. What else could I do? What else could I ever do?

Of course, my husband's name isn't really Lancelot Stebbins, because I am changing names and circumstances, as far as I can, to protect the guilty. However, the point is that even if I used real names you would not recognize my husband.

Lancelot had a talent in that respect—a talent for being passed over, for going unnoticed. His discoveries are invariably anticipated, or blurred by the presence of a greater discovery made simultaneously. At scientific conventions his papers are poorly attended because another paper of greater importance is being given in another section.

Naturally this has had its effect on him. It changed him.

When I first married him, twenty-five years ago, he was a sparkling catch. He was well-to-do through inheritance and already a trained physicist with an intense ambition and great promise. As for myself, I believe myself to have been pretty then, but that didn't last. What did last was my introversion and my failure to be the kind of social success an ambitious young faculty member needs for a wife.

Perhaps that was part of Lancelot's talent for going unnoticed. Had he married another kind of wife, she might have made him visible in her radiation.

Did he realize that himself after a while? Was that why he grew away from me after the first two or three reasonably happy years? Sometimes I believed this and bitterly blamed myself.

But then I would think it was only his thirst for fame, which grew for being unslaked. He left his position on the faculty and built a laboratory of his own far outside town, for the sake, he said, of cheap land and of isolation.

Money was no problem. In his field, the government was generous with its grants and those he could always get. On top of that, he used our own money without limit.

I tried to withstand him. I said, "But it's not necessary, Lancelot. It's not as though we have financial worries. It's not as though they're not willing to let you remain on the university staff. All I want are children and a normal life."

But there was a burning inside him that blinded him to everything else. He turned angrily on me. "There is something that must come first. The world of science must recognize me for what I am, for a—a—great investigator."

At that time, he still hesitated to apply the term genius to himself.

It didn't help. The fall of chance remained always and perpetually against him. His laboratory hummed with work; he hired assistants at excellent salaries; he drove himself roughly and pitilessly. Nothing came of it.

I kept hoping he would give up someday; return to the city; allow us to lead a normal, quiet life. I waited, but always when he might have admitted defeat, some new battle would be taken up, some new attempt to storm the bastions of fame. Each time he charged with such hope and fell back in such despair.

And always he turned on me; for if he was ground down by the world, he could always grind me in return. I am not a brave person, but I was coming to believe I must leave him.

And yet . . .

In this last year he had obviously been girding himself for another battle. A last one, I thought. There was something about him more intense, more a-quiver than I had ever seen before. There was the way he murmured to himself and laughed briefly at nothing. There were the times he went for days without food and nights without sleep. He even took to keeping laboratory notebooks in a bedroom safe as though he feared even his own assistants.

Of course I was fatalistically certain that this attempt of his would fail also. But surely, if it failed, then at his age, he would have to recognize that his last chance had gone. Surely he would have to give up.

So I decided to wait, as patiently as I could.

But the affair of the obituary at breakfast came as something of a jolt. Once, on an earlier occasion of the sort, I had remarked that at least he could count on a certain amount of recognition in his own obituary.

I suppose it wasn't a very clever remark, but then my remarks never are. I had meant it to be lighthearted, to pull him out of a gathering depression during which I knew, from experience, he would be most intolerable.

And perhaps there had been a little unconscious spite in it, too. I cannot honestly say.

At any rate, he turned full on me. His lean body shook and his dark eyebrows pulled down over his deep-set eyes as he shrieked at me in falsetto, "But I'll never read my obituary. I'll be deprived even of that."

And he spat at me. He deliberately spat at me.

I ran to my bedroom.

He never apologized, but after a few days in which I avoided him completely, we carried on our frigid life as before. Neither of us ever referred to the incident.

Now there was another obituary.

Somehow, as I sat there alone at the breakfast table, I felt it to be the last straw for him, the climax of his long-drawn-out failure.

I could sense a crisis coming and didn't know whether to fear or welcome it. Perhaps, on the whole, I would welcome it. Any change could not fail to be a change for the better.

Shortly before lunch, he came upon me in the living room, where a basket of unimportant sewing gave my hands something to do and a bit of television occupied my mind.

He said abruptly, "I will need your help."

It had been twenty years or more since he had said anything like that and involuntarily I thawed toward him. He looked unhealthily excited. There was a flush on his ordinarily pale cheeks.

I said, "Gladly, if there's something I can do for you."

"There is. I have given my assistants a month's vacation. They will leave Saturday and after that you and I will work

alone in the laboratory. I tell you now so that you will
refrain from making any other arrangements for the coming
week."

I shriveled a bit. "But Lancelot, you know I can't help
you with your work. I don't understand—"

"I know that," he said with complete contempt, "but you
don't have to understand my work. You need only follow a
few simple instructions and follow them carefully. The point
is that I have discovered something, finally, which will put
me where I belong—"

"Oh, Lancelot," I said involuntarily, for I had heard this
before a number of times.

"Listen to me, you fool, and for once try to behave like an
adult. This time I have done it. No one can anticipate me this
time because my discovery is based on such an unorthodox
concept that no physicist alive, except me, is genius enough
to think of it, not for a generation at least. And when my
work bursts on the world, I could be recognized as the
greatest name of all time in science."

"I'm sure I'm very glad for you, Lancelot."

"I said I *could* be recognized. I could not be, also. There
is a great deal of injustice in the assignment of scientific
credit. I've learned that often enough. So it will not be
enough merely to announce the discovery. If I do, everyone
will crowd into the field and after a while I'll just be a name
in the history books, with glory spread out over a number
of Johnny-come-latelies."

I think the only reason he was talking to me then, three
days before he could get to work on whatever it was he
planned to do, was that he could no longer contain himself.
He bubbled over and I was the only one who was nonentity
enough to be witness to that.

He said, "I intend my discovery to be so dramatized, to
break on mankind with so thunderous a clap, that there will
be no room for anyone else to be mentioned in the same
breath with me, ever."

He was going too far, and I was afraid of the effect of
another disappointment on him. Might it not drive him mad?
I said, "But Lancelot, why need we bother? Why don't we
leave all this? Why not take a long vacation? You have
worked hard enough and long enough, Lancelot. Perhaps
we can take a trip to Europe. I've always wanted to—"

He stamped his foot. *"Will* you stop your foolish meow-ing? Saturday, you will come into my laboratory with me."

I slept poorly for the next three nights. He had never been quite like this before, I thought, never quite as bad. Might he not be mad already, perhaps?

It could be madness now, I thought, a madness born of disappointment no longer endurable, and sparked by the obituary. He had sent away his assistants and now he wanted me in the laboratory. He had never allowed me there before. Surely he meant to do something to me, to make me the subject of some insane experiment, or to kill me outright.

During the miserable, frightened nights I would plan to call the police, to run away, to—to do anything.

But then morning would come and I would think surely he wasn't mad, surely he wouldn't offer me violence. Even the spitting incident was not truly violent and he had never actually tried to hurt me physically.

So in the end I waited and on Saturday I walked to what might be my death as meekly as a chicken. Together, silently, we walked down the path that led from our dwelling to the laboratory.

The laboratory was frightening just in itself, and I stepped about gingerly, but Lancelot only said, "Oh, stop staring about you as though something were going to hurt you. You just do as I say and look where I tell you."

"Yes, Lancelot." He had led me into a small room, the door of which had been padlocked. It was almost choked with objects of very strange appearance and with a great deal of wiring.

Lancelot said, "To begin with, do you see this iron crucible?"

"Yes, Lancelot." It was a small but deep container made out of thick metal and rusted in spots on the outside. It was covered by a coarse wire netting.

He urged me toward it and I saw that inside it was a white mouse with its front paws up on the inner side of the crucible and its small snout at the wire netting in quivering curiosity, or perhaps in anxiety. I am afraid I jumped, for to see a mouse without expecting to is startling, at least to me.

Lancelot growled, "It won't hurt you. Now just back against the wall and watch me."

My fears returned most forcefully. I grew horribly certain that from somewhere a lightning bolt would shoot out and incinerate me, or some monstrous thing of metal might emerge and crush me, or—or—

I closed my eyes.

But nothing happened; to me, at least. I heard only a phfft as though a small firecracker had misfired, and Lancelot said to me, "Well?"

I opened my eyes. He was looking at me, fairly shining with pride. I stared blankly.

He said, "Here, don't you see it, you idiot? Right here."

A foot to one side of the crucible was a second one. I hadn't seen him put it there.

"Do you mean this second crucible?" I asked.

"It isn't quite a second crucible, but a duplicate of the first one. For all ordinary purposes, they are the same crucible, atom for atom. Compare them. You'll find the rust marks identical."

"You made the second one out of the first?"

"Yes, but in a special way. To create matter would require a prohibitive amount of energy ordinarily. It would take the complete fission of a hundred grams of uranium to create one gram of duplicate matter, even granting perfect efficiency. The great secret I have stumbled on is that the duplication of an object at a point in future time requires very little energy if that energy is applied correctly. The essence of the feat, my—my dear, in my creating such a duplicate and bringing it back is that I have accomplished the equivalent of time travel."

It was the measure of his triumph and happiness that he actually used an affectionate term in speaking to me.

"Isn't that remarkable?" I said, for to tell the truth, I *was* impressed. "Did the mouse come too?"

I looked inside the second crucible as I asked that and got another nasty shock. It contained a white mouse—a dead white mouse.

Lancelot turned faintly pink. "That is a shortcoming. I can bring back living matter, but not as living matter. It comes back dead."

"Oh, what a shame. Why?"

"I don't know yet. I imagine the duplications are completely perfect on the atomic scale. Certainly there is no visible damage. Dissections show that."

"You might ask—" I stopped myself quickly as he glanced at me. I decided I had better not suggest a collaboration of any sort, for I knew from experience that in that case the collaborator would invariably get all the credit for the discovery.

Lancelot said with sour amusement, "I *have* asked. A trained biologist has performed autopsies on some of my animals and found nothing. Of course, they didn't know where the animal came from and I took care to take it back before anything would happen to give it away. Lord, even my assistants don't know what I've been doing."

"But why must you keep it so secret?"

"Just because I can't bring objects back alive. Some subtle molecular derangement. If I published my results, someone else might learn the method of preventing such derangement, add his slight improvement to my basic discovery, and achieve a greater fame, because he would bring back a living man who might give information about the future."

I saw that quite well. Nor need he say it "might" be done. It would be done. Inevitably. In fact, no matter what he did, he would lose the credit. I was sure of it.

"However," he went on, more to himself than to me, "I can wait no longer. I must announce this, but in such a way that it will be indelibly and permanently associated with me. There must be a drama about it so effective that thereafter there will be no way of mentioning time travel without mentioning me no matter what other men may do in the future. I am going to prepare that drama and you will play a part in it."

"But what do you want me to do, Lancelot?"

"You'll be my widow."

I clutched at his arm. "Lancelot, do you mean—" I cannot quite analyze the conflicting feelings that upset me at that moment.

He disengaged himself roughly. "Only temporarily. I am not committing suicide. I am simply going to bring myself back from three days in the future."

"But you'll be dead then."

"Only the 'me' that is brought back. The real 'me' will be

as alive as ever. Like that white rat." His eyes shifted to a dial and he said, "Ah, Zero time in a few seconds. Watch the second crucible and the dead mouse."

Before my eyes it disappeared and there was a phfft sound again.

"Where did it go?"

"Nowhere," said Lancelot. "It was only a duplicate. The moment we passed that instant in time at which the duplicate was formed, it naturally disappeared. It was the first mouse that was the original, and it remains alive and well. The same will be true of me. A duplicate 'me' will come back dead. The original 'me' will be alive. After three days, we will come to the instant at which the duplicate 'me' was formed, using the real 'me' as a model, and sent back dead. Once we pass that instant the dead duplicate 'me' will disappear and the live 'me' will remain. Is that clear?"

"It sounds dangerous."

"It isn't. Once my dead body appears, the doctor will pronounce me dead, the newspapers will report me dead, the undertaker will prepare to bury the dead. I will then return to life and announce how I did it. When that happens, I will be more than the discoverer of time travel; I will be the man who came back from the dead. Time travel and Lancelot Stebbins will be publicized so thoroughly and so intermingled, that nothing will extricate my name from the thought of time travel ever again."

"Lancelot," I said softly, "why can't we just announce your discovery? This is too elaborate a plan. A simple announcement will make you famous enough and then we can move to the city perhaps—"

"*Quiet!* You will do what I say."

I don't know how long Lancelot was thinking of all this before the obituary actually brought matters to a head. Of course, I don't minimize his intelligence. Despite his phenomenally bad luck, there is no questioning his brilliance.

He had informed his assistants before they had left of the experiments he intended to conduct while they were gone. Once they testified it would seem quite natural that he should be bent over a particular set of reacting chemicals and that he should be dead of cyanide poisoning to all appearances.

"So you see to it that the police get in touch with my assistants at once. You know where they can be reached. I want no hint of murder or suicide, or anything but accident, natural and logical accident. I want a quick death certificate from the doctor, a quick notification to the newspapers."

I said, "But Lancelot, what if they find the real you?"

"Why should they?" he snapped. "If you find a corpse, do you start searching for the living replica also? No one will look for me and I will stay quietly in the temporal chamber for the interval. There are toilet facilities and I can bring in enough sandwich fixings to keep me."

He added regretfully, "I'll have to make do without coffee, though, till it's over. I can't have anyone smelling unexplained coffee here while I'm supposed to be dead. Well, there's plenty of water and it's only three days."

I clasped my hands nervously and said, "Even if they do find you, won't it be the same thing anyway? There'll be a dead 'you' and a living 'you'—" It was myself I was trying to console, myself I was trying to prepare for the inevitable disappointment.

But he turned on me, shouting, "No, it won't be the same thing at all. It will all become a hoax that failed. I'll be famous, but only as a fool."

"But Lancelot," I said cautiously, "something always goes wrong."

"Not this time."

"But you always say 'not this time' and yet something *always*—"

He was white with rage and his irises showed clear all about their circle. He caught my elbow and hurt it terribly but I dared not cry out. He said, "Only one thing can go wrong and that is *you*. If you give it away, if you don't play your part perfectly, if you don't follow the instructions exactly, I—I—" He seemed to cast about for a punishment. "I'll *kill* you."

I turned my head away in sheer terror and tried to break loose, but he held on grimly. It was remarkable how strong he could be when he was in a passion. He said, "Listen to me! You have done me a great deal of harm by being you, but I have blamed myself for marrying you in the first place and for never finding the time to divorce you in the second. But now I have my chance, despite you, to turn my life into

a vast success. If you spoil even that chance, I will kill you.
I mean that literally."

I was sure he did. "I'll do everything you say," I whispered, and he let me go.

He spent a day on his machinery. "I've never transported more than a hundred grams before," he said, calmly thoughtful.

I thought: It won't work. How can it?

The next day he adjusted the device to the point where I needed only to close one switch. He made me practice that particular switch on a dead circuit for what seemed an interminable time.

"Do you understand now? Do you see exactly how it is done?"

"Yes."

"Then do it, when this light flashes and not a moment before."

It won't work, I thought. "Yes," I said.

He took his position and remained in stolid silence. He was wearing a rubber apron over a laboratory jacket.

The light flashed, and the practice turned out to be worth while for I pulled the switch automatically before thought could stop me or even make me waver.

For an instant there were two Lancelots before me, side by side, the new one dressed as the old one was but more rumpled. And then the new one collapsed and lay still.

"All right," cried the living Lancelot, stepping off the carefully marked spot. "Help me. Grab his legs."

I marveled at Lancelot. How, without wincing or showing any uneasiness, could he carry his own dead body, his own body of three days in the future? Yet he held it under its arms without showing any more emotion than if it had been a sack of wheat.

I held it by the ankles, my stomach turning at the touch. It was still blood-warm to the touch; freshly dead. Together we carried it through a corridor and up a flight of stairs, down another corridor and into a room. Lancelot had it already arranged. A solution was bubbling in a queer all-glass contraption inside a closed section, with a movable glass door partitioning it off.

Other chemical equipment was scattered about, calculated, no doubt, to show an experiment in progress. A bottle, boldly labeled "Potassium cyanide" was on the desk, prominent among the others. There was a small scattering of crystals on the desk near it; cyanide, I presume.

Carefully Lancelot crumpled the dead body as though it had fallen off the stool. He placed crystals on the body's left hand and more on the rubber apron; finally, a few on the body's chin.

"They'll get the idea," he muttered.

A last look-around and he said, "All right, now. Go back to the house now and call the doctor. Your story is that you came here to bring me a sandwich because I was working through lunch. There it is." And he showed me a broken dish and a scattered sandwich where, presumably, I had dropped it. "Do a little screaming, but don't overdo it."

It was not difficult for me to scream when the time came, or to weep. I had felt like doing both for days and now it was a relief to let the hysteria out.

The doctor behaved precisely as Lancelot had said he would. The bottle of cyanide was virtually the first thing he saw. He frowned. "Dear me, Mrs. Stebbins, he was a careless chemist."

"I suppose so," I said, sobbing. "He shouldn't have been working himself, but both his assistants are on vacation."

"When a man treats cyanide as though it were salt, it's bad." The doctor shook his head in grave moralistic fashion. "Now, Mrs. Stebbins, I will have to call the police. It's accidental cyanide poisoning, but it's a violent death and the police——"

"Oh, yes, yes, call them." And then I could almost have beaten myself for having sounded suspiciously eager.

The police came, and along with them a police surgeon, who grunted in disgust at the cyanide crystals on hand, apron, and chin. The police were thoroughly disinterested, asked only statistical questions concerning names and ages. They asked if I could manage the funeral arrangements. I said yes, and they left.

I then called the newspapers, and two of the press associations. I said I thought they would be picking up news of the death from the police records and I hoped they would not stress the fact that my husband was a careless chemist, with the tone of one who hoped nothing ill would be said of the dead. After all, I went on, he was a nuclear physicist rather than a chemist and I had a feeling lately he might be in some sort of trouble.

I followed Lancelot's line exactly in this and that also worked. A nuclear physicist in trouble? Spies? Enemy agents?

The reporters began to come eagerly. I gave them a youthful portrait of Lancelot and a photographer took pictures of the laboratory buildings. I took them through a few rooms of the main laboratory for more pictures. No one, neither the police nor the reporters, asked questions about the bolted room or even seemed to notice it.

I gave them a mass of professional and biographical material that Lancelot had made ready for me and told several anecdotes designed to show a combination of humanity and brilliance. In everything I tried to be letter-perfect and yet I could feel no confidence. Something would go wrong; *something* would go wrong.

And when it did, I knew he would blame me. And this time he had promised to kill me.

The next day I brought him the newspapers. Over and over again, he read them, eyes glittering. He had made a full box on the lower left of the New York *Times'* front page. The *Times* made little of the mystery of his death and so did the A.P., but one of the tabloids had a front-page scare headline: ATOM SAVANT IN MYSTERY DEATH.

He laughed aloud as he read that and when he completed all of them, he turned back to the first.

He looked up at me sharply. "Don't go. Listen to what they say."

"I've read them already, Lancelot."

"Listen, I tell you."

He read every one aloud to me, lingering on their praises of the dead, then said to me, aglow with self-satisfaction, "Do you still think something will go wrong?"

I said hesitantly, "If the police come back to ask why I thought you were in trouble . . ."

"You were vague enough. Tell them you had had bad dreams. By the time they decide to push investigations further, if they do, it will be too late."

To be sure, everything was working, but I could not hope that all would continue so. And yet the human mind is odd; it will persist in hoping even when it cannot hope.

I said, "Lancelot, when this is all over and you are famous, really famous, then after that, surely you can retire. We can go back to the city and live quietly."

"You are an imbecile. Don't you see that once I am recognized, I *must* continue? Young men will flock to me. This laboratory will become a great Institute of Temporal Investigation. I'll become a legend in my lifetime. I will pile my greatness so high that no one afterward will ever be able to be anything but an intellectual dwarf compared to me." He raised himself on tiptoe, eyes shining, as though he already saw the pedestal onto which he would be raised.

It had been my last hope of some personal shreds of happiness and a small one. I sighed.

I asked the undertaker that the body be allowed to remain in its coffin in the laboratories before burial in the Stebbins family plot on Long Island. I asked that it remain unembalmed, offering to keep it in a large refrigerated room with the temperature set at forty. I asked that it not be removed to the funeral home.

The undertaker brought the coffin to the laboratory in frigid disapproval. No doubt this was reflected in the eventual bill. My offered explanation that I wanted him near me for a last period of time and that I wanted his assistants to be given a chance to view the body was lame and sounded lame.

Still, Lancelot had been most specific in what I was to say.

Once the dead body was laid out, with the coffin lid still open, I went to see Lancelot.

"Lancelot," I said, "the undertaker was quite displeased. I think he suspects that something odd is going on."

"Good," said Lancelot with satisfaction.

"But—"

"We need only wait one more day. Nothing will be brought to a head out of mere suspicion before then. Tomorrow morning the body will disappear, or should."

"You mean it might not?" I knew it; I knew it.

"There could be some delay, or some prematurity. I have

never transported anything this heavy and I'm not certain how exactly my equations hold. To make the necessary observation is one reason I want the body here and not in a funeral parlor."

"But in the funeral parlor it would disappear before witnesses."

"And here you think they will suspect trickery?"

"Of course."

He seemed amused. "They will say: Why did he send his assistants away? Why did he run experiments himself that any child could perform and yet manage to kill himself running them? Why did the dead body happen to disappear without witnesses? They will say: There is nothing to this absurd story of time travel. He took drugs to throw himself in a cataleptic trance and doctors were hoodwinked."

"Yes," I said faintly. How did he come to understand all that?

"And," he went on, "when I continue to insist I have solved time travel and that I was indisputably pronounced dead and was not indisputably alive, orthodox scientists will heatedly denounce me as a fraud. Why, in one week, I will have become a household name to every man on Earth. They will talk of nothing else. I will offer to make a demonstration of time travel before any group of scientists who wish to see it. I will offer to make the demonstration on an intercontinental TV circuit. Public pressure will force scientists to attend, and the networks to give permission. It doesn't matter whether people will watch hoping for a miracle or for a lynching. They will watch! And *then* I will succeed and who in science will ever have had a more transcendent climax to his life?"

I was dazzled for a moment, but something unmoved within me said: Too long, too complicated; something will go wrong.

That evening, his assistants arrived and tried to be respectfully grieving in the presence of the corpse. Two more witnesses to swear they had seen Lancelot dead; two more witnesses to confuse the issue and help build events to their stratospheric peak.

By four the next morning, we were in the cold-room, bundled in overcoats and waiting for zero moment.

Lancelot, in high excitement, kept checking his instruments and doing I-know-not-what with them. His desk computer was working constantly, though how he could make his cold fingers jiggle the keys so nimbly, I am at a loss to say.

I, myself, was quite miserable. There was the cold, the dead body in the coffin, the uncertainty of the future.

We had been there for what seemed an eternity and finally Lancelot said, "It will work. It will work as predicted. At the most, disappearance will be five minutes late and this when seventy kilograms of mass are involved. My analysis of chronous forces is masterly indeed." He smiled at me, but he also smiled at his own corpse with equal warmth.

I noticed that his lab jacket, which he had been wearing constantly for three days now, sleeping in it I am certain, had become wrinkled and shabby. It was about as it had seemed upon the second Lancelot, the dead one, when it had appeared.

Lancelot seemed to be aware of my thoughts, or perhaps only of my gaze, for he looked down at his jacket and said, "Ah, yes, I had better put on the rubber apron. My second self was wearing it when it appeared."

"What if you didn't put it on?" I asked tonelessly.

"I would have to. It would be a necessity. Something would have reminded me. Else *it* would not have appeared in one." His eyes narrowed. "Do you still think something will go wrong?"

"I don't know," I mumbled.

"Do you think the body won't disappear, or that I'll disappear instead?"

When I didn't answer at all, he said in a half-scream, "Can't you see my luck has changed at last? Can't you see how smoothly and according to plan it is all working out? I will be the greatest man who ever lived. Come, heat up the water for the coffee." He was suddenly calm again. "It will serve as celebration when my double leaves us and I return to life. I haven't had any coffee for three days."

It was only instant coffee he pushed in my direction, but after three days that, too, would serve. I fumbled at the laboratory hot-plate with my cold fingers until Lancelot pushed me roughly to one side and set a beaker of water upon it.

"It'll take a while," he said, turning the control to "high."

He looked at his watch, then at various dials on the wall. "My double will be gone before the water boils. Come here and watch." He stepped to the side of the coffin.

I hesitated. "Come," he said peremptorily.

I came.

He looked down at himself with infinite pleasure and waited. We both waited, staring at a corpse.

There was the phfft sound and Lancelot cried out, "Less than two minutes off."

Without a blur or a wink, the dead body was gone.

The open coffin contained an empty set of clothes. The clothes, of course, had not been those in which the dead body had been brought back. They were real clothes and they stayed in reality. There they now were: underwear within shirt and pants; shirt within tie; tie within jacket. Shoes had turned over, dangling socks from within them. The body was gone.

I could hear water boiling.

"Coffee," said Lancelot. "Coffee first. Then we call the police and the newspapers."

I made the coffee for him and myself. I gave him the usual level teaspoon from the sugar bowl, neither heaping nor deficient. Even under these conditions, when I was sure for once it wouldn't matter to him, habit was strong.

I sipped at my coffee, which I drank without cream or sugar, as was my habit. Its warmth was most welcome.

He stirred his coffee. "All," he said softly, "all I have waited for." He put the cup to his grimly triumphant lips and drank.

Those were his last words.

Now that it was over, there was a kind of frenzy over me. I managed to strip him and dress him in the clothing from the coffin. Somehow I was able to heave his weight upward and place him in the coffin. I folded his arms across his chest as they had been.

I then washed out every trace of coffee in the sink in the room outside, and the sugar bowl, too. Over and over again I rinsed, until all the cyanide, which I had substituted for the sugar, was gone.

I carried his laboratory jacket and other clothes to the hamper where I had stored those the double had brought back. The second set had disappeared, of course, and I put the first set there.

Next I waited.

By that evening, I was sure the corpse was cold enough, and called the undertakers. Why should they wonder? They expected a dead body and there was the dead body. The same dead body. Really the same body. It even had cyanide in it as the first was supposed to have.

I suppose they might still be able to tell the difference between a body dead twelve hours and one dead three and a half days, even under refrigeration, but why should they dream of looking?

They didn't. They nailed down the coffin, took him away, and buried him. It was the perfect murder.

As a matter of fact, since Lancelot was legally dead at the time I killed him, I wonder if, strictly speaking, it was murder at all. Of course, I don't intend to ask a lawyer about this.

Life is quiet for me now; peaceful and contented. I have money enough. I attend the theater. I have made friends.

And I live without remorse. To be sure, Lancelot will never receive credit for time travel. Someday when time travel is discovered again, the name of Lancelot Stebbins will rest in Stygian darkness, unrecognized. But then, I told him that whatever his plans, he would end without the credit. If I hadn't killed him, something else would have spoiled things, and then he would have killed me.

No, I live without remorse.

In fact, I have forgiven Lancelot everything, everything but that moment when he spat at me. So it is rather ironic that he did have one happy moment before he died, for he was given a gift few could have, and he, above all men, savored it.

Despite his cry, when he spat at me, Lancelot managed to read his own obituary.

Star Light

Arthur Trent heard them quite clearly. The tense, angry words shot out of his receiver.

"Trent! You can't get away. We will intersect your orbit in two hours and if you try to resist we will blow you out of space."

Trent smiled and said nothing. He had no weapons and no need to fight. In far less than two hours the ship would make its Jump through hyperspace and they would never find him. He would have with him nearly a kilogram of Krillium, enough for the construction of the brain-paths of thousands of robots and worth some ten million credits on any world in the Galaxy—and no questions asked.

Old Brennmeyer had planned the whole thing. He had planned it for thirty years and more. It had been his life's work.

"It's the getaway, young man," he had said. "That's why I need you. You can lift a ship off the ground and out into space. I can't."

"Getting it into space is no good, Mr. Brennmeyer," Trent said. "We'll be caught in half a day."

"Not," said Brennmeyer craftily, "if we make the Jump. Not if we flash through hyperspace and end up light-years away."

"It would take half a day to plot the Jump and even if we could take the time, the police would alert all stellar systems."

"No, Trent, no." The old man's hand fell on his, clutching it in trembling excitement. "Not *all* stellar systems; only the dozen in our neighborhood. The Galaxy is big and the colonists of the last fifty thousand years have lost touch with each other."

He talked avidly, painting the picture. The Galaxy now

was like the surface of man's original planet—Earth, they had called it—in prehistoric times. Man had been scattered over all the continents but each group had known only the area immediately surrounding itself.

"If we make the Jump at random," Brennmeyer said, "we would be anywhere, even fifty thousand light-years away, and there would be no more chance of finding us than of finding a pebble in a meteor swarm."

Trent shook his head. "And we don't find ourselves, either. We wouldn't have the foggiest way of getting to an inhabited planet."

Brennmeyer's quick-moving eyes inspected the surroundings. No one was near him, but his voice sank to a whisper anyway. "I've spent thirty years collecting data on every habitable planet in the Galaxy. I've searched all the old records. I've traveled thousands of light-years, farther than any space pilot. And the location of every habitable planet is now in the memory store of the best computer in the world."

Trent lifted his eyebrows politely.

Brennmeyer said, "I design computers and I have the best. I've also plotted the exact location of every luminous star in the Galaxy, every star of spectral class of F, B, A, and O, and put that into the memory store. Once we've made the Jump the computer will scan the heavens spectroscopically and compare the results with the map of the Galaxy it contains. Once it finds the proper match, and sooner or later it will, the ship is located in space and it is then automatically guided through a second Jump to the neighborhood of the nearest inhabited planet."

"Sounds too complicated."

"It can't miss. All these years I've worked on it and it can't miss. I'll have ten years left yet to be a millionaire. But you're young; you'll be a millionaire much longer."

"When you Jump at random, you can end inside a star."

"Not one chance in a hundred trillion, Trent. We might also land so far from any luminous star that the computer can't find anything to match up against its program. We might find we've jumped only a light-year or two and the police are still on our trail. The chances of that are smaller still. If you want to worry, worry that you might die of a heart attack at the moment of takeoff. The chances for that are much higher."

"*You* might, Mr. Brennmeyer. You're older."

The old man shrugged. "I don't count. The computer will do everything automatically."

Trent nodded and remembered that. One midnight, when the ship was ready and Brennmeyer arrived with the Krillium in a briefcase—he had no difficulty for he was a greatly trusted man—Trent took the briefcase with one hand while his other moved quickly and surely.

A knife was still the best, just as quick as a molecular depolarizer, just as fatal, and much more quiet. Trent left the knife there with the body, complete with fingerprints. What was the difference? They wouldn't get him.

Deep in space now, with the police cruisers in pursuit, he felt the gathering tension that always preceded a Jump. No physiologist could explain it, but every space-wise pilot knew what it felt like.

There was a momentary inside-out feeling as his ship and himself for one moment of non-space and non-time, became non-matter and non-energy, then reassembled itself instantaneously in another part of the Galaxy.

Trent smiled. He was still alive. No star was too close and there were thousands that were close enough. The sky was alive with stars and the pattern was so different that he knew the Jump had gone far. Some of those stars had to be spectral class F and better. The computer would have a nice rich pattern to match against its memory. It shouldn't take long.

He leaned back in comfort and watched the bright pattern of star light move as the ship rotated slowly. A bright star came into view, a really bright one. It didn't seem more than a couple of light-years away and his pilot's sense told him it was a hot one, good and hot. The computer would use that as its base and match the pattern centered about it. Once again he thought: It shouldn't take long.

But it did. The minutes passed. Then an hour. And still the computer clicked busily and its lights flashed.

Trent frowned. Why didn't it find the pattern? The pattern had to be there. Brennmeyer had showed him his long years of work. He *couldn't* have left out a star or recorded it in the wrong place.

Surely stars were born and died and moved through space while in being, but these changes were slow, slow. In a million years the patterns that Brennmeyer had recorded couldn't—

A sudden panic clutched at Trent. No! It *couldn't* be. The chances for it were even smaller than Jumping into a star's interior.

He waited for the bright star to come into view again and, with trembling hands, brought it into telescopic focus. He put in all the magnification he could, and around the bright speck of light was the telltale fog of turbulent gases caught, as it were, in mid-flight.

It was a nova!

From dim obscurity the star had raised itself to bright luminosity, perhaps only a month ago. It had graduated from a spectral class low enough to be ignored by the computer, to one that would be most certainly taken into account.

But the nova that existed in space didn't exist in the computer's memory store because Brennmeyer had not put it there. It had not existed when Brennmeyer was collecting his data—at least not as a brightly luminous star.

"Don't count it," shrieked Trent. "Ignore it!"

But he was shouting at automatic machinery that would match the nova-centered pattern against the Galactic pattern and find it nowhere and continue, nevertheless, to match and match and match for as long as its energy supply held out.

The air supply would run out much sooner. Trent's life would ebb away much sooner.

Helplessly Trent slumped in his chair, watching the mocking pattern of star light and beginning the long and agonized wait for death.

If he had only kept the knife . . .

AFTERWORD

In recent years, several students in English Literature or in Library Science have taken to writing term papers, or even Master's theses, on my books and stories. *Very flattering*, of course, but very scary, too, for they find out all sorts of things about my literary life that I never knew existed.

For instance, there is a certain similarity between "Star Light" and "The Singing Bell" that I was not aware of until I went over both stories for this volume. And "The Dust of Death" resembles "The Singing Bell" in another fashion. I guess it comes from using the same aging brain for all three stories.

I'll bet anyone studying my literary output notices such resemblances at once, but lest they draw unwarranted conclusions, let me assure them that I remain blissfully ignorant of such things until I reread the stories in question in quick succession.

FOREWORD

This story was written under extremely pleasant circumstances. Joseph W. Ferman and Edward L. Ferman, father and son, and also publisher and editor of The Magazine of Fantasy and Science Fiction, *wanted to put out a special issue in my honor.*

I pretended to be overcome by modesty, but, in actual fact, the appeal to my vanity was absolutely overpowering. When they said they wanted a new story especially written for the issue, I agreed at once.

So I sat down and wrote a fourth Wendell Urth story, fully ten years after I had written the third. It was so nice to be back in harness, and so nice to see the special issue when it appeared. Ed Emshwiller, s.f. artist without peer, succeeded in drawing my portrait for the cover and in performing that incredible tour de force *of making it look, at one and the same time, like me and yet handsome. Now if I could have persuaded Doubleday to run that same portrait on the jacket of this book, you would have seen for yourself.**

Incidentally, in preparing this volume I saw that the level of technology on Earth and Moon in this story is far behind that described in "The Singing Bell." To which I shout, "Emerson!" (see page 73).

---

* A reference to the original hardcover edition.

The Key

Karl Jennings knew he was going to die. He had a matter of hours to live and much to do.

There was no reprieve from the death sentence, not here on the Moon, not with no communications in operation.

Even on Earth there were a few fugitive patches where, without radio handy, a man might die without the hand of his fellow man to help him, without the heart of his fellow man to pity him, without even the eye of his fellow man to discover the corpse. Here on the Moon, there were few spots that were otherwise.

Earthmen knew he was on the Moon, of course. He had been part of a geological expedition—no, selenological expedition! Odd, how his Earth-centered mind insisted on the "geo-."

Wearily he drove himself to think, even as he worked. Dying though he was, he still felt that artificially imposed clarity of thought. Anxiously he looked about. There was nothing to see. He was in the dark of the eternal shadow of the northern interior of the wall of the crater, a blackness relieved only by the intermittent blink of his flash. He kept that intermittent, partly because he dared not consume its power source before he was through and partly because he dared not take more than the minimum chance that it be seen.

On his left hand, toward the south along the nearby horizon of the Moon, was a crescent of bright white Sunlight. Beyond the horizon, and invisible, was the opposite lip of the crater. The Sun never peered high enough over the lip of his own edge of the crater to illuminate the floor immediately beneath his feet. He was safe from radiation—from that at least.

He dug carefully but clumsily, swathed as he was in his spacesuit. His side ached abominably.

The dust and broken rock did not take up the "fairy castle" appearance characteristic of those portions of the Moon's surface exposed to the alternation of light and dark, heat and cold. Here, in eternal cold, the slow crumbling of the crater wall had simply piled fine rubble in a heterogeneous mass. It would not be easy to tell there had been digging going on.

He misjudged the unevenness of the dark surface for a moment and spilled a cupped handful of dusty fragments. The particles dropped with the slowness characteristic of the Moon and yet with the appearance of a blinding speed, for there was no air resistance to slow them further still and spread them out into a dusty haze.

Jennings' flash brightened for a moment, and he kicked a jagged rock out of the way.

He hadn't much time. He dug deeper into the dust.

A little deeper and he could push the Device into the depression and begin covering it. Strauss must not find it.

Strauss!

The other member of the team. Half-share in the discovery. Half-share in the renown.

If it were merely the whole share of the credit that Strauss had wanted, Jennings might have allowed it. The discovery was more important than any individual credit that might go with it. But what Strauss wanted was something far more, something Jennings would fight to prevent.

One of the few things Jennings was willing to die to prevent.

And he was dying.

They had found it together. Actually, Strauss had found the ship; or, better, the remains of the ship; or, better still, what just conceivably might have been the remains of something analogous to a ship.

"Metal," said Strauss, as he picked up something ragged and nearly amorphous. His eyes and face could just barely be seen through the thick lead glass of the visor, but his rather harsh voice sounded clearly enough through the suit radio.

Jennings came drifting over from his own position half a mile away. He said, "Odd! There is no free metal on the Moon."

"There shouldn't be. But you know well enough they haven't explored more than one percent of the Moon's surface. Who knows what can be found on it?"

Jennings grunted assent and reached out his gauntlet to take the object.

It was true enough that almost anything might be found on the Moon for all anyone really knew. Theirs was the first privately financed selenographic expedition ever to land on the Moon. Till then, there had been only government-conducted shotgun affairs, with half a dozen ends in view. It was a sign of the advancing space age that the Geological Society could afford to send two men to the Moon for selenological studies only.

Strauss said, "It looks as though it once had a polished surface."

"You're right," said Jennings. "Maybe there's more about."

They found three more pieces, two of trifling size and one a jagged object that showed traces of a seam.

"Let's take them to the ship," said Strauss.

They took the small skim boat back to the mother ship. They shucked their suits once on board, something Jennings at least was always glad to do. He scratched vigorously at his ribs and rubbed his cheeks till his light skin reddened into welts.

Strauss eschewed such weakness and got to work. The laser beam pock-marked the metal and the vapor recorded itself on the spectrograph. Titanium-steel, essentially, with a hint of cobalt and molybdenum.

"That's artificial, all right," said Strauss. His broad-boned face was as dour and as hard as ever. He showed no elation, although Jennings could feel his own heart begin to race.

It may have been the excitement that trapped Jennings into beginning, "This is a development against which we must steel ourselves—" with a faint stress on "steel" to indicate the play on words.

Strauss, however, looked at Jennings with an icy distaste, and the attempted set of puns was choked off.

Jennings sighed. He could never swing it, somehow. Never could! He remembered at the University— Well, never mind. The discovery they had made was worth a far better pun than any he could construct for all Strauss's calmness.

Jennings wondered if Strauss could possibly miss the significance.

He knew very little about Strauss, as a matter of fact, except by selenological reputation. That is, he had read Strauss's papers and he presumed Strauss had read his. Although their ships might well have passed by night in their University days, they had never happened to meet until after both had volunteered for this expedition and had been accepted.

In the week's voyage, Jennings had grown uncomfortably aware of the other's stocky figure, his sandy hair and china-blue eyes, and the way the muscles over his prominent jawbones worked when he ate. Jennings, himself, much slighter in build, also blue-eyed, but with darker hair, tended to withdraw automatically from the heavy exudation of the other's power and drive.

Jennings said, "There's no record of any ship ever having landed on this part of the Moon. Certainly none has crashed."

"If it were part of a ship," said Strauss, "it should be smooth and polished. This is eroded and, without an atmosphere here, that means exposure to micrometeor bombardment over many years."

Then he *did* see the significance. Jennings said, with an almost savage jubilation, "It's a non-human artifact. Creatures not of Earth once visited the Moon. Who knows how long ago?"

"Who knows?" agreed Strauss dryly.

"In the report—"

"Wait," said Strauss imperiously. "Time enough to report when we have something to report. If it was a ship, there will be more to it than what we now have."

But there was no point in looking further just then. They had been at it for hours, and the next meal and sleep were overdue. Better to tackle the whole job fresh and spend hours at it. They seemed to agree on that without speaking.

The Earth was low on the eastern horizon, almost full in phase, bright and blue-streaked. Jennings looked at it while they ate and experienced, as he always did, a sharp homesickness.

"It looks peaceful enough," he said, "but there are six billion people busy on it."

Strauss looked up from some deep inner life of his own and said, "Six billion people ruining it!"

Jennings frowned. "You're not an Ultra, are you?"

Strauss said, "What the hell are you talking about?"

Jennings felt himself flush. A flush always showed against his fair skin, turning it pink at the slightest upset of the even tenor of his emotions. He found it intensely embarrassing.

He turned back to his food, without saying anything.

For a whole generation now, the Earth's population had held steady. No further increase could be afforded. Everyone admitted that. There were those, in fact, who said that "no higher" wasn't enough; the population had to drop. Jennings himself sympathized with that point of view. The globe of the Earth was being eaten alive by its heavy freight of humanity.

But *how* was the population to be made to drop? Randomly, by encouraging the people to lower the birth rate still further, as and how they wished? Lately there had been the slow rise of a distant rumble which wanted not only a population drop but a selected drop—the survival of the fittest, with the self-declared fit choosing the criteria of fitness.

Jennings thought: I've insulted him, I suppose.

Later, when he was almost asleep, it suddenly occurred to him that he knew virtually nothing of Strauss's character. What if it were his intention to go out now on a foraging expedition of his own so that he might get sole credit for—?

He raised himself on his elbow in alarm, but Strauss was breathing heavily, and even as Jennings listened, the breathing grew into the characteristic burr of a snore.

They spent the next three days in a single-minded search for additional pieces. They found some. They found more than that. They found an area glowing with the tiny phosphorescence of Lunar bacteria. Such bacteria were common enough, but nowhere previously had their occurrence been reported in concentration so great as to cause a visible glow.

Strauss said, "An organic being, or his remains, may have been here once. He died, but the micro-organisms within him did not. In the end they consumed him."

"And spread perhaps," added Jennings. "That may be the source of Lunar bacteria generally. They may not be native at all but may be the result of contamination instead—eons ago."

"It works the other way, too," said Strauss. "Since the bacteria are completely different in very fundamental ways from any Earthly form of micro-organism, the creatures they parasitized—assuming this was their source—must have been fundamentally different too. Another indication of extraterrestrial origin."

The trail ended in the wall of a small crater.

"It's a major digging job," said Jennings, his heart sinking. "We had better report this and get help."

"No," said Strauss somberly. "There may be nothing to get help for. The crater might have formed a million years after the ship had crash-landed."

"And vaporized most of it, you mean, and left only what we've found."

Strauss nodded.

Jennings said, "Let's try anyway. We can dig a bit. If we draw a line through the finds we've made so far and just keep on . . ."

Strauss was reluctant and worked halfheartedly, so that it was Jennings who made the real find. Surely that counted! Even though Strauss had found the first piece of metal, Jennings had found the artifact itself.

It *was* an artifact—cradled three feet underground under the irregular shape of a boulder which had fallen in such a way that it left a hollow in its contact with the Moon's surface. In that hollow lay the artifact, protected from everything for a million years or more; protected from radiation, from micrometeors, from temperature change, so that it remained fresh and new forever.

Jennings labeled it at once the Device. It looked not remotely similar to any instrument either had ever seen, but then, as Jennings said, why should it?

"There are no rough edges that I can see," he said. "It may not be broken."

"There may be missing parts, though."

"Maybe," said Jennings, "but there seems to be nothing movable. It's all one piece and certainly oddly uneven." He noted his own play on words, then went on with a not-altogether-successful attempt at self-control. "*This* is what we need. A piece of worn metal or an area rich in bacteria is only material for deduction and dispute. But this is the real thing—a Device that is clearly of extraterrestrial manufacture."

It was on the table between them now, and both regarded it gravely.

Jennings said, "Let's put through a preliminary report, now."

"No!" said Strauss, in sharp and strenuous dissent. "Hell, no!"

"Why not?"

"Because if we do, it becomes a Society project. They'll swarm all over it and we won't be as much as a footnote when all is done. No!" Strauss looked almost sly. "Let's do all we can with it and get as much out of it as possible before the harpies descend."

Jennings thought about it. He couldn't deny that he too wanted to make certain that no credit was lost. But still—

He said, "I don't know that I like to take the chance, Strauss." For the first time he had an impulse to use the man's first name, but fought it off. "Look, Strauss," he said, "it's not right to wait. If this is of extraterrestrial origin, then it must be from some other planetary system. There isn't a place in the Solar System, outside the Earth, that can possibly support an advanced life form."

"Not proven, really," grunted Strauss, "but what if you're right?"

"Then it would mean that the creatures of the ship had interstellar travel and therefore had to be far in advance, technologically, of ourselves. Who knows what the Device can tell us about their advanced technology? It might be the key to—who knows what? It might be the clue to an unimaginable scientific revolution."

"That's romantic nonsense. If this is the product of a technology far advanced over ours, we'll learn nothing from it. Bring Einstein back to life and show him a microprotowarp and what would he make of it?"

"We can't be certain that we won't learn."

"So what, even so? What if there's a small delay? What if we assure credit for ourselves? What if we make sure that we ourselves go along with this, that we don't let go of it?"

"But Strauss"—Jennings felt himself moved almost to tears in his anxiety to get across his sense of the importance of the Device—"what if we crash with it? What if we don't make it back to Earth? We can't risk this thing." He tapped it then, almost as though he were in love with it. "We should report it now and have them send ships out here to get it. It's too precious to—"

At the peak of his emotional intensity, the Device seemed to grow warm under his hand. A portion of its surface, half-hidden under a flap of metal, glowed phosphorescently.

Jennings jerked his hand away in a spasmodic gesture and the Device darkened. But it was enough; the moment had been infinitely revealing.

He said, almost choking, "It was like a window opening into your skull. I could see into your mind."

"I read yours," said Strauss, "or experienced it, or entered into it, or whatever you choose." He touched the Device in his cold, withdrawn way, but nothing happened.

"You're an Ultra," said Jennings angrily. "When I touched this"—And he did so. "It's happening again. I see it. Are you a madman? Can you honestly believe it is humanly decent to condemn almost all the human race to extinction and destroy the versatility and variety of the species?"

His hand dropped away from the Device again, in repugnance at the glimpses revealed, and it grew dark again. Once more, Strauss touched it gingerly and again nothing happened.

Strauss said, "Let's not start a discussion, for God's sake. This thing is an aid to communication—a telepathic amplifier. Why not? The brain cells have each their electric potentials. Thought can be viewed as a wavering electromagnetic field of microintensities—"

Jennings turned away. He didn't want to speak to Strauss. He said, "We'll report it now. I don't give a damn about credit. Take it all. I just want it out of our hands."

For a moment Strauss remained in a brown study. Then he said, "It's more than a communicator. It responds to emotion and it amplifies emotion."

"What are you talking about?"

"Twice it started at your touch just now, although you'd been handling it all day with no effect. It still has no effect when I touch it."

"Well?"

"It reacted to you when you were in a state of high emotional tension. That's the requirement for activation, I suppose. And when you raved about the Ultras while you were holding it just now, I felt as you did, for just a moment."

"So you should."

"But, listen to me. Are you sure *you're* so right? There isn't a thinking man on Earth that doesn't know the planet would be better off with a population of one billion rather than six billion. If we used automation to the full—as now the hordes won't allow us to do—we could probably have a completely efficient and viable Earth with a population of no more than, say, five million. Listen to me, Jennings. Don't turn away, man."

The harshness in Strauss's voice almost vanished in his effort to be reasonably winning. "But we can't reduce the population democratically. You know that. It isn't the sex urge, because uterine inserts solved the birth control problem long ago; you know that. It's a matter of nationalism. Each ethnic group wants other groups to reduce themselves in population first, and I agree with them. I want my ethnic group, *our* ethnic group, to prevail. I want the Earth to be inherited by the elite, which means by men like ourselves. We're the true men, and the horde of half-apes who hold us down are destroying us all. They're doomed to death anyway; why not save ourselves?"

"No," said Jennings strenuously. "No one group has a monopoly on humanity. Your five million mirror-images, trapped in a humanity robbed of its variety and versatility, would die of boredom—and serve them right."

"Emotional nonsense, Jennings. You don't believe that. You've just been trained to believe it by our damn-fool equalitarians. Look, this Device is just what we need. Even if we can't build any others or understand how this one works, this one Device might do. If we could control or influence the minds of key men, then little by little we can superimpose our views on the world. We already have an organization. You must know that if you've seen my mind. It's better motivated and better designed than any other organization on Earth. The brains of mankind flock to us daily. Why not you too? This instrument is a key, as you see, but not just a key to a bit more knowledge. It is a key to the final solution of men's problems. Join us! Join us!" He had reached an earnestness that Jennings had never heard in him.

Strauss's hand fell on the Device, which flickered a second or two and went out.

Jennings smiled humorlessly. He saw the significance of that. Strauss had been deliberately trying to work himself into an emotional state intense enough to activate the Device and had failed.

"You can't work it," said Jennings. "You're too darned supermannishly self-controlled and can't break down, can you?" He took up the Device with hands that were trembling, and it phosphoresced at once.

"Then *you* work it. Get the credit for saving humanity."

"Not in a hundred million years," said Jennings, gasping and barely able to breathe in the intensity of his emotion. "I'm going to report this now."

"No," said Strauss. He picked up one of the table knives. "It's pointed enough, sharp enough."

"You needn't work so hard to make your point," said Jennings, even under the stress of the moment conscious of the pun. "I can see your plans. With the Device you can convince anyone that I never existed. You can bring about an Ultra victory."

Strauss nodded. "You read my mind perfectly."

"But you won't," gasped Jennings. "Not while I hold this." He was willing Strauss into immobility.

Strauss moved raggedly and subsided. He held the knife out stiffly and his arm trembled, but he did not advance.

Both were perspiring freely.

Strauss said between clenched teeth, "You can't keep it—up all—day."

The sensation was clear, but Jennings wasn't sure he had the words to describe it. It was, in physical terms, like holding a slippery animal of vast strength, one that wriggled incessantly. Jennings had to concentrate on the feeling of immobility.

He wasn't familiar with the Device. He didn't know how to use it skillfully. One might as well expect someone who had never seen a sword to pick one up and wield it with the grace of a musketeer.

"Exactly," said Strauss, following Jennings' train of thought. He took a fumbling step forward.

Jennings knew himself to be no match for Strauss's mad

determination. They both knew that. But there was the skim boat. Jennings had to get away. With the Device.

But Jennings had no secrets. Strauss saw his thought and tried to step between the other and the skim boat.

Jennings redoubled his efforts. Not immobility, but unconsciousness. Sleep, Strauss, he thought desperately. Sleep!

Strauss slipped to his knees, heavy-lidded eyes closing.

Heart pounding, Jennings rushed forward. If he could strike him with something, snatch the knife—

But his thoughts had deviated from their all-important concentration on sleep, so that Strauss's hand was on his ankle, pulling downward with raw strength.

Strauss did not hesitate. As Jennings tumbled, the hand that held the knife rose and fell. Jennings felt the sharp pain and his mind reddened with fear and despair.

It was the very access of emotion that raised the flicker of the Device to a blaze. Strauss's hold relaxed as Jennings silently and incoherently screamed fear and rage from his own mind to the other.

Strauss rolled over, face distorted.

Jennings rose unsteadily to his feet and backed away. He dared do nothing but concentrate on keeping the other unconscious. Any attempt at violent action would block out too much of his own mind force, whatever it was; too much of his unskilled bumbling mind force that could not lend itself to really effective use.

He backed toward the skim boat. There would be a suit on board—bandages—

The skim boat was not really meant for long-distance runs. Nor was Jennings, any longer. His right side was slick with blood despite the bandages. The interior of his suit was caked with it.

There was no sign of the ship itself on his tail, but surely it would come sooner or later. Its power was many times his own; it had detectors that would pick up the cloud of charge concentration left behind by his ion-drive reactors.

Desperately Jennings had tried to reach Luna Station on his radio, but there was still no answer, and he stopped in despair. His signals would merely aid Strauss in pursuit.

He might reach Luna Station bodily, but he did not think he could make it. He would be picked off first. He would die and crash first. He wouldn't make it. He would have to hide the Device, put it away in a safe place, *then* make for Luna Station.

The Device . . .

He was not sure he was right. It might ruin the human race, but it was infinitely valuable. Should he destroy it altogether? It was the only remnant of non-human intelligent life. It held the secrets of an advanced technology; it was an instrument of an advanced science of the mind. Whatever the danger, consider the value—the potential value—

No, he must hide it so that it could be found again—but only by the enlightened Moderates of the government. Never by the Ultras . . .

The skim boat flickered down along the northern inner rim of the crater. He knew which one it was, and the Device could be buried here. If he could not reach Luna Station thereafter, either in person or by radio, he would have to at least get away from the hiding spot; well away, so that his own person would not give it away. And he would have to leave *some* key to its location.

He was thinking with an unearthly clarity, it seemed to him. Was it the influence of the Device he was holding? Did it stimulate his thinking and guide him to the perfect message? Or was it the hallucination of the dying, and would none of it make any sense to anyone? He didn't know, but he had no choice. He had to try.

For Karl Jennings knew he was going to die. He had a matter of hours to live and much to do.

H. Seton Davenport of the American Division of the Terrestrial Bureau of Investigation rubbed the star-shaped scar on his left cheek absently. "I'm aware, sir, that the Ultras are dangerous."

The Division Head, M. T. Ashley, looked at Davenport narrowly. His gaunt cheeks were set in disapproving lines. Since he had sworn off smoking once again, he forced his groping fingers to close upon a stick of chewing gum, which he shelled, crumpled, and shoved into his mouth morosely. He was getting old, and bitter, too, and his short iron-gray mustache rasped when he rubbed his knuckles against it.

He said, "You don't know how dangerous. I wonder if

anyone does. They are small in numbers, but strong among the powerful who, after all, are perfectly ready to consider themselves the elite. No one knows for certain who they are or how many."

"Not even the Bureau?"

"The Bureau is held back. We ourselves aren't free of the taint, for that matter. Are you?"

Davenport frowned. "I'm not an Ultra."

"I didn't say you were," said Ashley. "I asked if you were free of the taint. Have you considered what's been happening to the Earth in the last two centuries? Has it never occurred to you that a moderate decline in population would be a good thing? Have you never felt that it would be wonderful to get rid of the unintelligent, the incapable, the insensitive, and leave the rest? *I* have, damn it."

"I'm guilty of thinking that sometimes, yes. But considering something as a wish-fulfillment idea is one thing, but planning it as a practical scheme of action to be Hitlerized through is something else."

"The distance from wish to action isn't as great as you think. Convince yourself that the end is important enough, that the danger is great enough, and the means will grow increasingly less objectionable. Anyway, now that the Istanbul matter is taken care of, let me bring you up to date on this matter. Istanbul was of no importance in comparison. Do you know Agent Ferrant?"

"The one who's disappeared? Not personally."

"Well, two months ago, a stranded ship was located on the Moon's surface. It had been conducting a privately financed selenographic survey. The Russo-American Geological Society, which had sponsored the flight, reported the ship's failure to report. A routine search located it without much trouble within a reasonable distance of the site from which it had made its last report.

"The ship was not damaged but its skim boat was gone and with it one member of the crew. Name—Karl Jennings. The other man, James Strauss, was alive but in delirium. There was no sign of physical damage to Strauss, but he was quite insane. He still is, and that's important."

"Why?" put in Davenport.

"Because the medical team that investigated him reported neurochemical and neuroelectrical abnormalities of unprecedented nature. They'd never seen a case like it. Nothing human could have brought it about."

A flicker of a smile crossed Davenport's solemn face. "You suspect extraterrestrial invaders?"

"Maybe," said the other, with no smile at all. "But let me continue. A routine search in the neighborhood of the stranded ship revealed no signs of the skim boat. Then Luna Station reported receipt of weak signals of uncertain origin. They had been tabbed as coming from the western rim of Mare Imbrium, but it was uncertain whether they were of human origin or not, and no vessel was believed to be in the vicinity. The signals had been ignored. With the skim boat in mind, however, the search party headed out for Imbrium and located it. Jennings was aboard, dead. Knife wound in one side. It's rather surprising he had lived as long as he did.

"Meanwhile the medicos were becoming increasingly disturbed at the nature of Strauss's babbling. They contacted the Bureau and our two men on the Moon—one of them happened to be Ferrant—arrived at the ship.

"Ferrant studied the tape recordings of the babblings. There was no point in asking questions, for there was, and is, no way of reaching Strauss. There is a high wall between the universe and himself—probably a permanent one. However, the talk in delirium, although heavily repetitious and disjointed, can be made to make sense. Ferrant put it together like a jigsaw puzzle.

"Apparently Strauss and Jennings had come across an object of some sort which they took to be of ancient and non-human manufacture, an artifact of some ship wrecked eons ago. Apparently it could somehow be made to twist the human mind."

Davenport interrupted. "And it twisted Strauss's mind? Is that it?"

"That's exactly it. Strauss was an Ultra—we can say 'was' for he's only technically alive—and Jennings did not wish to surrender the object. Quite right, too. Strauss babbled of using it to bring about the self-liquidation, as he called it, of the undesirable. He wanted a final, ideal population of five million. There was a fight in which only Jennings, apparently, could handle the mind-thing, but in which Strauss had a knife. When Jennings left, he was knifed, but Strauss's mind had been destroyed."

"And where was the mind-thing?"

"Agent Ferrant acted decisively. He searched the ship and the surroundings again. There was no sign of anything that was neither a natural Lunar formation nor an obvious product of human technology. There was nothing that could be the mind-thing. He then searched the skim boat and its surroundings. Again nothing."

"Could the first search team, the ones who suspected nothing—could they have carried something off?"

"They swore they did not, and there is no reason to suspect them of lying. Then Ferrant's partner—"

"Who was he?"

"Gorbansky," said the District Head.

"I know him. We've worked together."

"I know you have. What do you think of him?"

"Capable and honest."

"All right. Gorbansky found something. Not an alien artifact. Rather, something most routinely human indeed. It was an ordinary white three-by-five card with writing on it, spindled, and in the middle finger of the right gauntlet. Presumably Jennings had written it before his death and, also presumably, it represented the key to where he had hidden the object."

"What reason is there to think he had hidden it?"

"I said we had found it nowhere."

"I mean, what if he had destroyed it, as something too dangerous to leave intact?"

"That's highly doubtful. If we accept the conversation as reconstructed from Strauss's ravings—and Ferrant built up what seems a tight word-for-word record of it—Jennings thought the mind-thing to be of key importance to humanity. He called it 'the clue to an unimaginable scientific revolution.' He wouldn't destroy something like that. He would merely hide it from the Ultras and try to report its whereabouts to the government. Else why leave a clue to its whereabouts?"

Davenport shook his head, "You're arguing in a circle, chief. You say he left a clue because you think there is a hidden object, and you think there is a hidden object because he left a clue."

"I admit that. Everything is dubious. Is Strauss's delirium meaningful? Is Ferrant's reconstruction valid? Is Jennings' clue really a clue? Is there a mind-thing, or a Device, as Jennings called it, or isn't there? There's no use asking such questions. Right now, we must act on the assumption that there is such a Device and that it must be found."

"Because Ferrant disappeared?"

"Exactly."

"Kidnapped by the Ultras?"

"Not at all. The card disappeared with him."

"Oh—I see."

"Ferrant has been under suspicion for a long time as a secret Ultra. He's not the only one in the Bureau under suspicion either. The evidence didn't warrant open action; we can't simply lay about on pure suspicion, you know, or we'll gut the Bureau from top to bottom. He was under surveillance."

"By whom?"

"By Gorbansky, of course. Fortunately Gorbansky had filmed the card and sent the reproduction to the headquarters on Earth, but he admits he considered it as nothing more than a puzzling object and included it in the information sent to Earth only out of a desire to be routinely complete. Ferrant—the better mind of the two, I suppose—did see the significance and took action. He did so at great cost, for he has given himself away and has destroyed his future usefulness to the Ultras, but there is a chance that there will be no need for future usefulness. If the Ultras control the Device—"

"Perhaps Ferrant has the Device already."

"He was under surveillance, remember. Gorbansky swears the Device did not turn up anywhere."

"Gorbansky did not manage to stop Ferrant from leaving with the card. Perhaps he did not manage to stop him from obtaining the Device unnoticed, either."

Ashley tapped his fingers on the desk between them in an uneasy and uneven rhythm. He said at last, "I don't want to think that. If we find Ferrant, we may find out how much damage he's done. Till then, we must search for the Device. If Jennings hid it, he must have tried to get away from the hiding place. Else why leave a clue? It wouldn't be found in the vicinity."

"He might not have lived long enough to get away."

Again Ashley tapped, "The skim boat showed signs of having engaged in a long, speedy flight and had all but crashed at the end. That is consistent with the view that Jennings was trying to place as much space as possible between himself and some hiding place."

"Can you tell from what direction he came?"

"Yes, but that's not likely to help. From the condition of the side vents, he had been deliberately tacking and veering."

Davenport sighed. "I suppose you have a copy of the card with you."

"I do. Here it is." He flipped a three-by-five replica toward Davenport. Davenport studied it for a few moments. It looked like this:

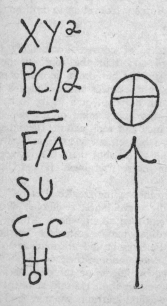

$$\frac{XY^2}{PC/2} = \frac{F/A}{SU}$$

$$C-C$$

Davenport said, "I don't see any significance here."

"Neither did I, at first, nor did those I first consulted. But consider. Jennings must have thought that Strauss was in pursuit; he might not have known that Strauss had been put out of action, at least, not permanently. He was deadly afraid, then, that an Ultra would find him before a Moderate would. He dared not leave a clue too open. This"—and the Division Head tapped the reproduction—"must represent a clue that is opaque on the surface but clear enough to anyone sufficiently ingenious."

"Can we rely on that?" asked Davenport doubtfully. "After all, he was a dying, frightened man, who might have been subjected to this mind-altering object himself. He need not have been thinking clearly, or even humanly. For instance, why didn't he make an effort to reach Lunar Station? He ended half a circumference away almost. Was he too twisted to think clearly? Too paranoid to trust even the Station? Yet he must have tried to reach them at first since they picked up signals. What I'm saying is that this card, which looks as though it is covered with gibberish, *is* covered with gibberish."

Ashley shook his head solemnly from side to side, like a tolling bell. "He was in panic, yes. And I suppose he lacked the presence of mind to try to reach Lunar Station. Only the need to run and escape possessed him. Even so this can't be gibberish. It hangs together too well. Every notation on the card can be made to make sense, and the whole can be made to hang together."

"Where's the sense, then?" asked Davenport.

"You'll notice that there are seven items on the left side and two on the right. Consider the left-hand side first. The third one down looks like an equals sign. Does an equals sign mean anything to you, anything in particular?"

"An algebraic equation."

"That's general. Anything particular?"

"No."

"Suppose you consider it as a pair of parallel lines?"

"Euclid's fifth postulate?" suggested Davenport, groping.

"Good! There is a crater called Euclides on the Moon—the Greek name of the mathematician we call Euclid."

Davenport nodded. "I see your drift. As for F/A, that's force divided by acceleration, the definition of mass by Newton's second law of motion—"

"Yes, and there is a crater called Newton on the Moon also."

"Yes, but wait awhile, the lowermost item is the astronomic symbol for the planet Uranus, and there is certainly no crater—or any other lunar object, so far as I know—that is named Uranus."

"You're right there. But Uranus was discovered by William Herschel, and the H that makes up part of the astronomic symbol is the initial of his name. As it happens, there is a crater named Herschel on the Moon—three of them, in fact, since one is named for Caroline Herschel, his sister, and another for John Herschel, his son."

Davenport thought awhile, then said, "PC/2—Pressure times half the speed of light. I'm not familiar with that equation."

"Try craters. Try P for Ptolemaeus and C for Copernicus."

"And strike an average? Would that signify a spot exactly between Ptolemaeus and Copernicus?"

"I'm disappointed, Davenport," said Ashley sardonically. "I thought you knew your history of astronomy better than that. Ptolemy, or Ptolemaeus in Latin, presented a geocentric picture of the Solar System with the Earth at the center, while Copernicus presented a heliocentric one with the Sun at the center. One astronomer attempted a compromise, a picture halfway between that of Ptolemy and Copernicus—"

"Tycho Brahe!" said Davenport.

"Right. And the crater Tycho is the most conspicuous feature on the Moon's surface."

"All right. Let's take the rest. The C-C is a common way of writing a common type of chemical bond, and I think there is a crater named Bond."

"Yes, named for an American astronomer, W. C. Bond."

"The item on top, XY^2. Hmm. XYY. An X and two Y's. Wait! Alfonso X. He was the royal astronomer in medieval Spain who was called Alfonso the Wise. X the Wise. XYY. The crater Alphonsus."

"Very good. What's SU?"

"That stumps me, chief."

"I'll tell you one theory. It stands for Soviet Union, the old name for the Russian Region. It was the Soviet Union that first mapped the other side of the Moon, and maybe it's a crater there. Tsiolkovsky, for instance. You see, then, the symbols on the left can each be interpreted as standing for a crater: Alphonsus, Tycho, Euclides, Newton, Tsiolkovsky, Bond, Herschel."

"What about the symbols on the right-hand side?"

"That's perfectly transparent. The quartered circle is the astronomic symbol for the Earth. An arrow pointing to it indicates that Earth must be directly overhead."

"Ah," said Davenport, "the Sinus Medii—the Middle Bay —over which the Earth is perpetually at zenith. That's not a crater, so it's on the right-hand side, away from the other symbols."

"All right," said Ashley. "The notations all make sense, or they can be made to make sense, so there's at least a good chance that this isn't gibberish and that it is trying to tell us something. But what? So far we've got seven craters and a non-crater mentioned, and what does that mean? Presumably, the Device can only be in one place."

"Well," said Davenport heavily, "a crater can be a huge place to search. Even if we assume he hugged the shadow to avoid Solar radiation, there can be dozens of miles to examine in each case. Suppose the arrow pointing to the symbol for the Earth defines the crater where he hid the Device, the place from which the Earth can be seen nearest the zenith."

"That's been thought of, old man. It cuts out one place and leaves us with seven pinpointed craters, the southernmost extremity of those north of the Lunar equator and the northernmost extremity of those south. But which of the seven?"

Davenport was frowning. So far, he hadn't thought of anything that hadn't already been thought of. "Search them all," he said brusquely.

Ashley crackled into brief laughter. "In the weeks since this has all come up, we've done exactly that."

"And what have you found?"

"Nothing. We haven't found a thing. We're still looking, though."

"Obviously one of the symbols isn't interpreted correctly."

"Obviously!"

"You said yourself there were three craters named Herschel. The symbol SU, if it means the Soviet Union and therefore the other side of the Moon, can stand for any crater on the other side: Lomonosov, Jules Verne, Joliot-Curie, any of them. For that matter, the symbol of the Earth might stand for the crater Atlas, since he is pictured as supporting the Earth in some versions of the myth. The arrow might stand for the Straight Wall."

"There's no argument there, Davenport. But even if we

get the right interpretation for the right symbol, how do we recognize it from among all the wrong interpretations, or from among the right interpretations of the wrong symbols? Somehow there's got to be something that leaps up at us from this card and gives us so clear a piece of information that we can tell it at once as the real thing from among all the red herrings. We've all failed and we need a fresh mind, Davenport. What do you see here?"

"I'll tell you one thing we could do," said Davenport reluctantly. "We can consult someone I— Oh, my God!" He half-rose.

Ashley was all controlled excitement at once. "What do you see?"

Davenport could feel his hand trembling. He hoped his lips weren't. He said, "Tell me, have you checked on Jennings' past life?"

"Of course."

"Where did he go to college?"

"Eastern University."

A pang of joy shot through Davenport, but he held on. That was not enough. "Did he take a course in extraterrology?"

"Of course, he did. That's routine for a geology major."

"All right, then, don't you know who teaches extraterrology at Eastern University?"

Ashley snapped his fingers. "That oddball. What's-his-name —Wendell Urth."

"Exactly, an oddball who is a brilliant man in his way. An oddball who's acted as a consultant for the Bureau on several occasions and given perfect satisfaction every time. An oddball I was going to suggest we consult this time and then noticed that this card was *telling* us to do so. An arrow pointing to the symbol for the Earth. A rebus that couldn't mean more clearly 'Go to Urth,' written by a man who was once a student of Urth and would know him."

Ashley stared at the card, "By God, it's possible. But what could Urth tell us about the card that we can't see for ourselves?"

Davenport said, with polite patience, "I suggest we ask him, sir."

Ashley looked about curiously, half-wincing as he turned

from one direction to another. He felt as though he had found himself in some arcane curiosity shop, darkened and dangerous, from which at any moment some demon might hurtle forth squealing.

The lighting was poor and the shadows many. The walls seemed distant, and dismally alive with book-films from floor to ceiling. There was a Galactic Lens in soft three-dimensionality in one corner and behind it were star charts that could dimly be made out. A map of the Moon in another corner might, however, possibly be a map of Mars.

Only the desk in the center of the room was brilliantly lit by a tight-beamed lamp. It was littered with papers and opened printed books. A small viewer was threaded with film, and a clock with an old-fashioned round-faced dial hummed with subdued merriment.

Ashley found himself unable to recall that it was late afternoon outside and that the sun was quite definitely in the sky. Here, within, was a place of eternal night. There was no sign of any window, and the clear presence of circulating air did not spare him a claustrophobic sensation.

He found himself moving closer to Davenport, who seemed insensible to the unpleasantness of the situation.

Davenport said in a low voice, "He'll be here in a moment, sir."

"Is it always like this?" asked Ashley.

"Always. He never leaves this place, as far as I know, except to trot across the campus and attend his classes."

"Gentlemen! Gentlemen!" came a reedy, tenor voice. "I am so glad to see you. It is good of you to come."

A round figure of a man bustled in from another room, shedding shadow and emerging into the light.

He beamed at them, adjusting round, thick-lensed glasses upward so that he might look through them. As his fingers moved away, the glasses slipped downward at once to a precarious perch upon the round nubbin of his snub nose. "I am Wendell Urth," he said.

The scraggly gray Van Dyke on his pudgy, round chin did not in the least add to the dignity which the smiling face and the stubby ellipsoidal torso so noticeably lacked.

"Gentlemen! It is good of you to come," Urth repeated, as he jerked himself backward into a chair from which his legs dangled with the toes of his shoes a full inch above the floor. "Mr. Davenport remembers, perhaps, that it is a matter of—uh—some importance to me to remain here. I do not like to travel, except to walk, of course, and a walk across the campus is quite enough for me."

Ashley looked baffled as he remained standing, and Urth stared at him with a growing bafflement of his own. He pulled a handkerchief out and wiped his glasses, then replaced them, and said, "Oh, I see the difficulty. You want chairs. Yes. Well, just take some. If there are things on them, just push them off. Push them off. Sit down, please."

Davenport removed the books from one chair and placed them carefully on the floor. He pushed the chair toward Ashley. Then he took a human skull off a second chair and placed the skull even more carefully on Urth's desk. Its mandible, insecurely wired, unhinged as he transferred it, and it sat there with jaw askew.

"Never mind," said Urth, affably, "it will not hurt. Now tell me what is on your mind, gentlemen?"

Davenport waited a moment for Ashley to speak, then, rather gladly, took over. "Dr. Urth, do you remember a student of yours named Jennings? Karl Jennings?"

Urth's smile vanished momentarily with the effort of recall. His somewhat protuberant eyes blinked. "No," he said at last. "Not at the moment."

"A geology major. He took your extraterrology course some years ago. I have his photograph here, if that will help."

Urth studied the photograph handed him with nearsighted concentration, but still looked doubtful.

Davenport drove on. "He left a cryptic message which is the key to a matter of great importance. We have so far failed to interpret it satisfactorily, but this much we see—it indicates we are to come to you."

"Indeed? How interesting! For what purpose are you to come to me?"

"Presumably for your advice on interpreting the message."

"May I see it?"

Silently Ashley passed the slip of paper to Wendell Urth. The extraterrologist looked at it casually, turned it over, and stared for a moment at the blank back. He said, "Where does it say to ask me?"

Ashley looked startled, but Davenport forestalled him by

saying, "The arrow pointing to the symbol of the Earth. It seems clear."

"It is clearly an arrow pointing to the symbol for the planet Earth. I suppose it might literally mean 'go to the Earth' if this were found on some other world."

"It was found on the Moon, Dr. Urth, and it could, I suppose, mean that. However, the reference to you seemed clear once we realized that Jennings had been a student of yours."

"He took a course in extraterrology here at the University?"

"That's right."

"In what year, Mr. Davenport?"

"In '18."

"Ah. The puzzle is solved."

"You mean the significance of the message?" said Davenport.

"No, no. The message has no meaning to me. I mean the puzzle of why it is that I did not remember him, for I remember him now. He was a very quiet fellow, anxious, shy, self-effacing—not at all the sort of person anyone would remember. Without this"—and he tapped the message—"I might never have remembered him."

"Why does the card change things?" asked Davenport.

"The reference to me is a play on words. Earth—Urth. Not very subtle, of course, but that is Jennings. His unattainable delight was the pun. My only clear memory of him is his occasional attempts to perpetrate puns. I enjoy puns, I adore puns, but Jennings—yes, I remember him well now—was atrocious at it. Either that, or distressingly obvious at it, as in this case. He lacked all talent for puns, yet craved them so much—"

Ashley suddenly broke in. "This message consists entirely of a kind of wordplay, Dr. Urth. At least, we believe so, and that fits in with what you say."

"Ah!" Urth adjusted his glasses and peered through them once more at the card and the symbols it carried. He pursed his plump lips, then said cheerfully, "I make nothing of it."

"In that case—" began Ashley, his hands balling into fists.

"But if you tell me what it's all about," Urth went on, "then perhaps it might mean something."

Davenport said quickly, "May I, sir? I am confident that this man can be relied on—and it may help."

"Go ahead," muttered Ashley. "At this point, what can it hurt?"

Davenport condensed the tale, giving it in crisp, telegraphic sentences, while Urth listened carefully, moving his stubby fingers over the shining milk-white desktop as though he were sweeping up invisible cigar ashes. Toward the end of the recital, he hitched up his legs and sat with them crossed like an amiable Buddha.

When Davenport was done, Urth thought a moment, then said, "Do you happen to have a transcript of the conversation reconstructed by Ferrant?"

"We do," said Davenport. "Would you like to see it?"

"Please."

Urth placed the strip of microfilm in a scanner and worked his way rapidly through it, his lips moving unintelligibly at some points. Then he tapped the reproduction of the cryptic message. "And this, you say, is the key to the entire matter? The crucial clue?"

"We think it is, Dr. Urth."

"But it is not the original. It is a reproduction."

"That is correct."

"The original has gone with this man, Ferrant, and you believe it to be in the hands of the Ultras."

"Quite possibly."

Urth shook his head and looked troubled. "Everyone knows my sympathies are not with the Ultras. I would fight them by all means, so I don't want to seem to be hanging back, but—what is there to say that this mind-affecting object exists at all? You have only the ravings of a psychotic and your dubious deductions from the reproduction of a mysterious set of marks that may mean nothing at all."

"Yes, Dr. Urth, but we can't take chances."

"How certain are you that this copy is accurate? What if the original has something on it that this lacks, something that makes the message quite clear, something without which the message must remain impenetrable?"

"We are certain the copy is accurate."

"What about the reverse side? There is nothing on the back of this reproduction. What about the reverse of the original?"

"The agent who made the reproduction tells us that the back of the original was blank."

"Men can make mistakes."

"We have no reason to think he did, and we must work on the assumption that he didn't. At least until such time as the original is regained."

"Then you assure me," said Urth, "that any interpretation to be made of this message must be made on the basis of exactly what one sees here."

"We think so. We are virtually certain," said Davenport with a sense of ebbing confidence.

Urth continued to look troubled. He said, "Why not leave the instrument where it is? If neither group finds it, so much the better. I disapprove of any tampering with minds and would not contribute to making it possible."

Davenport placed a restraining hand on Ashley's arm, sensing the other was about to speak. Davenport said, "Let me put it to you, Dr. Urth, that the mind-tampering aspect is not the whole of the Device. Suppose an Earth expedition to a distant primitive planet had dropped an old-fashioned radio there, and suppose the native population had discovered electric current but had not yet developed the vacuum tube.

"The population might discover that if the radio was hooked up to a current, certain glass objects within it would grow warm and would glow, but of course they would receive no intelligible sound, merely, at best, some buzzes and crackles. However, if they dropped the radio into a bathtub while it was plugged in, a person in that tub might be electrocuted. Should the people of this hypothetical planet therefore conclude that the device they were studying was designed solely for the purpose of killing people?"

"I see your analogy," said Urth. "You think that the mind-tampering property is merely an incidental function of the Device?"

"I'm sure of it," said Davenport earnestly. "If we can puzzle out its real purpose, earthly technology may leap ahead centuries."

"Then you agree with Jennings when he said"—here Urth consulted the microfilm—"'It might be the key to—who knows what? It might be the clue to an unimaginable scientific revolution.'"

"Exactly!"

"And yet the mind-tampering aspect is there and is infinitely dangerous. Whatever the radio's purpose, it *does* electrocute."

"Which is why we can't let the Ultras get it."

"Or the government either, perhaps?"

"But I must point out that there is a reasonable limit to caution. Consider that men have always held danger in their hands. The first flint knife in the old Stone Age; the first wooden club before that could kill. They could be used to bend weaker men to the will of stronger ones under threat of force and that, too, is a form of mind-tampering. What counts, Dr. Urth, is not the Device itself, however dangerous it may be in the abstract, but the intentions of the men who make use of the Device. The Ultras have the declared intention of killing off more than 99.9 per cent of humanity. The government, whatever the faults of the men composing it, would have no such intention."

"What *would* the government intend?"

"A scientific study of the Device. Even the mind-tampering aspect itself could yield infinite good. Put to enlightened use, it could educate us concerning the physical basis of mental function. We might learn to correct mental disorders or cure the Ultras. Mankind might learn to develop greater intelligence generally."

"How can I believe that such idealism will be put into practice?"

"*I* believe so. Consider that you face a possible turn to evil by the government if you help us, but you risk the certain and declared evil purpose of the Ultras if you don't."

Urth nodded thoughtfully. "Perhaps you're right. And yet I have a favor to ask of you. I have a niece who is, I believe, quite fond of me. She is constantly upset over the fact that I steadfastly refuse to indulge in the lunacy of travel. She states that she will not rest content until someday I accompany her to Europe or North Carolina or some other outlandish place—"

Ashley leaned forward earnestly, brushing Davenport's restraining gesture to one side. "Dr. Urth, if you help us find the Device and if it can be made to work, then I assure you that we will be glad to help you free yourself of your phobia against travel and make it possible for you to go with your niece anywhere you wish."

Urth's bulging eyes widened and he seemed to shrink

within himself. For a moment he looked wildly about as though he were already trapped. *"No!"* he gasped. "Not at all! Never!"

His voice dropped to an earnest, hoarse whisper. "Let me explain the nature of my fee. If I help you, if you retrieve the Device and learn its use, if the fact of my help becomes public, then my niece will be on the government like a fury. She is a terribly headstrong and shrill-voiced woman who will raise public subscriptions and organize demonstrations. She will stop at nothing. And yet you must not give in to her. You must *not!* You must resist all pressures. I wish to be left alone exactly as I am now. That is my absolute and minimum fee."

Ashley flushed. "Yes, of course, since that is your wish."

"I have your word?"

"You have my word."

"Please remember. I rely on you too, Mr. Davenport."

"It will be as you wish," soothed Davenport. "And now, I presume, you can interpret the items?"

"The items?" asked Urth, seeming to focus his attention with difficulty on the card. "You mean these markings, XY^2 and so on?"

"Yes. What do they mean?"

"I don't know. Your interpretations are as good as any, I suppose."

Ashley exploded. "Do you mean that all this talk about helping us is nonsense? What was this maundering about a fee, then?"

Wendell Urth looked confused and taken aback. "I would like to help you."

"But you don't know what these items mean."

"I—I don't. But I know what this message means."

"You do?" cried Davenport.

"Of course. Its meaning is transparent. I suspected it halfway through your story. And I was sure of it once I read the reconstruction of the conversations between Strauss and Jennings. You would understand it yourself, gentlemen, if you would only stop to think."

"See here," said Ashley in exasperation, "you said you don't know what the items mean."

"I don't. I said I know what the *message* means."

"What is the message if it is not the items? Is it the paper, for Heaven's sake?"

"Yes, in a way."

"You mean invisible ink or something like that?"

"No! Why is it so hard for you to understand, when you yourself stand on the brink?"

Davenport leaned toward Ashley and said in a low voice, "Sir, will you let me handle it, please?"

Ashley snorted, then said in a stifled manner, "Go ahead."

"Dr. Urth," said Davenport, "will you give us your analysis?"

"Ah! Well, all right." The little extraterrologist settled back in his chair and mopped his damp forehead on his sleeve. "Let's consider the message. If you accept the quartered circle and the arrow as directing you to me, that leaves seven items. If these indeed refer to seven craters, six of them, at least, must be designed merely to distract, since the Device surely cannot be in more than one place. It contained no movable or detachable parts—it was all one piece.

"Then, too, none of the items are straightforward. SU might, by your interpretation, mean any place on the other side of the Moon, which is an area the size of South America. Again PC/2 can mean 'Tycho,' as Mr. Ashley says, or it can mean 'halfway between Ptolemaeus and Copernicus,' as Mr. Davenport thought, or for that matter 'halfway between Plato and Cassini.' To be sure, XY^2 could mean 'Alfonsus'—very ingenious interpretation, that—but it could refer to some co-ordinate system in which the Y co-ordinate was the square of the X co-ordinate. Similarly C-C could mean 'Bond' or it could mean 'halfway between Cassini and Copernicus.' F-A could mean 'Newton' or it could mean 'between Fabricius and Archimedes.'

"In short, the items have so many meanings that they are meaningless. Even if one of them had meaning, it could not be selected from among the others, so that it is only sensible to suppose that all the items are merely red herrings.

"It is necessary, then, to determine what about the message is completely unambiguous, what is perfectly clear. The answer to that can only be that it *is* a message, that it *is* a clue to a hiding place. That is the one thing we are certain about, isn't it?"

Davenport nodded, then said cautiously, "At least, we think we are certain of it."

"Well, you have referred to this message as the key to the whole matter. You have acted as though it were the crucial clue. Jennings himself referred to the Device as a key or a clue. If we combine this serious view of the matter with Jennings' penchant for puns, a penchant which may have been heightened by the mind-tampering Device he was carrying— So let me tell you a story.

"In the last half of the sixteenth century, there lived a German Jesuit in Rome. He was a mathematician and astronomer of note and helped Pope Gregory XIII reform the calendar in 1582, performing all the enormous calculations required. This astronomer admired Copernicus but he did not accept the heliocentric view of the Solar System. He clung to the older belief that the Earth was the center of the Universe.

"In 1650, nearly forty years after the death of this mathematician, the Moon was mapped by another Jesuit, the Italian astronomer, Giovanni Battista Riccioli. He named the craters after astronomers of the past and since he too rejected Copernicus, he selected the largest and most spectacular craters for those who placed the Earth at the center of the Universe—for Ptolemy, Hipparchus, Alfonso X, Tycho Brahe. The biggest crater Riccioli could find he reserved for his German Jesuit predecessor.

"This crater is actually only the second largest of the craters visible from Earth. The only larger crater is Bailly, which is right on the Moon's limb and is therefore very difficult to see from the Earth. Riccioli ignored it, and it was named for an astronomer who lived a century after his time and who was guillotined during the French Revolution."

Ashley was listening to all this restlessly. "But what has this to do with the message?"

"Why, everything," said Urth, with some surprise. "Did you not call this message the key to the whole business? Isn't it the crucial clue?"

"Yes, of course."

"Is there any doubt that we are dealing with something that is a clue or key to something else?"

"No, there isn't," said Ashley.

"Well, then— The name of the German Jesuit I have been speaking of is Christoph Klau—pronounced 'klow.' Don't you see the pun? Klau—clue?"

Ashley's entire body seemed to grow flabby with disappointment. "Farfetched," he muttered.

Davenport said anxiously, "Dr. Urth, there is no feature on the Moon named Klau as far as I know."

"Of course not," said Urth excitedly. "That is the whole point. At this period of history, the last half of the sixteenth century, European scholars were Latinizing their names. Klau did so. In place of the German 'u', he made use of the equivalent letter, the Latin 'v'. He then added an 'ius' ending typical of Latin names and Christoph Klau became Christopher Clavius, and I suppose you are all aware of the giant crater we call Clavius."

"But—" began Davenport.

"Don't 'but' me," said Urth. "Just let me point out that the Latin word 'clavis' means 'key.' *Now* do you see the double and bilingual pun? Klau—clue, Clavius—clavis—key. In his whole life, Jennings could never have made a double, bilingual pun, without the Device. Now he could, and I wonder if death might not have been almost triumphant under the circumstances. And he directed you to me because he knew I would remember his penchant for puns and because he knew I loved them too."

The two men of the Bureau were looking at him wide-eyed.

Urth said solemnly, "I would suggest you search the shaded rim of Clavius, at that point where the Earth is nearest the zenith."

Ashley rose. "Where is your videophone?"

"In the next room."

Ashley dashed. Davenport lingered behind. "Are you sure, Dr. Urth?"

"Quite sure. But even if I am wrong, I suspect it doesn't matter."

"What doesn't matter?"

"Whether you find it or not. For if the Ultras find the Device, they will probably be unable to use it."

"Why do you say that?"

"You asked me if Jennings had ever been a student of mine, but you never asked me about Strauss, who was also a geologist. He was a student of mine a year or so after Jennings. I remember him well."

"Oh?"

"An unpleasant man. Very cold. It is the hallmark of the Ultras, I think. They are all very cold, very rigid, very sure of themselves. They can't empathize, or they wouldn't speak of killing off billions of human beings. What emotions they possess are icy ones, self-absorbed ones, feelings incapable of spanning the distance between two human beings."

"I think I see."

"I'm sure you do. The conversation reconstructed from Strauss's ravings showed us he could not manipulate the Device. He lacked the emotional intensity, or the type of necessary emotion. I imagine all Ultras would. Jennings, who was not an Ultra, could manipulate it. Anyone who could use the Device would, I suspect, be incapable of deliberate cold-blooded cruelty. He might strike out of panic fear as Jennings struck at Strauss, but never out of calculation, as Strauss tried to strike at Jennings. In short, to put it tritely, I think the Device can be actuated by love, but never by hate, and the Ultras are nothing if not haters."

Davenport nodded. "I hope you're right. But then—why were you so suspicious of the government's motives if you felt the wrong men could not manipulate the Device?"

Urth shrugged. "I wanted to make sure you could bluff and rationalize on your feet and make yourself convincingly persuasive at a moment's notice. After all, you may have to face my niece."

This story has even pleasanter memories for me than the one before. At the Twenty-fourth World Science Fiction Convention, held in Cleveland over the Labor Day weekend in 1966, I was one of those who received a Hugo (the "Oscar" of science fiction fandom), under conditions of great satisfaction to myself, and with my wife and children in the audience to see. (I am grinning foolishly for sheer joy of recall as I type this.)

The science fiction magazine IF also won a Hugo and its editor set about collecting promises from other Hugo winners to write stories for a special Hugo issue. I would have had to have a heart of obsidian not to promise—so I did.

This is the result. It is the only story I know of to combine the mystery form with Einstein's General Theory of Relativity.

The Billiard Ball

James Priss—I suppose I ought to say Professor James Priss, though everyone is sure to know whom I mean even without the title—always spoke slowly.

I know. I interviewed him often enough. He had the greatest mind since Einstein, but it didn't work quickly. He admitted his slowness often. Maybe it was *because* he had so great a mind that it didn't work quickly.

He would say something in slow abstraction, then he would think, and then he would say something more. Even over trivial matters, his giant mind would hover uncertainly, adding a touch here and then another there.

Would the Sun rise tomorrow, I can imagine him wondering. What do we mean by "rise"? Can we be certain that tomorrow will come? Is the term "Sun" completely unambiguous in this connection?

Add to this habit of speech a bland countenance, rather pale, with no expression except for a general look of uncertainty; gray hair, rather thin, neatly combed; business suits of an invariably conservative cut; and you have what Professor James Priss was—a retiring person, completely lacking in magnetism.

That's why nobody in the world, except myself, could possibly suspect him of being a murderer. And even I am not sure. After all, he *was* slow-thinking; he was *always* slow-thinking. Is it conceivable that at one crucial moment he managed to think quickly and act at once?

It doesn't matter. Even if he murdered, he got away with it. It is far too late now to try to reverse matters and I wouldn't succeed in doing so even if I decided to let this be published.

Edward Bloom was Priss's classmate in college, and an associate, through circumstance, for a generation afterward. They were equal in age and in their propensity for the bachelor life, but opposites in everything else that mattered.

Bloom was a living flash of light; colorful, tall, broad, loud, brash, and self-confident. He had a mind that resembled a meteor strike in the sudden and unexpected way it could seize the essential. He was no theoretician, as Priss was; Bloom had neither the patience for it, nor the capacity to concentrate intense thought upon a single abstract point. He admitted that; he boasted of it.

What he did have was an uncanny way of seeing the application of a theory; of seeing the manner in which it could be put to use. In the cold marble block of abstract structure, he could see, without apparent difficulty, the intricate design of a marvelous device. The block would fall apart at his touch and leave the device.

It is a well-known story, and not too badly exaggerated, that nothing Bloom ever built had failed to work, or to be patentable, or to be profitable. By the time he was forty-five, he was one of the richest men on Earth.

And if Bloom the Technician were adapted to one particular matter more than anything else, it was to the way of thought of Priss the Theoretician. Bloom's greatest gadgets were built upon Priss's greatest thoughts, and as Bloom grew wealthy and famous, Priss gained phenomenal respect among his colleagues.

Naturally it was to be expected that when Priss advanced his Two-Field Theory, Bloom would set about at once to build the first practical anti-gravity device.

My job was to find human interest in the Two-Field Theory for the subscribers to *Tele-News Press,* and you get that by trying to deal with human beings and not with abstract ideas. Since my interviewee was Professor Priss, that wasn't easy.

Naturally, I was going to ask about the possibilities of anti-gravity, which interested everyone; and not about the Two-Field Theory, which no one could understand.

"Anti-gravity?" Priss compressed his pale lips and considered. "I'm not entirely sure that it is possible, or ever will be. I haven't—uh—worked the matter out to my satisfaction. I don't entirely see whether the Two-Field equations would have a finite solution, which they would have to have, of course, if—" And then he went off into a brown study.

I prodded him. "Bloom says he thinks such a device can be built."

Priss nodded. "Well, yes, but I wonder. Ed Bloom has had an amazing knack at seeing the unobvious in the past. He has an unusual mind. It's certainly made him rich enough."

We were sitting in Priss's apartment. Ordinary middle-class. I couldn't help a quick glance this way and that. Priss was not wealthy.

I don't think he read my mind. He saw me look. And I think it was on *his* mind. He said, "Wealth isn't the usual reward for the pure scientist. Or even a particularly desirable one."

Maybe so, at that, I thought. Priss certainly had his own kind of reward. He was the third person in history to win two Nobel Prizes, and the first to have both of them in the sciences and both of them unshared. You can't complain about that. And if he wasn't rich, neither was he poor.

But he didn't sound like a contented man. Maybe it wasn't Bloom's wealth alone that irked Priss; maybe it was Bloom's fame among the people of Earth generally; maybe it was the fact that Bloom was a celebrity wherever he went, whereas Priss, outside scientific conventions and faculty clubs, was largely anonymous.

I can't say how much of all this was in my eyes or in the way I wrinkled the creases in my forehead, but Priss went on to say, "But we're friends, you know. We play billiards once or twice a week. I beat him regularly."

(I never published that statement. I checked it with Bloom, who made a long counterstatement that began: "He beats *me* at billiards. That jackass—" and grew increasingly personal thereafter. As a matter of fact, neither one was a novice at billiards. I watched them play once for a short while, after the statement and counterstatement, and both handled the cue with professional aplomb. What's more, both played for blood, and there was no friendship in the game that I could see.)

I said, "Would you care to predict whether Bloom will manage to build an anti-gravity device?"

"You mean would I commit myself to anything? Hmm. Well, let's consider, young man. Just what do we mean by anti-gravity? Our conception of gravity is built around Einstein's General Theory of Relativity, which is now a century and a half old but which, within its limits, remains firm. We can picture it—"

I listened politely. I'd heard Priss on the subject before, but if I was to get anything out of him—which wasn't certain —I'd have to let him work his way through in his own way.

"We can picture it," he said, "by imagining the Universe to be a flat, thin, superflexible sheet of untearable rubber. If we picture mass as being associated with weight, as it is on the surface of the Earth, then we would expect a mass, resting upon the rubber sheet, to make an indentation. The greater the mass, the deeper the indentation.

"In the actual Universe," he went on, "all sorts of masses exist, and so our rubber sheet must be pictured as riddled with indentations. Any object rolling along the sheet would dip into and out of the indentations it passed, veering and changing direction as it did so. It is this veer and change of direction that we interpret as demonstrating the existence of a force of gravity. If the moving object comes close enough to the center of the indentation and is moving slowly enough, it gets trapped and whirls round and round that indentation. In the absence of friction, it keeps up that whirl forever. In other words, what Isaac Newton interpreted as a force, Albert Einstein interpreted as geometrical distortion."

He paused at this point. He had been speaking fairly fluently—for him—since he was saying something he had said often before. But now he began to pick his way.

He said, "So in trying to produce anti-gravity, we are trying to alter the geometry of the Universe. If we carry on our metaphor, we are trying to straighten out the indented rubber sheet. We could imagine ourselves getting under the indenting mass and lifting it upward, supporting it so as to prevent it from making an indentation. If we make the rubber sheet flat in that way, then we create a Universe—or at least a portion of the Universe—in which gravity doesn't exist. A rolling body would pass the non-indenting mass without altering its direction of travel a bit, and we could interpret this as meaning that the mass was exerting no gravitational force. In order to accomplish this feat, however, we need a mass equivalent to the indenting mass. To produce anti-gravity on Earth in this way, we would have to make use of a mass equal to that of Earth and poise it above our heads, so to speak."

I interrupted him. "But your Two-Field Theory—"

"Exactly. General Relativity does not explain both the gravitational field and the electromagnetic field in a single set of equations. Einstein spent half his life searching for that single set—for a Unified Field Theory—and failed. All who followed Einstein also failed. I, however, began with the assumption that there were two fields that could not be unified and followed the consequences, which I can explain, in part, in terms of the 'rubber sheet' metaphor."

Now we came to something I wasn't sure I had ever heard before. "How does that go?" I asked.

"Suppose that, instead of trying to lift the indenting mass, we try to stiffen the sheet itself, make it less indentable. It would contract, at least over a small area, and become flatter. Gravity would weaken, and so would mass, for the two are essentially the same phenomenon in terms of the indented Universe. If we could make the rubber sheet completely flat, both gravity and mass would disappear altogether.

"Under the proper conditions, the electromagnetic field could be made to counter the gravitational field, and serve to stiffen the indented fabric of the Universe. The electromagnetic field is tremendously stronger than the gravitational field, so the former could be made to overcome the latter."

I said uncertainly, "But you say 'under the proper conditions.' Can those proper conditions you speak of be achieved, Professor?"

"That is what I don't know," said Priss thoughtfully and slowly. "If the Universe were really a rubber sheet, its stiffness would have to reach an infinite value before it could be expected to remain completely flat under an indenting mass. If that is also so in the real Universe, then an infinitely intense electromagnetic field would be required and that would mean anti-gravity would be impossible."

"But Bloom says—"

"Yes, I imagine Bloom thinks a finite field will do, if it can be properly applied. Still, however ingenious he is," and Priss smiled narrowly, "we needn't take him to be infallible. His grasp on theory is quite faulty. He—he never earned his college degree, did you know that?"

I was about to say that I knew that. After all, everyone did. But there was a touch of eagerness in Priss's voice as he said it and I looked up in time to catch animation in his eye, as though he were delighted to spread that piece of news. So I nodded my head as if I were filing it for future reference.

"Then you would say, Professor Priss," I prodded again, "that Bloom is probably wrong and that anti-gravity is impossible?"

And finally Priss nodded and said, "The gravitational field can be weakened, of course, but if by anti-gravity we mean a true zero-gravity field—no gravity at all over a significant volume of space—then I suspect anti-gravity may turn out to be impossible, despite Bloom."

And I had, after a fashion, what I wanted.

I wasn't able to see Bloom for nearly three months after that, and when I did see him he was in an angry mood.

He had grown angry at once, of course, when the news first broke concerning Priss's statement. He let it be known that Priss would be invited to the eventual display of the anti-gravity device as soon as it was constructed, and would even be asked to participate in the demonstration. Some reporter—not I, unfortunately—caught him between appointments and asked him to elaborate on that and he said:

"I'll have the device eventually; soon, maybe. And you can be there, and so can anyone else the press would care to have there. And Professor James Priss can be there. He can represent Theoretical Science and after I have demonstrated anti-gravity, he can adjust his theory to explain it. I'm sure he will know how to make his adjustments in masterly fashion and show exactly why I couldn't possibly have failed. He might do it now and save time, but I suppose he won't."

It was all said very politely, but you could hear the snarl under the rapid flow of words.

Yet he continued his occasional game of billiards with Priss and when the two met they behaved with complete propriety. One could tell the progress Bloom was making by their respective attitudes to the press. Bloom grew curt and even snappish, while Priss developed an increasing good humor.

When my umpteenth request for an interview with Bloom was finally accepted, I wondered if perhaps that meant a break in Bloom's quest. I had a little daydream of him announcing final success to me.

It didn't work out that way. He met me in his office at Bloom Enterprises in upstate New York. It was a wonderful setting, well away from any populated area, elaborately landscaped, and covering as much ground as a rather large industrial establishment. Edison at his height, two centuries ago, had never been as phenomenally successful as Bloom.

But Bloom was not in a good humor. He came striding in ten minutes late and went snarling past his secretary's desk with the barest nod in my direction. He was wearing a lab coat, unbuttoned.

He threw himself into his chair and said, "I'm sorry if

I've kept you waiting, but I didn't have as much time as I had hoped." Bloom was a born showman and knew better than to antagonize the press, but I had the feeling he was having a great deal of difficulty at that moment in adhering to this principle.

I made the obvious guess. "I am given to understand, sir, that your recent tests have been unsuccessful."

"Who told you that?"

"I would say it was general knowledge, Mr. Bloom."

"No, it isn't. Don't say that, young man. There is no general knowledge about what goes on in my laboratories and workshops. You're stating the Professor's opinions, aren't you? Priss's, I mean."

"No, I'm—"

"Of course you are. Aren't you the one to whom he made that statement—that anti-gravity is impossible?"

"He didn't make the statement that flatly."

"He never says anything flatly, but it was flat enough for him, and not as flat as I'll have his damned rubber-sheet Universe before I'm finished."

"Then does that mean you're making progress, Mr. Bloom?"

"You know I am," he said with a snap. "Or you should know. Weren't you at the demonstration last week?"

"Yes, I was."

I judged Bloom to be in trouble or he wouldn't be mentioning that demonstration. It worked but it was not a world beater. Between the two poles of a magnet a region of lessened gravity was produced.

It was done very cleverly. A Mössbauer-Effect Balance was used to probe the space between the poles. If you've never seen an M-E Balance in action, it consists primarily of a tight monochromatic beam of gamma rays shot down the low-gravity field. The gamma rays change wavelength slightly but measurably under the influence of the gravitational field and if anything happens to alter the intensity of the field, the wavelength-change shifts correspondingly. It is an extremely delicate method for probing a gravitational field and it worked like a charm. There was no question but that Bloom had lowered gravity.

The trouble was that it had been done before by others. Bloom, to be sure, had made use of circuits that greatly increased the ease with which such an effect had been achieved—his system was typically ingenious and had been duly patented—and he maintained that it was by this method that anti-gravity would become not merely a scientific curiosity but a practical affair with industrial applications.

Perhaps. But it was an incomplete job and he didn't usually make a fuss over incompleteness. He wouldn't have done so this time if he weren't desperate to display *something*.

I said, "It's my impression that what you accomplished at that preliminary demonstration was 0.82 *g*, and better than that was achieved in Brazil last spring."

"That so? Well, calculate the energy input in Brazil and here, and then tell me the difference in gravity decrease per kilowatt-hour. You'll be surprised."

"But the point is, can you reach 0 *g*—zero gravity? That's what Professor Priss thinks may be impossible. Everyone agrees that merely lessening the intensity of the field is no great feat."

Bloom's fist clenched. I had the feeling that a key experiment had gone wrong that day and he was annoyed almost past endurance. Bloom hated to be balked by the Universe.

He said, "Theoreticians make me sick." He said it in a low, controlled voice, as though he were finally tired of not saying it, and he was going to speak his mind and be damned. "Priss has won two Nobel Prizes for sloshing around a few equations, but what has he done with it? Nothing! I *have* done something with it and I'm going to do more with it, whether Priss likes it or not.

"*I*'m the one people will remember. *I*'m the one who gets the credit. He can keep his damned title and his Prizes and his kudos from the scholars. Listen, I'll tell you what gripes him. Plain old-fashioned jealousy. It kills him that I get what I get for doing. He wants it for *thinking*.

"I said to him once—we play billiards together, you know—"

It was at this point that I quoted Priss's statement about billiards and got Bloom's counterstatement. I never published either. That was just trivia.

"We play billiards," said Bloom, when he had cooled down, "and I've won my share of games. We keep things friendly enough. What the hell—college chums and all that—though how he got through, I'll never know. He made it in physics, of course, and in math, but he got a bare pass—out of pity, I think—in every humanities course he ever took."

"You did not get your degree, did you, Mr. Bloom?" That was sheer mischief on my part. I was enjoying his eruption.

"I quit to go into business, damn it. My academic average, over the three years I attended, was a strong B. Don't imagine anything else, you hear? Hell, by the time Priss got his Ph.D., I was working on my second million."

He went on, clearly irritated, "Anyway, we were playing billiards and I said to him, 'Jim, the average man will never understand why you get the Nobel Prize when I'm the one who gets the results. Why do you need two? Give me one!' He stood there, chalking up his cue, and then he said in his soft namby-pamby way, 'You have two billions, Ed. Give me one.' So you see, he wants the money."

I said, "I take it you don't mind his getting the honor?"

For a minute I thought he was going to order me out, but he didn't. He laughed instead, waved his hand in front of him, as though he were erasing something from an invisible blackboard in front of him. He said, "Oh, well, forget it. All that is off the record. Listen, do you want a statement? Okay. Things didn't go right today and I blew my top a bit, but it will clear up. I think I know what's wrong. And if I don't, I'm going to know.

"Look, you can say that *I* say that we *don't* need infinite electromagnetic intensity; we *will* flatten out the rubber sheet; we *will* have zero gravity. And when we get it, I'll have the damndest demonstration you ever saw, exclusively for the press and for Priss, and you'll be invited. And you can say it won't be long. Okay?"

Okay!

I had time after that to see each man once or twice more. I even saw them together when I was present at one of their billiard games. As I said before, both of them were *good*.

But the call to the demonstration did not come as quickly as all that. It arrived six weeks less than a year after Bloom gave me his statement. And at that, perhaps it was unfair to expect quicker work.

I had a special engraved invitation, with the assurance of a cocktail hour first. Bloom never did things by halves and he was planning to have a pleased and satisfied group of reporters on hand. There was an arrangement for trimensional TV, too. Bloom felt completely confident, obviously; confident enough to be willing to trust the demonstration in every living room on the planet.

I called up Professor Priss, to make sure he was invited too. He was.

"Do you plan to attend, sir?"

There was a pause and the professor's face on the screen was a study in uncertain reluctance. "A demonstration of this sort is most unsuitable where a serious scientific matter is in question. I do not like to encourage such things."

I was afraid he would beg off, and the dramatics of the situation would be greatly lessened if he were not there. But then, perhaps, he decided he dared not play the chicken before the world. With obvious distaste he said, "Of course, Ed Bloom is not really a scientist and he must have his day in the sun. I'll be there."

"Do you think Mr. Bloom can produce zero gravity, sir?"

"Uh . . . Mr. Bloom sent me a copy of the design of his device and . . . and I'm not certain. Perhaps he can do it, if . . . uh . . . he says he can do it. Of course"—he paused again for quite a long time—"I think I would like to see it."

So would I, and so would many others.

The staging was impeccable. A whole floor of the main building at Bloom Enterprises—the one on the hilltop—was cleared. There were the promised cocktails and a splendid array of hors d'oeuvres, soft music and lighting, and a carefully dressed and thoroughly jovial Edward Bloom playing the perfect host, while a number of polite and unobtrusive menials fetched and carried. All was geniality and amazing confidence.

James Priss was late and I caught Bloom watching the corners of the crowd and beginning to grow a little grim about the edges. Then Priss arrived, dragging a volume of colorlessness in with him, a drabness that was unaffected by the noise and the absolute splendor (no other word would describe it—or else it was the two martinis glowing inside me) that filled the room.

Bloom saw him and his face was illuminated at once. He bounced across the floor, seized the smaller man's hand and dragged him to the bar.

"Jim! Glad to see you! What'll you have? Hell, man, I'd have called it off if you hadn't showed. Can't have this thing without the star, you know." He wrung Priss's hand. "It's your theory, you know. We poor mortals can't do a thing without you few, you damned *few* few, pointing the way."

He was being ebullient, handing out the flattery, because he could afford to do so now. He was fattening Priss for the kill.

Priss tried to refuse a drink, with some sort of mutter, but a glass was pressed into his hand and Bloom raised his voice to a bull roar.

"Gentlemen! A moment's quiet, please. To Professor Priss, the greatest mind since Einstein, two-time Nobel Laureate, father of the Two-Field Theory, and inspirer of the demonstration we are about to see—even if he didn't think it would work, and had the guts to say so publicly."

There was a distinct titter of laughter that quickly faded out and Priss looked as grim as his face could manage.

"But now that Professor Priss is here," said Bloom, "and we've had our toast, let's get on with it. Follow me, gentlemen!"

The demonstration was in a much more elaborate place than had housed the earlier one. This time it was on the top floor of the building. Different magnets were involved—smaller ones, by heaven!—but as nearly as I could tell, the same M-E Balance was in place.

One thing was new, however, and it staggered everybody, drawing much more attention than anything else in the room. It was a billiard table, resting under one pole of the magnet. Beneath it was the companion pole. A round hole, about a foot across, was stamped out of the very center of the table and it was obvious that the zero-gravity field, if it was to be produced, would be produced through that hole in the center of the billiard table.

It was as though the whole demonstration had been designed, surrealist fashion, to point up the victory of Bloom over Priss. This was to be another version of their everlasting billiards competition and Bloom was going to win.

I don't know if the other newsmen took matters in that fashion, but I think Priss did. I turned to look at him and saw that he was still holding the drink that had been forced into his hand. He rarely drank, I knew, but now he lifted the glass to his lips and emptied it in two swallows. He stared at that billiard ball and I needed no gift of ESP to realize that he took it as a deliberate snap of fingers under his nose.

Bloom led us to the twenty seats that surrounded three sides of the table, leaving the fourth free as a working area. Priss was carefully escorted to the seat commanding the most convenient view. Priss glanced quickly at the trimensional cameras which were now working. I wondered if he were thinking of leaving but deciding that he couldn't in the full glare of the eyes of the world.

Essentially, the demonstration was simple; it was the production that counted. There were dials in plain view that measured the energy expenditure. There were others that transferred the M-E Balance readings into a position and a size that were visible to all. Everything was arranged for easy trimensional viewing.

Bloom explained each step in a genial way, with one or two pauses in which he turned to Priss for a confirmation that had to come. He didn't do it often enough to make it obvious, but just enough to turn Priss upon the spit of his own torment. From where I sat I could look across the table and see Priss on the other side.

He had the look of a man in Hell.

As we all know, Bloom succeeded. The M-E Balance showed the gravitational intensity to be sinking steadily as the electromagnetic field was intensified. There were cheers when it dropped below the 0.52 g mark. A red line indicated that on the dial.

"The 0.52 g mark, as you know," said Bloom confidently, "represents the previous record low in gravitational intensity. We are now lower than that at a cost in electricity that is less than ten per cent what it cost at the time that mark was set. And we will go lower still."

Bloom—I think deliberately, for the sake of the suspense —slowed the drop toward the end, letting the trimensional cameras switch back and forth between the gap in the billiard table and the dial on which the M-E Balance reading was lowering.

Bloom said suddenly, "Gentlemen, you will find dark goggles in the pouch on the side of each chair. Please put them on now. The zero-gravity field will soon be established and it will radiate a light rich in ultraviolet."

He put goggles on himself, and there was a momentary rustle as others went on too.

I think no one breathed during the last minute, when the dial reading dropped to zero and held fast. And just as that happened a cylinder of light sprang into existence from pole to pole through the hole in the billiard table.

There was a ghost of twenty sighs at that. Someone called out, "Mr. Bloom, what is the reason for the light?"

"It's characteristic of the zero-gravity field," said Bloom smoothly, which was no answer, of course.

Reporters were standing up now, crowding about the edge of the table. Bloom waved them back. "Please, gentlemen, stand clear!"

Only Priss remained sitting. He seemed lost in thought and I have been certain ever since that it was the goggles that obscured the possible significance of everything that followed. I didn't see his eyes. I couldn't. And that meant neither I nor anyone else could even begin to make a guess as to what was going on behind those eyes. Well, maybe we couldn't have made such a guess, even if the goggles hadn't been there, but who can say?

Bloom was raising his voice again. "Please! The demonstration is not yet over. So far, we've only repeated what I have done before. I have now produced a zero-gravity field and I have shown it can be done practically. But I want to demonstrate something of what such a field can do. What we are going to see next will be something that has never been seen, not even by myself. I have not experimented in this direction, much as I would have liked to, because I have felt that Professor Priss deserved the honor of—"

Priss looked up sharply. "What—what—"

"Professor Priss," said Bloom, smiling broadly, "I would like you to perform the first experiment involving the interaction of a solid object with a zero-gravity field. Notice that the field has been formed in the center of a billiard table. The world knows your phenomenal skill in billiards, Professor, a talent second only to your amazing aptitude in theoretical physics. Won't you send a billiard ball into the zero-gravity volume?"

Eagerly he was handing a ball and cue to the professor. Priss, his eyes hidden by the goggles, stared at them and only very slowly, very uncertainly, reached out to take them.

I wonder what his eyes were showing. I wonder, too, how much of the decision to have Priss play billiards at the demonstration was due to Bloom's anger at Priss's remark about their periodic game, the remark I had quoted. Had I been, in my way, responsible for what followed?

"Come, stand up, Professor," said Bloom, "and let me have your seat. The show is yours from now on. Go ahead!"

Bloom seated himself, and still talked, in a voice that grew more organlike with each moment. "Once Professor Priss sends the ball into the volume of zero gravity, it will no longer be affected by Earth's gravitational field. It will remain truly motionless while the Earth rotates about its axis and travels about the Sun. In this latitude, and at this time of day, I have calculated that the Earth, in its motions, will sink downward. We will move with it and the ball will stand still. To us it will seem to rise up and away from the Earth's surface. Watch."

Priss seemed to stand in front of the table in frozen paralysis. Was it surprise? Astonishment? I don't know. I'll never know. Did he make a move to interrupt Bloom's little speech, or was he just suffering from an agonized reluctance to play the ignominious part into which he was being forced by his adversary?

Priss turned to the billiard table, looking first at it, then back at Bloom. Every reporter was on his feet, crowding as closely as possible in order to get a good view. Only Bloom himself remained seated, smiling and isolated. He, of course, was not watching the table, or the ball, or the zero-gravity field. As nearly as I could tell through the goggles, he was watching Priss.

Priss turned to the table and placed his ball. He was going to be the agent that was to bring final and dramatic triumph to Bloom and make himself—the man who said it couldn't be done—the goat to be mocked forever.

Perhaps he felt there was no way out. Or perhaps—

With a sure stroke of his cue, he set the ball into motion. It was not going quickly, and every eye followed it. It struck the side of the table and caromed. It was going even slower now as though Priss himself were increasing the suspense and making Bloom's triumph the more dramatic.

I had a perfect view, for I was standing on the side of the table opposite from that where Priss was. I could see the ball moving toward the glitter of the zero-gravity field and beyond it I could see those portions of the seated Bloom which were not hidden by that glitter.

The ball approached the zero-gravity volume, seemed to hang on the edge for a moment, and then was gone, with a streak of light, the sound of a thunderclap, and the sudden smell of burning cloth.

We yelled. We all yelled.

I've seen the scene on television since—along with the rest of the world. I can see myself in the film during that fifteen-second period of wild confusion, but I don't really recognize my face.

Fifteen seconds!

And then we discovered Bloom. He was still sitting in the chair, his arms still folded, but there was a hole the size of a billiard ball through forearm, chest, and back. The better part of his heart, as it later turned out under autopsy, had been neatly punched out.

They turned off the device. They called in the police. They dragged off Priss, who was in a state of utter collapse. I wasn't much better off, to tell the truth, and if any reporter then on the scene ever tried to say he remained a cool observer of that scene, then he's a cool liar.

It was some months before I got to see Priss again. He had lost some weight but seemed well otherwise. Indeed, there was color in his cheeks and an air of decision about him. He was better dressed than I had ever seen him to be.

He said, "I know what happened *now*. If I had had time to think, I would have known then. But I am a slow thinker, and poor Ed Bloom was so intent on running a great show and doing it so well that he carried me along with him. Naturally, I've been trying to make up for some of the damage I unwittingly caused."

"You can't bring Bloom back to life," I said soberly.

"No, I can't," he said, just as soberly. "But there's Bloom Enterprises to think of, too. What happened at the demonstra-

tion, in full view of the world, was the worst possible advertisement for zero gravity, and it's important that the story
be made clear. That is why *I* have asked to see *you*."

"Yes?"

"If I had been a quicker thinker, I would have known Ed
was speaking the purest nonsense when he said that the billiard ball would slowly rise in the zero-gravity field. It *couldn't*
be so! If Bloom hadn't despised theory so, if he hadn't been
so intent on being proud of his own ignorance of theory,
he'd have known it himself.

"The Earth's motion, after all, isn't the only motion involved, young man. The Sun itself moves in a vast orbit
about the center of the Milky Way Galaxy. And the Galaxy
moves too, in some not very clearly defined way. If the billiard
ball were subjected to zero gravity, you might think of it as
being unaffected by any of these motions and therefore of
suddenly falling into a state of absolute rest—when there is
no such thing as absolute rest."

Priss shook his head slowly. "The trouble with Ed, I think,
was that he was thinking of the kind of zero gravity one gets
in a spaceship in free fall, when people float in mid-air. He
expected the ball to float in mid-air. However, in a spaceship,
zero gravity is not the result of an absence of gravitation, but
merely the result of two objects, a ship and a man within the
ship, falling at the same rate, responding to gravity in
precisely the same way, so that each is motionless with respect
to the other.

"In the zero-gravity field produced by Ed, there was a
flattening of the rubber-sheet Universe, which means an actual
loss of mass. Everything in that field, including molecules of
air caught within it, and the billiard ball I pushed into it, was
completely massless as long as it remained with it. A completely massless object can move in only one way."

He paused, inviting the question. I asked, "What motion
would that be?"

"Motion at the speed of light. Any massless object, such
as a neutrino or a photon, must travel at the speed of light
as long as it exists. In fact, light moves at that speed only
because it is made up of photons. As soon as the billiard ball
entered the zero-gravity field and lost its mass, it too assumed
the speed of light at once and left."

I shook my head. "But didn't it regain its mass as soon as it left the zero-gravity volume?"

"It certainly did, and at once it began to be affected by the gravitational field and to slow up in response to the friction of the air and the top of the billiard table. But imagine how much friction it would take to slow up an object the mass of a billiard ball going at the speed of light. It went through the hundred-mile thickness of our atmosphere in a thousandth of a second and I doubt that it was slowed more than a few miles a second in doing so, a few miles out of 186,282 of them. On the way, it scorched the top of the billiard table, broke cleanly through the edge, went through poor Ed and the window too, punching out neat circles because it had passed through before the neighboring portions of something even as brittle as glass had a chance to split and splinter.

"It is extremely fortunate we were on the top floor of a building set in a countrified area. If we were in the city, it might have passed through a number of buildings and killed a number of people. By now that billiard ball is off in space, far beyond the edge of the Solar System, and it will continue to travel so forever, at nearly the speed of light, until it happens to strike an object large enough to stop it. And then it will gouge out a sizable crater."

I played with the notion and was not sure I liked it. "How is that possible? The billiard ball entered the zero-gravity volume almost at a standstill. I saw it. And you say it left with an incredible quantity of kinetic energy. Where did the energy come from?"

Priss shrugged. "It came from nowhere! The law of conservation of energy only holds under the conditions in which general relativity is valid; that is, in an indented-rubber-sheet universe. Wherever the indentation is flattened out, general relativity no longer holds, and energy can be created and destroyed freely. That accounts for the radiation along the cylindrical surface of the zero-gravity volume. That radiation, you remember, Bloom did not explain, and, I fear, could not explain. If he had only experimented further first; if he had only not been so foolishly anxious to put on his show—"

"What accounts for the radiation, sir?"

"The molecules of air inside the volume. Each assumes the speed of light and comes smashing outward. They're only molecules, not billiard balls, so they're stopped, but the kinetic energy of their motion is converted into energetic radiation. It's continuous because new molecules are always drifting in, and attaining the speed of light and smashing out."

"Then energy is being created continuously?"

"Exactly. And that is what we must make clear to the public. Anti-gravity is not primarily a device to lift spaceships or to revolutionize mechanical movement. Rather, it is the source of an endless supply of free energy, since part of the energy produced can be diverted to maintain the field that keeps that portion of the Universe flat. What Ed Bloom invented, without knowing it, was not just anti-gravity, but the first successful perpetual-motion machine of the first class —one that manufactures energy out of nothing."

I said slowly, "Any one of us could have been killed by that billiard ball, is that right, Professor? It might have come out in any direction."

Priss said, "Well, massless photons emerge from any light source at the speed of light in any direction; that's why a candle casts light in all directions. The massless air molecules come out of the zero-gravity volume in all directions, which is why the entire cylinder radiates. But the billiard ball was only one object. It could have come out in any direction, but it had to come out in some one direction, chosen at random, and the chosen direction happened to be the one that caught Ed."

That was it. Everyone knows the consequences. Mankind had free energy and so we have the world we have now. Professor Priss was placed in charge of its development by the board of Bloom Enterprises, and in time he was as rich and famous as ever Edward Bloom had been. And Priss still has two Nobel Prizes in addition.

Only . . .

I keep thinking. Photons smash out from a light source in all directions because they are created at the moment and there is no reason for them to move in one direction more than in another. Air molecules come out of a zero-gravity field in all directions because they enter it in all directions.

But what about a single billiard ball, entering a zero-gravity field from one particular direction? Does it come out in the same direction or in any direction?

I've inquired delicately, but theoretical physicists don't seem to be sure, and I can find no record that Bloom Enterprises, which is the only organization working with zero-gravity fields, has ever experimented in the matter. Someone at the organization once told me that the uncertainty principle guarantees the random emersion of an object entering in any direction. But then why don't they try the experiment?

Could it be, then . . .

Could it be that for once Priss's mind had been working quickly? Could it be that, under the pressure of what Bloom was trying to do to him, Priss had suddenly seen everything? He had been studying the radiation surrounding the zero-gravity volume. He might have realized its cause and been certain of the speed-of-light motion of anything entering the volume.

Why, then, had he said nothing?

One thing is certain. *Nothing* Priss would do at the billiard table could be accidental. He was an expert and the billiard ball did exactly what he wanted it to. I was standing right there. I saw him look at Bloom and then at the table as though he were judging angles.

I watched him hit that ball. I watched it bounce off the side of the table and move into the zero-gravity volume, heading in one particular direction.

For when Priss sent that ball toward the zero-gravity volume—and the tri-di films bear me out—it was *already* aimed directly at Bloom's heart!

Accident? Coincidence?

. . . Murder?

AFTERWORD

A friend of mine after reading the above story suggested I change the title to "Dirty Pool." I have been tempted to do so but have refrained, for it seems too flippant a title for so grave a story—or perhaps I am just corroded with jealousy at not having thought of it first.

But in either case, now that all the stories in this volume have been gone over, and I have experienced the memories to which each gave rise, all I can say is, "Gee, it's great to be a science fiction writer."

Isaac asimov

☐ BEFORE THE GOLDEN AGE, Book I	C2913	1.95
☐ BEFORE THE GOLDEN AGE, Book II	Q2452	1.50
☐ BEFORE THE GOLDEN AGE, Book III	Q2525	1.50
☐ THE BEST OF ISAAC ASIMOV	23018-X	1.75
☐ BUY JUPITER AND OTHER STORIES	23062-7	1.50
☐ THE CAVES OF STEEL	Q2858	1.50
☐ THE CURRENTS OF SPACE	P2495	1.25
☐ EARTH IS ROOM ENOUGH	Q2801	1.50
☐ THE END OF ETERNITY	Q2832	1.50
☐ THE GODS THEMSELVES	X2883	1.75
☐ I, ROBOT	Q2829	1.50
☐ THE MARTIAN WAY	23158-5	1.50
☐ THE NAKED SUN	Q2648	1.50
☐ NIGHTFALL AND OTHER STORIES	23188-7	1.75
☐ NINE TOMORROWS	Q2688	1.50
☐ PEBBLE IN THE SKY	Q2828	1.50
☐ THE STARS, LIKE DUST	Q2780	1.50
☐ WHERE DO WE GO FROM HERE?—Ed.	X2849	1.75